A VERY
HUMAN PLACE

A VERY
HUMAN PLACE

PTG MAN

M. WITHNAIL PRESS
SYDNEY, AUSTRALIA

Copyright © 2016 by **PTG Man**

All rights reserved. Without limiting the rights of the copyright reserved above, no part of this publication may be reproduced, stored in or introduced into a retrieval system, or transmitted, in any form or by any means (electronic, mechanical, photocopying, recording, or otherwise), without the prior written permission of the copyright owner.

The scanning, uploading, and distribution of this book via the Internet or via any other means without the permission of the publisher is illegal and punishable by law. Please purchase only authorized electronic editions and do not participate in or encourage electronic piracy of copyrightable materials. Your support of the author's rights is appreciated. This is a work of fiction. Names, characters, places and incidents are the products of the author's imagination or are used fictitiously. Any resemblance to actual events, or persons, living or dead, is entirely coincidental.

Cover Image: Wild boar Ukrainian traditional tribal art in karakoko style © Karakotsya Shutterstock

All section illustrations from Shutterstock

Sharon Downes. Worm turns for cotton pest as Australia breeds in resistance. The Conversation. Australian Ed; 28 June 2013, 2.14pm AEST

Barricades and Brickwalls; Lyrics Kasey Chambers, 2001.

XXXX Gold – The Queensland Beer Advertisement (Lyrics: Beautiful Queensland, Tex Morton)

M. Withnail Press

A Very Human Place. -- 1st ed.

ISBN 978-0-9874316-3-9 PRINT
ISBN 978-0-9874316-2-2 EBOOK

CONTENTS

PROLOGUE	2
OVERTURE	4
GUBURNBURNIN	8
WORROBOBO	76
GUBURNBURNIN	98
THE DUCK POND 1862	152
HO HO HO	162
CARLO	176
INTERMISSION	196
STRAYADAY	212
ALL THE PRETTY FLOWERS	232
THE METAMORPHOSIS	260
A NEW DAY	280
EPILOGUE	290

PROLOGUE

For He said to him, "Come out of the man, unclean spirit!" Then He asked him, "What is your name?" And he answered, saying, "My name is Legion; for we are many." . . . Now a large herd of swine was feeding there near the mountains. So all the demons begged Him, saying, "Send us to the swine, that we may enter them." And at once He gave them permission. Then the unclean spirits went out and entered the swine (there were about two thousand); and the herd ran violently down the steep place into the sea, and drowned.

-Mark 5:8-13

But some of the pigs could swim.

OVERTURE

The camera settled back to the balloon-lipped presenter—a Botox-paralyzed face straining to transmit her distaste for those feral neighbors, exposed by hidden cameras, exposed as dole bludgers, school dropouts, drug users, festering in and around the good citizens who watched and listened to her fat lips.

"You left school at 13?"

"So what's that to you?"

"You roam the streets, we have the footage."

"Why wouldja follow me? What've I done to you?"

"Your neighbors complained about the noise, about the foul language in the middle of the night."

"How's that your business?"

"Don't tell me my business, I've been reporting stories like yours for many years."

"Who gives a shit?"

"Look at these pictures. Why do you roam the streets during the day?"

"Nothin' else to do."

"Get a job. What about that?"

"I tried. Nobody'll give me one."

"Look at this footage. We showed this last week."

Black and white images of a wide suburban street, the Pizza store, the closed down furniture store—Charlie's Sofas—the young man's accused face, real time, in the corner of the screen. *"Is that you?"*

"Who gives a shit?"

"What are you buying from that man?"

"Why's his face blurred and not mine?"

"He's selling drugs under cover for our program. Don't worry. They weren't real. You didn't get high did you?"

"Who gives a shit?"

"Why do you take them? Tell me—no, tell the audience, tell Australia, why do you waste your time roaming the streets during the day, causing a disturbance at night, and taking drugs?"

"I'm bored."

"You're bored?"

"You deaf?"

"No, just perplexed. Yes, I'm very perplexed."

"Who the shit cares what you think?"

"Well your language is consistent."

"What'd you follow me and set me up for? What've I done to you, you piece of shit?"

"This is what you wanted to tell me? This is what you wanted to tell Australia?"

"Yeah. You're all shits."

"So you're bored? And your response to being bored is taking drugs and shouting out abuse to your neighbors . . . and Australia."

"Never got on with the neighbors. We've fought for years."

"Really, what about."

"What business is that of yours?"

"I think I know my business, we've established that. Let's look at some more footage we showed two weeks ago." An infrared image of a house, a high timber fence. Dogs barking. Expletives deleted. The wide shot of suburbia exposed in lime and black. More expletives deleted. Little else. And fade out.

"You recognize that house?"

"Yeah."

"Well, that footage was taken just after midnight."

"My dog barks. They shouted over the fence for him to stop. How do you stop a dog barking? Tell me."

"You sounded drunk."

"What's it to you?"

"Well you can understand your neighbors' view. I think our audience understands. Obscenities over a fence in the early hours of the morning. Who would want to live around that?"

"I told you, they started it."

"That's not how we saw it, or Australia saw it."

"Yeah, but you're all shits."

"You really are making an impression."

"Why would I care what you think?"

"What Australia thinks?"

"Who gives a shit what Australia thinks?"

"Anyway, thank you for coming in and giving up your valuable time and telling us your version of the story." Pan to the smiling fat-lipped presenter. *"Well Australia, there you have it—the defense. Make of it what you will. And that's the show for this evening. Thanks for your company, and good night."*

"A real turd."

GUBURNBURNIN

ONE

They sat on a dirt road the color of old blood. It was noon, and the summer sky was cloudless. Wheat fields reached out in flat plains on either side, and from where they were seated, they could see nothing but the yellow-gold of the land, and the blood road that cut it in two.

"Shouldn't be long now," Lil said. A wide straw hat shaded her face.

"You said that already."

"Did I?" She turned to him. "You should wear a proper hat. You'll get burnt with that baseball cap and then whine all night."

"I think the locals call it whinge. It's a cricket cap. And it doesn't look like I'll burn like you."

"A black man would burn in this sun." She picked at a sore on her freckled arm. "Why on earth do I have skin like this?"

"Perhaps black would have been a better color?" He grinned but kept staring at the wheat.

"Too much bother, Sam. We'd get no cooperation from the townspeople."

"It'd be more of a challenge."

"I'm long past challenges, you know that." She watched him swipe at flies that sidled his face. "Why don't you get one of those hats with hanging corks. They were high fashion at Worrobobo."

Sam removed the cricket cap and combed black hair away from his high forehead, the oil shining silver over his scalp. "I think I have a touch of Aboriginal in me. Good for the dexterity."

"A touch is okay, but a decent dose is far too much trouble for the both of us." Lil picked at her skin again and held her arm under his chin. "What do you think of this? I might need to get it attended to when we arrive."

"Stop fiddling with it and it'll go away."

"It bleeds on its own, doctor."

"Then I'd recommend a biopsy."

"Thank you, doctor. Can you do this for me?"

"I could bite it off and spit it on the road."

"Not very professional, doctor."

"Or in your face."

"Charming, Sam."

He swiped at another fly.

"I liked Worrobobo," she said.

He turned to her but didn't speak.

"How long were we there?"

"Long enough for you to go through the entire town a couple of times."

"Don't exaggerate, Sam. You're so prone to exaggeration these days."

"I can count eight in the cricket team alone."

"How many in a team?"

"Eleven, but we only had ten."

"Did you count Kylie?" she said.

"I did. In the team count, and yours."

"I liked Kylie, she was such a dear."

He turned to her again, combing his slicked-back mane. "You're picking up some of the local vernacular I see."

"I always do, Sam, you know that too. Some words linger on, deep in this old brain of mine, often I don't remember where from."

"I notice you stopped saying shamayim a while back . . . but you said it yesterday."

"Shamayim," she said the word slowly in an accent of thick phlegm. "Brings back memories, hey Sam?"

He kept his stare on the wheat but with a hint of a smile.

"Shamayim. You were my rescuer then, Sam. My hero." She turned to him. "Why, I haven't thought about those days for as long as I can remember." She picked at the sore of her arm and it started to bleed. "Shouldn't be long now."

They sat on their suitcases so the blood road wouldn't stain their clothes. There was no wind, and the dirt settled still at their feet, and the flies kept on at their faces. In front, heat lifted off the plains like shallow waves in a pool, and the hot, dry air pinched at their skin.

"We might try and stay longer this time," Lil said.

"We might."

"I liked Worrobobo."

"You already said that."

"Well, try and not lose your temper so much."

"Then don't keep repeating yourself."

"I mean, try not to lose your temper like you did in Worrobobo." She turned to him. "Sam, will you try?"

"Yes."

"Good boy." She swiped at a fly. "You can be a good boy, you know that."

"Good to whom?"

"To me, of course. Who else?"

"Tov."

"Yes, good. Sometimes." She smiled. "But you weren't exactly good at Worrobobo."

"We could have stayed if you wanted."

"Don't be ridiculous, Sam."

A low flying crow circled over the field and landed at the edge of the road just up from them. Sam studied the bird and didn't reply.

"We could have stayed . . . Shamayim!" The crow hopped towards them and she kicked dust in its direction. "Now you've got me saying shamayim again. I'm sure that amuses you."

He looked ahead with a smile but kept on quiet.

"How could we have stayed there, Sam?"

"We didn't need an invitation. It was Worrobobo, not Zǐjinchéng."

"Sam, may I make a suggestion?"

"Could I stop you?"

"No. Before you plan on any flamboyant exhibitions, any of your more high spirited demonstrations of frustration, revelations for want of a better word . . .would you have the courtesy of discussing those plans with me first?"

"You would have said no."

"Not necessarily. Of course, in the case of Worrobobo, I would have said no. But there have been times when these exhibitions were called for. And not just the early days."

He turned to her. "Really? Such as when?"

"Paris, for instance."

"That was some time ago."

"I haven't forgotten. Definitely Paris, but not Worrobobo, Sam. Do you see the difference between the two?"

He watched the crow turn back and hop towards their feet, pecking into the red dust as it went. "Not really."

Lil stared at him. "Not really, Sam? Let me summarize for you then. In Paris you had a group wanting to cut off your head. A clean separation of the head from the shoulders. You were rightly annoyed about this."

"Thank you."

"Your response may have been a little theatrical. I can attribute that to your Carlo years. They were still fresh."

"They still are."

"I'm glad you admit it. Carlo is your favorite. He's a part of you."

He kept staring out front.

"But you were understandably very theatrical at that time."

"You liked me more then."

"Don't be a baby. But what you did in response—despite the circus tricks, the fireworks—what you did was completely understandable." She looked down at the crow that hopped a few steps closer. "In Worrobobo, no one wanted to remove your head."

"That you know of."

"Rather, the local grocer called you a poof."

"Poofter."

"My apologies. Poof-ter." She swatted away another fly. "Nevertheless, can you spot any difference in the severity of these situations?"

He threw up a hint of a smile. "You've been known for some flamboyant exhibitions in your time."

"But I think it's safe to say I've a bit more sense of restraint than you. Worrobobo was not an act that you should be proud of."

Sam smiled and watched the heat rise off the plains.

Lil kicked at the black crow, which lifted itself off the ground, flapping clumsily with its neck arched back, throwing itself rather than flying, before landing thirty feet down the way.

They sat still on their cases looking out at the shimmering wheat and the sun fell down on them without any respite.

And Lil said, "Shouldn't be long now."

* * *

Where the stream snaked its course, the land turned green for a bit. Boulders of granite as high as men, painted with patches of gray lichens, sprouted jagged-edged around the place. Tall grasses burgeoned in their crevices, and larger eucalypts rose up where the stones splayed away.

The wallaby's body was shaped like a small boulder, the same color as the lichen-stained stone, only its tiny pointed head and forelegs to reveal it. And, in the late afternoon, when the light fashioned shadows on the place, not even an experienced native might be expected to see it.

Close to where the wallaby chewed at the grass, a thin tree branch lay on the ground, too long for a walking stick, too thick for a spear, its shaft twisted into a gentle S in the middle, one side a strip of dark olive, the other tarnished silver from the reflected sun.

The fatter tip of the branch lifted off the earth.

And before the wallaby had swallowed, the branch flung itself forward, wrapping its shaft around the gray-brown fur, round and around its neck, the striped head of the wallaby squeezed out and tilted to one side, its pointed ears twitching, its pink tongue beginning to protrude, and its wide eyes seeming to look at nothing—a straight-on, patient stare.

And patience was needed. For it would take the Olive python two hours to swallow the wallaby whole. And seven days to digest it.

* * *

The car, spraying a cloud of blood dust in its wake, veered across the road toward the couple. Bob watched as they stood to greet him, and he slowed on approach. When he stopped, his window was an arm's length from their faces. He rolled the window down, but only a third of the way, and lifted himself higher in the seat so his mouth reached the open space.

"You folks okay?"

The woman practically sung her reply in a thick crow twang. "Oh darling! Sweetness! You are a liife saaver. How can we thank you for stoppin'?"

"You need a lift?"

"Sweetness, we do!"

The driver glanced at the man who stood back a step—silent, tall, standing as if waiting for a bus. At his feet were two old leather suitcases the same color as the road—just enough for a week's journey.

"I can take you to town if it's in the right direction for you." He bent down and released the boot lock. "You can put those cases in the back if you like."

"You haave come from the heavens, dearest. You truly haave!"

He watched them enter the cool of the car, slumping on the black upholstery as slick as the hair of the silent passenger.

"What is that de-liightful smell?" the woman asked.

"Air conditioning deodorant. Pine meadow."

"Piiiine meadow. Sam, have you ever smelled anything as niice?"

"Never," Sam said, deadpan.

In the rear mirror, Bob watched the younger man preen his hair, one hand flattening as it followed the comb down.

"I don't know why people don't use it more often . . . deodorant for air conditioners. Why don't they, Sam? And look at these blinds at the back. I swear I could live in this car." The woman bent forward and spoke softer into his ear. "The way you look after this . . . I bet you're proud, 'ey." She slumped back and played with the venetians.

"It's a '77 Holden Statesman Deville. My father bought it new. It has three hundred kays on the clock but never missed a service. The books are in perfect order."

"A Statesman Dee-ville!" She crowed a high-pitched laugh. "Did you hear that, Sam? How dee-licious."

The car rolled on, puffing up a trail of haze.

"What are you folks doing on this road? You're far from anything here. This is still part of the Simpson's farm. It was just luck I came by."

"You a Simpson then?" Sam said.

Bob twisted to face the back. "No."

"Visiting the Simpsons?"

"Well, no."

"Then what are you doing on this road?"

He shone a confused face at Sam.

"To rescue us, Saaam!" The woman bent forward and touched his shoulder. "Where would you be taking us to . . . ?"

"Bob."

"Dearest, Bob. Where would you be taking us to?"

"Guburnburnin."

"Gu . . . burn . . . burnin. Sounds deelicious, doesn't it, Sam."

"Delicious," Sam said, still deadpan.

He twisted to face the back, but Sam kept his stare on the passing yellow wheat.

"Don't worry about my son, Bob. Nothing seems to excite him these days. Tell us about Guburnburnin. Tell us . . . everything!"

Bob kept his eyes on the road that aimed straight through the plains. "Not much to tell really. It's a small town. This is wheat and cotton country, there's not much else around. Most people live on the farms, so the town's tiny—a stopover more like. But it won the Tidy Town award last year . . . that's for all of Queensland."

"The Tidy Town of Queensland. I think we've struck gold, Sam."

Bob turned and looked at the odd woman uneasily.

"I'm being perfectly genuine. My son and I don't care for cities much. We like the simple life."

"Well, simple is what you'll get in Guburnburnin."

"Simple and tidy, I'm told. And where would you suggest we stay in this tidy town of yours?"

"Only one option, really. The Coral Waters. A funny name I know, since we're five hundred kays inland." He looked at Sam in the rear-vision mirror, who finally turned his gaze to him.

"Do you have a cricket team?" Sam asked.

"As a matter of fact, Pete, the local publican, just put one together."

"My boy likes cricket." The woman grinned at the passing checkerboard plains. "And I must say, I don't mind it myself—as a spectator of course. Any women in the team?"

"My wife, actually."

"This is a daaay of co-incidences. Shamayim!" Phlegm collected in the soft lining of the woman's throat.

"Does your wife bat or bowl?" Sam asked.

"Neither. To be honest, she's never played in any sporting team before. She just does it to get out of the house for a bit."

The woman leaned and touched his shoulder. "Do you play, Bob?"

"No. I'm a bit beyond that. Sharon—"

"Sharon's the little missus?"

"Yes. Sharon's a fair bit younger than me."

"Of course she is, Bob." Her crow twang suddenly transformed into the calm voice of a newsreader. "Of course she is."

The blood route ended at a T intersection with a tarred single lane road. As they moved on, meeting oncoming traffic only every five minutes or so, the land stayed flat but turned into a patchwork of green, ochre and yellow rectangles. Wrought iron windmills and homesteads were scattered, haphazard. And wire fences strung on frayed timber poles—leaning whichever way, but never upright.

They drove steadily on with the scent of pine meadow though gums were the only trees in sight; the tilt of the venetians keeping the sun off their faces. In a half an hour they reached Guburnburnin, the *Welcome to a Tidy Town of Queensland* sign fresh off the production line, the fifty-kilometer speed limit sign smaller and back a bit.

Bob looked at the town anew, through the visitors' eyes. It spanned a single stretch of road no more than a couple of hundred meters in length. No need of side streets. A post office, petrol station and corner store without the corner, all housed in one edifice; a pub, the Guburnburnin Hotel, although Pete the owner hadn't rented a room for as long as he could remember; and the Coral Waters Motel, with its green vacancy sign out front that never changed, even if the rooms were full. In between, little fibro shacks of houses sat with cars, children's swing sets, farm equipment, all rusting in long paspalum, cut at least once a month by town decree—a stipulation of the tidy town award. No zebra crossings. No traffic lights.

The Deville pulled up in front of the Coral Waters. "Is it okay to leave you here?"

"Sweetness, angel, what can we do to repay you?"

He turned around to look at the woman with her ragged strawberry mop of hair—unkempt as the town grass, now that the award was in hand—her freckled face dotted with red scaly crusts, a dowager's hump rolling thick to her neck, and a grin that took up most of her face.

"Give us your price, Bob."

"It was nothing, really."

"Sam, did you hear that. What a maan is our Bob!"

Sam opened the door and didn't reply.

"I hope we'll see each other again." She rested a hand on his shoulder. "Perhaps at the pub, if that's to your fancy?"

"Well, that might be nice . . ."

"I'm Lil, Bob. And you keep your promise, you hear? I'll be waiting." She sung a crow laugh that filled up the Holden, opened the door, and lifted her heavy-boned body out of the car. By the time she had composed herself, Sam was standing on the grass path with a suitcase in each hand.

"He's such a good boy, is my Sam," the woman said to him through the half turned down window. "You know, it's his thirtieth birthday today." She lowered her voice. "He's always grumpy on his birthday."

"Happy birthday, Sam," he said, raising his chin to the open window.

"Thank you, Bob."

And he drove away, leaving the town's two latest strangers to themselves.

Lil waved, and before the boxy, lumbering car was beyond the *You are leaving a Tidy Town of Queensland* sign said, not with a crow twang inflection, but in her newsreader drawl of no particular accent, a brogue just for Sam's ears, or special times, "Sam, why don't you make like a good son and find us a room." She turned to him and said without a flicker of a smile, "So I can have a long bath to remove the fucking stench of pine meadow from my skin."

* * *

The electronic toad croaked twice.

Gordon wiped the pasty crumbs from his mouth, his tongue scavenging any lingering bits, lifted himself from the dining table, and went through the beaded curtain doorway into the front office.

"Welcome to the Coral Waters," he said.

"I'd like to look at your rooms."

He looked down over the desk at the old suitcases at the man's feet and thought them odd, though he couldn't say why. "We have four rooms to choose from, but they're pretty well the same."

"I'd like to look at them."

He took the master key from under the table. "Number four is further from the road and the last in the block . . . so a bit quieter. They're all double brick though, so sound isn't usually a problem."

They went out into the open day. Eight small rooms at ground level, all with light blue doors, a white plastic chair, a hanging fern on the wall, and a painted piece of coral stuck to each door.

Gordon slipped the key in number four. "You by yourself?"

"My mother too."

"You need a twin then?"

The dark haired man didn't answer.

He opened number four. The inside was clean and small, an unadorned space except for a digital television, twin beds, and three bits of coral flying in formation next to a painting of The Great Barrier Reef––identified by an engraved faux-brass plate on the bottom of the frame.

"The kitchenette has everything you'd need. A carton of milk in the fridge, tea and coffee . . . all on the house. The shower takes a bit to warm up in the morning, but in this heat most don't bother."

"You have cable?"

"Just the local stations."

"You get the cricket?"

"Channel nine."

The dark-haired man nodded. "I'll take two rooms. Can you make this one into a double bed?"

"How many nights you need?"

The man ignited the TV and flicked through the stations. "A month. Maybe longer."

"We'll get to know each other pretty well then. I'm Gordon."

The newcomer looked at him blankly. "You play in the cricket team?"

"The pub team? No." The white uniforms on the green oval of The Gabba moved across the TV screen. He studied the man and felt a strange unease. "We might get the paper work organized so you can get settled."

The oiled-haired man nodded but kept his gaze at the TV.

"I'll meet you back at the front desk, then."

But the man seemed not to hear.

Gordon went back to the office. A month's guaranteed two-room occupancy should make him dance, but he didn't even skip. It'd look good on the books—nice for a prospective buyer, but he knew that the chances of selling The Coral were one in a million. He should phone Sally to tell her there was a regular cleaning job if she wanted. Otherwise he would do it himself.

He was sitting behind the desk when the toad croaked twice.

"You must be Gordon!"

All he could see was a mop of red hair and a smile that filled the room. "Welcome to the Coral Waters."

She had a bag of groceries in her hand. "I've just visited that niice store down the road. There's quite a gourmet selection there."

"It's pretty good for a town this size."

"I'm goin' to luv this town, Gordon. I can feel it deep in my womb."

He smiled at her mop of hair.

"I see my son has left the suitcases here. He is so absent miinded these daays." She leaned in and whispered, "You know, I think he must be in luv." She cackled up loudly. "What about you, Gordon?"

"Me?"

"Yes, you."

He kept silent but with a smile that showed all his teeth.

"Don't keep me in suspense. Are . . . you . . . in luv?"

"I can't say that I am . . . "

"It's Lil. And I'm so pleased to hear that!" She cackled even louder. "Now, I'm going to take these bags to my boy, and chastise him for leaving them here. Has he spoken to you about them?"

He looked down at the strange cases. They seemed to be made of some kind of old, pale leather. Almost like an untanned hide.

"Gordon, I can see in your eyes he hasn't. I think I'll have to give him a good smack." She softened her voice. "Now, I wonder if it would be possible, for privacy, which I'm sure you understand being a motel owner, if you could instruct the cleaner not to touch these cases."

"Absolutely, Lil. But I'd suggest leaving any valuables in the office safe."

"No need for that. I perfectly trust the Tidy Town of Guburnburnin and your staarf to keep our belongings secure."

"I will let Sally know not to touch the cases."

"You are a maan of action." She put the groceries next to the suitcases. "How old are you Gordon, if you don't mind me askin'?"

"Fifty-eight," he lied.

"Bull shit!" She put her hand up to her mouth. "Pardon the French, but fifty-aate . . . forty was my guess . . . maybe forty-fiiive, but fifty-aate? Never."

"And you, Lil?"

"Gordon, you should know better. Never ask a lady her age." She laughed again. "But let's just say we're of a similar vintage."

"I wonder, Lil, perhaps I could trouble you to fill out the paper work?"

"He hasn't even done that?" She shook her head. "What do you need?"

"Just the basics, and a credit card imprint."

"Why don't we just pay it all up front? Clean the slate."

"That's not necessary."

"Gordon, don't argue with a lady." She handed him a credit card that looked as strange as the suitcases.

He studied the black plastic card. A small hologram logo was in the center, but he couldn't make out the shape. The magnetic strip looked barely used. Otherwise, there were no markings on the card of any kind, no name, no expiration date, nothing.

"I'm afraid we only take Visa or MasterCard."

"Go on, give it a try."

"Sometimes our connection isn't good. Satellite problems, the bank tells me."

"We've never had a problem. Give it a go."

He swiped the card, and the machine made its thinking noise. "I'm not optimistic, Lil."

"Have faith, handsome Gordon."

He felt his cheeks flush and lowered his gaze, smiling at the thinking machine. "Is sixty a night for each room okay by you, Lil?"

"A real baargun from what I've seen. You must want me to staay on, hey?"

He looked up at Lil with her raised up brow, the whites of her eyes wide like her grin, the freckled face with little red scales, some with tiny blood crusts. She looked older than him, with her sun-soaked Queensland face.

"You'll catch a fly with that open mouth of yours, Gordon."

He felt his cheeks flush red hot again as the machine jumped into its processing tune. "Well, I'll be damned."

She laughed. "What a lovely expression."

He tore the merchant copy for Lil to sign. "I just put a week's worth on. I usually take an imprint, to cover . . . " He faltered.

"Damages, Gordon?"

"But not for you, Lil."

She signed the paper. "You need anything else from me?"

His pulse kept up its race. "Maybe an address?"

Lil smiled and picked up the suitcases and grocery bag. "That's easy, Gordon. Our address is here."

She waddled out through the door. As she went he peered at her large ass. And, when she was out of frame, he started to whistle.

Just like the old days.

* * *

Sharon heard the crunching gravel before the red Holden crept past the kitchen window. The door of the car opened and closed, the front door of the house as well, both with the same gentle force. Never a bang, just a reserved dull thud.

The same every time.

She rinsed the last of the dishes and wiped down the sink.

"I'm home," he said from the bedroom, same as he always did.

She peeled her gloves off and dangled them over the tap. Examined her white crinkled fingers, crinkled palms, and pushed dollops of moisturizer into them from a bottle that sat next to the detergent.

"I thought we might go out tonight," he said from the bedroom.

That was new. She looked out through the window, wiping the cream into her hands. The low sun lit the cotton crop lime green.

Bob came into the kitchen and kissed her forehead in the same way. "I met some new folks in town. I thought we might have a drink to welcome them."

"I've already put some meat out to thaw."

"Well, it'll keep 'til tomorrow."

"I thawed it out this morning."

"I'm sure it'll be fine, just stick it back in the fridge."

"You aren't supposed to eat meat more than a day after you thaw it."

"Then we'll have it for breakfast."

She put the plastic bag of chops back into the fridge, the door closing louder than the front and car door had been. She heard him sigh.

"Who are these people then?" she asked.

"Mother and son. But I must say, I couldn't see much of a resemblance. She's a red head, and his hair is as black as tar."

"Red hair can skip a generation."

"Well, the father must have some mighty red-repellant genes in him."

"Where'd you meet them?"

"On the Simpson's road. Gave them a lift."

"What you doin' over there?" Sharon looked out at Aka, their pet Alsatian, licking ferociously at his testicles. A boy running to smack the dog, little Jamie, but he didn't stop the dog because he wasn't really there. She had been imagining little Jamie taking out the garbage just minutes before the red Holden had interrupted it all.

She waited for the licking to stop before turning. "Bob, you a taxi driver now?"

"I just happened to pass by."

"The Simpson's?"

He sighed again and started to get a corrugated frown that could stay permanent if she wasn't careful. She knew she shouldn't be the schoolteacher so much. But she seemed less able to control it lately.

"What's the difference anyway? I picked them up and brought them to the Coral, and they're going to the pub. So, I thought we could go in for a drink and a bite to eat."

"Okay. I'll get made up."

"No need, baby."

"I'm not going out looking like this."

"You look pretty good to me, Sharon."

She went over and gave him a kiss. "I'll be thirty minutes. There're some bills to be paid on the table. And can you feed the dog before he eats his balls?"

Her summer frock was a bit too tight in the waist, but for the pub crowd it would do. She sat in front of the dressing table and looked at herself; pouting her lips, pink like the flowers on her dress, then gave a smile until fine lines circled her mouth. Not age lines—they had been there since her teens. No crows feet either. A few little freckles, but she couldn't help that. They were from childhood too.

She combed her fringe with her fingers. She was lucky with her hair—more on the blonde side of strawberry blonde, just like her mother and Nan. She gave up another smile, lips closed, bringing those lines into view again, and held the pose.

"We'll be late, Sharon," Bob said from the kitchen.

She stood up and moved back from the dresser, turned to the side, inspecting her little waist and the little bottom that was hidden under the frock. Bent her knee to bring her lithe calf up into the scene. No stockings. There was no need to cover her best feature.

Bob broke into the corner of the scene. "Here's my little Miss Queensland."

"Guburnburnin."

"Not a big enough trophy, Miss Guburnburnin. I think you can take on the State."

"Well, tonight it's just Miss Guburnburnin Hotel."

She laughed into the mirror and watched him stare at her. She liked it when he stared.

* * *

It was Friday night so the U shaped bar was cluttered with bunched hats. The hotel was a low lit, old-fashioned timber establishment, painted every shade of brown, and the warm, still air was dank with a mix of Castlemaine XXXX and the land that clung to the shirts of the hunched over men. The pub reeked of hops and grime, and the men settled in it like pigs in mud.

Bob held the door open and Sharon entered, pink and white and strawberry blonde like a piece of candy. She saw the heads turn; perhaps a wolf whistle, but it may have been the wind. The cluttered bar made up its welcome with muffled nods, lifting of hands. Bob pulled out a heavy stool for her and they sat together at the bar.

"Two middies, Pete. One light."

The publican nodded and gave Sharon a wink. "The light for you, Bob?" He drew the XXXX on tap.

She watched Bob scan the room. "What time did they say they were coming?"

"We didn't set a time."

She shrugged and didn't much care.

"A mother and son hasn't come in yet, Pete?"

The publican set the middies on coasters and shook his head. Bob kept restless on his stool.

The publican leaned forward, and she could smell the booze on his breath. "You ready for the practice tomorrow, Shaz?"

"Not really."

"I might have another one for the team," Bob said. "Young fella asked about it today."

"We're full up. I had to knock back Teddy. He was gutted."

"So, why am I in the team and not Teddy?" she said.

"He hasn't got legs like yours, Shaz."

She heard some laughter further down but didn't bother to see which of the dusty hats it was from.

"I see you're goin' bald, Bob," Pete said.

"I'm thinning a bit."

"More than a bit from where I'm standing."

She heard some more of the same laughter upstream. "What do I wear, then?"

He wiped a glass. "Just a little skirt will do fine, Shaz."

"In your dreams, Pete."

The publican smiled. "Long pants, white if you've got 'em. I've got the shirts already made up . . . the Guburnburnin Hooters . . . I thought of the name myself."

A burst of upstream laughter. "Good one, Pete," someone proffered.

"You must have work-shopped that for a week," Sharon said.

"I should've been in advertisin'." He wiped another glass. "Say, Bob, Robbo said he heard you were talkin' to that Chink mining company."

"I haven't seen Robbo for ages," she said.

"He's kept his head down since his missus got sick. She's in the hospital at Banga. Touch and go, I think."

"That's sad. I've never met her, but if you see Robbo say hello for me."

"Will do, Shaz." He kept on wiping the same clean glass. "So, Bob, cat got your tongue?"

She watched her man with his little boys' eyes sipping his beer and decided to come to his rescue. "We talk to lots of people, Pete. We're very social."

"Ted sold off his farm to 'em. Has the cash in the bank."

"So did Macka," a voice came from upstream.

"Bullshit! I don't believe it. That farm is three generations."

"Ain't never gonna be a fourth."

"These Chinks need their gas . . . to cook all that fried rice of theirs."

"Good one, Pete." Applause from downstream this time.

"So, Bobby boy, is Shaz doin' the talkin' for ya now, or would you like to educate us with a reply."

Bob turned and waved up an arm to the entrance. She twisted and saw a red mop of hair and the tall, dark figure walk toward them.

"Bob, you kept your promise," the red mop cackled up. "And so soon."

She smiled at the woman, who seemed nice, with a large, encompassing good humor—if first impressions were anything to go on.

Bob made the introductions and dragged two stools over from an empty table. "You haven't eaten I hope?"

"Not a morsel."

"The steak is the special of the night. Chips with salad or veges."

"Sounds mouthwatering."

He talked like a schoolboy, which was a strange affect in him. He was usually not the animated type.

He smiled like a schoolboy, as well. "Can I get you both a drink? They have wine if you like, Lil."

"Sam and I are both non-drinkers."

"No worries. What about a lemon, lime, and bitters?"

"I'm sure they can make a choice for themselves, honey," Sharon said.

"Lemon, lime and bitters will be just fine, Bob."

The Guburnburnin pub settled into the early evening—brown hats, faces, schooner-filled glasses—a sepia vista, lit orange-blonde from grimy shades, halos filtered through layers of insect bits on frosted glass. A campfire space that gave shelter away from the large, empty plains of wheat and cotton and furrowed land.

The drinks came and Bob raised his glass. "Happy birthday, Sam. The big three O, that's a milestone." Bob put his arms around her. "My little lady turned the same corner just a year back. I, on the other hand, turned the next corner even longer ago than that."

She looked at Sam, who had yet to speak. His forehead was large with his hair combed back. The oil was a bit odd, old fashioned, even for

Guburnburnin, yet his high forehead made him seem thoughtful, or smart—like a poet. If she had her way, it would be parted over with a long tongue of fringe, Hugh Grant style. He was good looking, though. And she wondered about him.

"Bob," Lil said, "tell me. Is there a doctor close by?"

"Thirty-five kays away. I'm happy to take you if you need a ride."

She thought about her taxi driver comment that riled him up at home. "It takes a week to get an appointment. And that's if they're taking new patients, honey."

"Doc owes me a favor for getting that irrigation quote for him. You let me organize it, Lil."

"This maan of yours is something, Sharon."

She smiled at Lil's XXXX accent, Austrayun, and turned to the dark silent one. "I hear you like cricket, Sam."

He hadn't looked at her since he arrived, but this seemed to get his attention. "You play, I've been told," he said.

"Just starting. Nothing serious. For a giggle, really."

"My Sam is unfortunately very serious about the game, luv. I had to drag him away from TV to attend to more important duties before . . . didn't I?"

"I would like to play in the team too," he said.

She felt a sudden unease. The team was full, she knew that, yet she had brought up the topic when she should have left it alone. Mum was right—she could be a real bitch sometimes. But she didn't like it about herself.

"We are playing a practice game tomorrow. You can come along if you like." She felt Bob squeeze at her thigh.

"I'll be there."

"We can pick you up before the game." After she said it, she thought about the taxi driver comment again.

Sam nodded his dark eyes at her. And she wondered if his eyes signaled anything more than his love of cricket.

"Bob, does this Doc of yours work on a Saturday?" Lil asked.

"He does. Perhaps they can play cricket while you and I attend to more serious matters."

Lil lifted her hands to the table. "Sweetness, please. If you ever want to share this maan of yours, I am the first in line."

She smiled, to her surprise, and so did Bob.

Lil picked at a sore on her forearm.

"Leave it alone," Sam said.

"There's no need to get angry, since this lump is clearly your fault."

Sam turned to his mother. "It's your rule . . ."

"Well you can choose better . . . as I do for you," Lil said.

Sharon found it strange how Lil's broad Australian twang shifted into something else without warning. "That looks nasty, Lil," she said. "You make sure Doc has a look at it."

"Thank you for the concern. I don't get much sympathy from . . . you know who."

"Doc's good with skin," she said. "He keeps an eye on my mole for me." She rubbed at the large birthmark on her forearm. "Bob calls it my map of Australia. There's no Tasmania though."

Lil cackled loud. "Sam, look at Sharon's mole . . . it does look like Austraya, doesn't it."

"I don't like the hairs in it. When I was a kid I used to pluck them out . . . 'Gorilla arm,' they called me."

"Kids, they find ways to torment. But what would they say looking at you now, Sharon. You could be on a postcard for Hollywood . . . couldn't she, Sam?" Lil touched her arm, sliding her fingers to touch the Australia-shaped mole.

Sharon felt heat rise in her cheeks.

"How do you like your steak, Lil?"

"Just this side of burnt, luv."

Bob took the food order of well-done steaks to Pete.

"It's such a niice place, your tidy town," Lil said. "The people seem friendly, too. This road trip of ours was such a good idea, 'ey? Leaving Cairns behind to look after itself. Sam and I thought we'd take off . . . and heaven help anyone who gets in our way." Lil shone up a laugh. "Shamayim!"

They moved over to the bistro garden at the rear of the pub. The night was still, cicadas chirping in the dark stretch of bush lit wan silver from a slice of moon. When the food arrived, Sharon noticed the first smile on Sam's face—though it didn't seem to sit right with him.

"What is this, Bob?" Lil pointed at the potato wrapped in foil.

"You don't like potatoes?"

"It's what's on it," Sam said. "An old habit of my mother's that she can't seem to break."

Lil pointed to the sour cream. "You can't boil a kid in its mother's milk, Bob."

Sam lifted a scoop of cream on his finger and smeared it onto his steak.

She smiled. "My son has never had a problem breaking old habits. But some old ways of mine, I just can't seem to move on from. It amuses Sam, doesn't it, luv?"

Sam smiled for the second time. It still didn't fit.

"I wonder, Bob, could you get them to do my steak again? I should have told the chef, but I just didn't expect this little surprise with a green salad. Everyone, please start." She paused. "Except for you, Sam. You wouldn't want to eat without your old mum, now, 'ey?"

Sharon watched him put his knife and fork down. He had stopped smiling and looked more comfortable for it.

* * *

"He gets these projects into his head, Sharon. Then he goes at it like a dog with a bone."

The men were playing the pokies, leaving them to some quiet women time.

"There could be worse hobbies than cricket, Lil." She looked to the bar of slouched-over men—arms folded, some still in their work gear, the sweat-soil smell of the earth not hidden by their roll-on Lynx. Some made an effort with a fresh collared shirt—short sleeves of course—a stripe of color somewhere, an advert for something to drink or drive on their backs. Friday night was family night, so the women sat all dolled up, long stints with the makeup kit, just as she had, their faces blushed with rouge, eyes lined another color, hair set into peroxide-streaked curls since the 80's had returned to Guburnburnin for a bit. They sat all pristine and shining like their men's cars after a Saturday polish. Pretty dolls with their not so pretty men.

"You have a man, Lil?"

"Sweetness, I do okay."

She grinned. "I'm sure you do. Sam's father around?"

"I've had two husbands, luv. The first was a brief encounter." She clicked her fingers. "Like that, it went. I was young. Mistakes, sweetness. We women can make mistakes."

She liked how Lil always spoke with a smile.

"He was a pig of course. Wanted his own way. Wanted to be the boss." Lil moved her hand over and touched Sharon's map of Australia. "You know, luv, I can barely remember what he looked like." Lil fingered the east coast of her mole. "He was a head taller than me, I remember that . . . and loud, he could sure shout I'll tell'ya . . . but I can barely see his face . . . A-dum." The last word said in an oily brogue. She bent closer in a whisper. "That's the second time today I've thought of him. But don't let Sam know we've talked about him, he gets so easily annoyed by the topic."

"You never kept in contact with him?"

"He's long gone, darl. Long gone." She cackled up a high screech. "But he left his mark, did that man of mine. He will be remembered!" She finished off the dregs of her soft drink, leaving a lipstick imprint at the end of the straw. "Promise me something, sweetness. Don't ever get stuck in an arranged marriage." Lil gave a shake to Sharon's arm. "What are we sayin'? With a maan like Bob, you can't go wrong, 'ey."

They turned to locate the source of a cheer that rose up behind them. She saw Pete and others circling where Bob and Sam were seated. Some peered over shoulders to strain a glance at the poker machine. One of the girls took a photo with a mobile. She heard Pete say to Bob, "You're a lucky bastard. It's been ten or more years since I've seen that." And Pete shook his head and moved away with a jealous sneer that she had become well accustomed to over the years.

Bob came on over after the back patting died down. He kissed her and then Lil and he stood there waiting with his schoolboy face on.

"I gather you had a win," she said.

"Five golden bananas. I've only seen three before. Ted reckons he's seen four. Pete, of course, said he's seen five, but I doubt he has."

"These boys with their games, Sharon."

"Games, Lil? This is big business tonight. Five thousand dollars in earnings . . . tax free."

"Jesus, honey."

He kissed them both again and went back to the jealous huddle.

Lil looked over and smiled, placing her hand again on Sharon's map of Australia that seemed to be a magnet for her finger. "It looks to me like Sam has taken a shining to your Bob." Lil turned back in their direction. "And he doesn't take a shining to many people luv, let me tell ya."

TWO

It was just before sunrise and the wheat field was the color of burnt sugar. Billy and his little sister had sneaked out to avoid the morning chores and planned to follow the path to the river, letting time run there for a spell.

When he first heard it, they were walking at the edge of the crop that rose up taller than their heads.

"What is it?" Sissy whispered.

They stopped, and Billy took her hand. "It's a lady," he said.

They kept there a minute before moving, still with hands held, following the sound into the caramel wheat. They didn't move far before stopping again.

"It might be an angel, Billy."

"There ain't no such things."

"There are too. Mrs. Shipping says I sing like an angel."

"You don't sing like that, I've heard you. Ain't nobody I know sings like that."

They stood holding hands and listened some more at the song that flowed through the grain; the dawn-lit wheat as if seen through brown frosted glass.

The children moved closer to where it came from, parting the wheat from their faces, then stopped again.

"She must be beautiful, Billy. To sing like that, she just has to be."

Sissy pulled him forward, but he kept anchored down. He wanted to listen, and the grain shifting around made too much noise.

They stood and listened some more—to a voice so light it seemed could float away, yet never fade.

"She might be a bird, Billy. Like the nightingale."

"Shoosh. That's just a story."

"How do you know? The nightingale could talk, remember." She let go of his hand. "Come on. I'm going closer."

They moved on deeper into the field, much further than they expected, as the nightingale sang up the high notes, clearer and more exquisite with every step. The brown frosted light started to yellow up, the song rising with the morning light.

They stopped again and listened a bit without talking. The lady seemed very close to them now.

"What is she singing about, Billy?"

"She's foreign, I can't understand it."

"She might be from She Lanka, like Mrs. Viddysinga."

They stood some more, but eventually the song drew them on. When they came to the edge of a tiny cleared space it was as clear as if the singer were in their living room. Standing in this open space, with a curtain of wheat circling around, the nightingale stood with raised arms and rolling head, as the song fell down and over them. Billy and Sissy looked on, with hands held, through a gap in the curtain of wheat at the edge of the space.

Neither of them dared to make a sound.

And Sam kept on with his song, as if they weren't there at all.

* * *

"It's a skin cancer, Lil. I think it's best we cut it out in one hit, without taking a biopsy."

"You better give me the details, Doc. My son always asks questions."

"A BCC . . . basal cell carcinoma. I'll write it down for you. And while you're here, I should take a look at the rest of your skin."

"Always happy to oblige."

She went behind the curtain as he made his notes.

"Take everything off except undies and bra, Lil."

"I'm ready for ya, luv."

He pulled the curtain away and she lay sprawled on her back, naked. He kept quiet about it. Experience had taught him this was best.

"Well, I can see where your skin has seen the sun, and where it hasn't." He took the liquid nitrogen canister in his hand. "I should spray some of these sun spots off as I find them."

"Very thorough of you, luv."

He lifted her freckled arm and sprayed the red scales a white freeze. Then her face, neck and other arm. The skin of her breasts and abdomen were a clean, pale white so he started down at her feet, moving slowly up, finding more scales to treat. As he moved up to her thighs, he saw her legs splay open an inch or two. He kept his focus on the spot he was examining, mid-thigh, even as her thighs parted further.

"You're very professional, luv."

He kept quiet and started on the other leg, down at her foot, moving higher, and as he did, her thighs drifted further apart and he found himself too distracted to continue.

"Very professional," she said in a different voice than before, richer, unaccented.

"Turn over on your stomach for me, Lil."

She rolled her large body over, the sheet of the examination couch bunching where the folds of fat resisted the move. He started at the calves and inched his way up, her legs now wide open, he was very aware of it, but he kept his focus on the red scales that had faded away by the time he reached the crease of her buttocks.

"Find anything interesting, luv?" Her crow twang returned.

"Nothing dangerous so far."

He moved to examine her back, finding an odd spot at the level of her left scapula. He took up his examination lamp that magnified the view—a small triangle of skin, a pedicle that lifted from the base like a tiny finger, without any features of a mole, or for that matter any skin tumor, at least in the books he had read. As he scanned the rest of her back, he saw the same type of spot, in the same location over her right scapula. The examination lamp confirmed their identical nature, a mirror image of each other.

"Nothing dangerous, luv?"

"How long have you had these two spots on your back?"

"Don't worry about those, darl. I've had them since birth . . . they run in the family." She laughed. "Call it a family curse."

He studied them under the bright lamp. "They're not getting bigger?"

"Actually, over the years they are getting smaller and smaller." She lifted her head to gaze at him. "I'm not tryin' to tell you your business, Doc, but it would be best just to leave'm be."

He pulled the curtain around and went back to his desk. "You're all clear to get dressed, Lil." And he completed the notes in her file.

She came out from the curtain and sat back down.

"You staying long in town, Lil?"

"We nomads don't have any fixed plans, luv." She rubbed at one of the frozen welts. "I've never had this done before." She smiled. "You've hurt me."

He looked at her arm and the old white scars that he knew were from previous treatments with the same technique he had just performed. "You've never had this done, Lil?"

"Not that I can remember."

He scratched some notes. "Perhaps, if you are planning on staying in town, I could do a more thorough check on you some time?"

"An oil change and grease, luv." She laughed. "Might be a good idea. This old body of mine hasn't been well cared for."

She uncrossed her legs and he saw she wasn't wearing any underwear. He tried to keep his gaze away. He noticed he was sweating. It didn't make any sense, this crossing over the line that pulled his gaze down—a well-defined, gold plated line that he had never crossed before.

It didn't make any sense at all.

Yet he kept his stare where it shouldn't have been.

* * *

The cricket oval was a rectangle of sprouting weeds and clods of red earth. The footy season had dug its way into the turf, leaving the heat of summer to fashion it dry and mottled. In the center, a twenty-two-yard strip had been plucked of all its grass and flattened into a pitch of baked clay. The oval was an open treeless space without a fence, and when the ball was well struck it would spill onto the road or vanish into the wheat fields that kept on as far as you could see.

"We're full up, Shaz," Pete said. "I told you yesterday and nothin's changed overnight."

Sharon looked over at Sam, who stood away from the others, tossing a red ball a few feet into the air and catching it again like a one armed juggler. "Pete, he looks so eager to play."

The publican grinned. "What's it worth for me?"

"The chance to do something nice for a change."

"That's not what I had in mind."

"I know what you have in mind, but that's where it's going to stay."

"And what about Teddy? I told him there was no spot for him. You gunna tell him we let a stranger play instead."

"If you let Sam play, I'll talk to Teddy."

"You're a sweet talkin tease, Shaz. You always were."

She walked away from the spite in his eyes and heard him shout out, "You owe me, Shaz. And I'm gunna collect."

Pete's guttural chuckle sprayed down on the back of her neck.

The rest of the Guburnburnin Hooters were men and boys, all of a drinking age. Most had played before in some way, a few just on mowed pitches in the backyards of their childhood, not tiny high-fenced spaces like in the city, where a broken window and over the fence is out, but in yards that sprawled into adjoining paddocks, no limit on how far you could hit a ball, no six and out. Most had played at school, some just in primary, though Tommy Richards had a long stint with the District under 21's.

They played haphazard in the rising heat of the day, each given some batting time and a bowl if they wanted. When it was Sharon's turn, she flung the bat at the first delivery and failed to connect.

"You're bowling too fast."

"Keep your eye on the ball," Pete shouted from his umpire's position.

The pads were heavy and hot on her legs, and she found it difficult to move the way she would like. She patted the pitch with her bat like she saw them do on the telly and took her stance again.

The ball flashed past her bat and she heard the stumps rattle apart. "Shit!"

"You're standin' too far away from the stumps, Shaz."

She struck at the next ball which caught the inside edge of the bat and ran down past the wicketkeeper into the wheat.

"Four!" She laughed, waving her arm in a long horizontal arc across her body as an umpire would.

Some of the players applauded, and she smiled and felt something just short of a thrill. For the rest of the innings she swung at the ball and connected as many times as the ball hit the stumps. There was no escape from the heat of the cloudless sky, and the sweat-mixed sunscreen stung at her eyes. But she was glad to be out—away from the kitchen and the dog that licked its balls too much.

When it was lunchtime, they took a break.

"I brought us a picnic lunch." She looked at Sam but he seemed preoccupied with dark eyed thoughts. "I hope you like chicken."

He nodded.

They sat away from the others and she knew it would raise eyebrows, but she didn't much care. She flattened the blanket down with her hand and took out the plastic plates and forks. Cold roast chicken and potato salad and slices of tomato fresh from the garden. Orange and mango juice.

"You play well," she said.

"How do you know?"

"The way you throw the ball. Very accurate."

He shrugged.

"I'm sure you'll get to bowl or bat after lunch."

"I hope to."

The truth was she wasn't too sure he would get a go. Pete was capable of letting him play out in the sun without touching the bat, just to niggle at her. And them sitting away from the others probably didn't help his chances either.

She studied Sam's poet face. "I like your mother."

"Most do."

"And what about her son?"

"Most don't," he said with no hint of bitterness.

She tasted the potato salad and was pleased—just enough garlic and celery salt. "And why is that, Sam?"

He shrugged again.

"Hey, maybe you talk too much." She watched his gaze move to the wheat field. "So tell me, are you a better batter or bowler?"

Sam moved his stare away from the plains, his eyes dancing with the question. "I was, at the beginning, better at batting. But my bowling technique has moved ahead a fair bit. My googly is well hidden, I think."

She laughed. "You keep your googlies well hidden, Sam. No displaying of the googlies, you hear me."

She watched him chomp into a chicken leg without any hint of a smile. The perfect symmetry of his face. His slicked back hair. Oiled. And those eyes.

"What's a googly, then?" she said.

"The ball spins off the pitch in the opposite way the batsman thinks it will."

"Sounds tricky."

"Takes practice."

"You got a girl, Sam?"

"You don't play well." He said this as he chewed at the meat.

She laughed. "I should be insulted."

"But you might play well, with practice." He put his plate down. "He doesn't know much."

"Pete?"

"He talks a lot but he doesn't know much. He is sort of right about watching the ball, but you have to watch it in the bowler's hand. By the time it's in the air, it's too late then. Every time you face up, watch the ball in his hand. Watch it leave his fingers. In time, you'll work out when and where it'll bounce, and once you've worked that out . . . you'll see it move off the pitch . . . its direction … for the speed is already known to you . . . and then you'll hit it in the middle of the bat. And eventually, you'll hit it where you want it to go."

She looked at his poet face, rapt with the joy of cricket, but kept quiet.

"If I were you, I wouldn't bother learning to bowl. Bat and field. Keep it simple. Bowling takes time to master—the synchronized movement of the feet and arms, the fingers, to hide your intentions. That's the key—to hide your intentions from the batsman. But it takes a lot of practice. Dedication and time."

In the distance, far off from where they were seated, a wide band of heavy clouds threw rain slantwise onto the wheat; the skyline painted with every shade of gray above the orange plain. By the time they had finished their lunch the low clouds had moved over to them, the rain raising steam off the asphalt of the road and the baked earth of the pitch.

And so, on this particular summer's day in Guburnburnin, no further play was had.

* * *

The toad croaked twice.

"Good arvo, Gordon." Lil's head poked through the open wire door. She covered her face with one hand. "Don't look at me, I'm such a mess after what that Doc of yours just did to me."

"He gave you a good spray over, by the looks of it."

"I look like a swarm of bees have fucked my face. Pardon the French."

"You should ask him for this cream he's got. It takes the layers off your skin, but you look ten years younger after it."

"And what age would that be, Gordon?"

Gordon studied her for a moment. "Twenty one."

She cackled. "You are a smooth one."

He looked at her welt-livid face and her grin and her dress that clung loose on her wide hips, and he tried to imagine her standing without a stitch of it on.

"Have you settled in okay, Lil?"

"Like a pig in the proverbial."

"And your son?"

"The same, Gordon. We are both very satisfied with your little abode."

He shuffled some papers on the desk, keeping his eyes low. "I hope I'm not sounding too . . . forward, Lil . . ." He felt a stammer building; this fat lip talk often came when he was flustered.

"Speak up, luv . . . don't ya get shy on me now."

He stacked the papers into a neat pile. "Well . . . seeing it's Saturday and I'm making some extra stew tonight—I always do a big pot on Saturdays and eat it over the next few days—"

"I bet you're a real gourmet, luv."

He knew he was babbling, but he didn't know how to stop himself. "Well, I'm partial to slow cooking, the heat way down, the veges, the beef, cooking slow in its juices. The meat falls off the bone when it's done right."

"You're makin' me salivaate, Gordon. I'm dripping."

He looked up at her grin and noticed some of the welts on her face were oozing clear liquid. "So, only if you are free, of course . . . I was wondering . . . whether you might like to share the stew. This evening."

"I must say, Gordon, you've takin' ya time with the invite." Her tight cheeks squeezed out more of the ooze as she laughed. "What time do you want me?"

Her voice grew sultry as she said this, and he felt his cock harden. "The great thing about slow cooking is we can eat whenever it pleases us."

"Then I'll freshen up and see you around seven. How's that sound to ya?" Her crow twang returned full force.

"That sounds just fine, Lil. It would just be . . . the two of us then?"

"I think we can keep Sam occupied elsewhere, don't you, luv?"

He watched her turn back out the door and the sun shone light through the thin cotton of her dress, showing the cheeks of her ass, round and heavy, and his breath kept held and he whistled with his swollen lips now gone, and his cock ached just like the old days.

* * *

"Billy, it's him."

"Shoosh, and don't point."

"But it's him, Billy. The nightingale."

Billy watched the nightingale move down the aisle of the store with a basket of groceries. When he turned in their direction they twisted their heads away and the boy grabbed a can of soup from the shelf and examined the label.

"Heinz classic mine-strony soup. I think we'll get this Sissy, you like mine-strony soup, don't ya?"

"I never had mine-strony soup, Billy."

"Yes you have, it's your favorite."

"No it's not . . . I like tomato best."

Billy kept his eyes low at the can as the nightingale moved past them. When he saw the long legs move further down the aisle he put the soup back on the shelf and lifted his gaze up at the man's tall, turned-away head.

"He bought Cheezels," Sissy said. "Two boxes. Get me some . . . it might be good for singin'."

"Don't be stupid . . . and keep your voice down."

"Well, I'm goin' to see what else is in his basket."

"Stay here, Sissy."

She followed the nightingale down the aisle, stopping just a few steps from him, then stood on her toes to gain a better view in the basket. Sam kept to his shopping as if she was invisible.

"Sissy," Billy stage whispered, "I'll get ya tomato if you come back now."

"I like Cheezels, too," she said looking up at the man.

His dark eyes kept on studying the shelves.

"I like Twisties more. Chicken the most." She came off her toes and looked at the same shelf as the nightingale. "Billy likes salt 'n vinegar chips . . . but they make me thirsty."

Sam moved a few steps down the aisle.

She followed him and watched him squeezing the fruit. "I like bananas and peaches but not apples. Apples are too hard on my tooth." She flashed a full set of teeth at him, wiggling one of the front ones with a finger.

From back where he had stayed, Billy hissed up again, "I'll get you Cheezels, Sissy . . . if you come back right now."

She turned and thought about going back but decided against it. Sam took some red apples from the shelf and added them to the basket.

"Mrs. Shipping says I sing like an angel."

His dark eyes finally swung away from the apples and down at her.

"If apples make me sing good, I can chew'm at the back. Do they make you sing good?"

"No."

"Then I won't get any." She raised herself on her toes and looked back into his shopping. "Do Cheezels make you sing good?"

"No."

"Anything in that basket make you sing good?"

"This makes you sing good." He pointed to his chest and up to the lump on his throat. "And here." He tapped his temple with a finger.

"Mrs. Shipping says it comes from the stumuck. She says to keep your back straight like a soldier. And to smile."

"Does she?"

"Yep. She says if you smile, you like doin' it. And if you like doin' it, you'll be good at it. Billy smiles, but only pretends to sing . . . nothin' ever comes out of his mouth. Billy's my brother, that's him over there. He says nobody sings as good as you."

The boy watched the nightingale's dark eyes move over to him and he felt a bit strange. He wanted to go over but his legs didn't seem to agree.

"You goin' to sing in McCarthy's farm again, Mister . . . ?"

"I might."

"Can you sing in the afternoon, after school's out?"

"No."

"Can you teach me to sing like you?"

"No."

"Can we come and see you sing again?"

He stole one of the black grapes and chewed into it, spitting the pips into his palm. "I sing too early for you."

"No you don't. We're up before dark every mornin'. I feed the chickens and Billy cuts the wood and we both change the hay, although Billy does most of it."

He looked down at her. "Just the two of you. No one else."

"Rusty might follow. He's our dog."

"If anyone else comes, I will get annoyed. You understand?"

"Rusty might come. We can't tie him up because he keeps the foxes from killin' the chickens. That's his job . . . but he ain't that good at it."

"I mean other people."

"Okay, Mister, nobody else but us. I promise." She bent down and picked a grape and chewed it like Sam, spitting bits of pip and grape into her hand. "Who taught you to sing, Mister?"

"A man . . . when I was a boy."

"I didn't know men could sing before I heard you. Neither did Billy."

He turned to stare at Billy. The stare made him feel even more like he wanted to crawl away. But he still couldn't move.

"How old is your brother?"

"Ten. I'm five, but'll be six on my birthday cumin' up. You want to come to my party?"

"No." He kept his gaze at the boy. "Do you have horses?"

"Yep. I have a pony called Black Beauty. Billy's is a grown horse, but it's old. Dad reckons he'll be dead soon. My name is Sarah Anne McConachy."

Sam looked down at Sissy like she was a packet of biscuits.

"I'm might be goin' now, Mister."

Sissy moved back down the aisle to Billy, still standing dumb in front of the soup cans. "Billy, the nightingale said he would teach us to sing if we don't bring anyone else assept Rusty." She grabbed his hand. "And can you get me a box of chicken Twisties. He said they make you sing good."

* * *

The skin of the basted chicken crinkled into orange-brown dimples over the bird, the baked potatoes and pumpkin cut into healthy chunks, the gravy made with the pan juices and a touch of brandy like Gran used to use.

Sharon wiped her hands against her apron and laid the rest of the table. She hummed as she did it—Denim and Lace—93.5 Sunny Day

FM having played hits of the seventies this week, that brought Guburnburnin a decade ahead of where it was currently living, which was two decades or more from everywhere else in the world. She wiped the rinsed glasses and looked out the kitchen window at the cotton field that had shifted to a dim olive in the dusk. Little Jamie hadn't shown up at all today, not even when she woke before Bob to get everything right for cricket. Little Jamie always popped into her bed when she woke. But not this morning.

Denim and lace, rich or poor or come what may, I'm gonna have you anyway, dressed in denim and lace. She danced with the glass and felt light from the wine she had drunk while the gravy was simmering. The napkins completed the table and she called out to Bob that everything was ready for him. *Dressed in denim and lace.*

They sat together on the large dining table.

"I love Saturday roast, don't you, Bob? We always had it on Sundays at Mum's, but I don't think I could do without it on Saturday."

"You might have to, if cricket doesn't get washed out."

"Pete went on about us going back to the pub after the game. I think I understand his motivation for starting the team."

He cut thin slices of chicken breast onto Sharon's plate. "Pete is always looking to make an extra quid." He smiled. "Did you see his face when I won that jackpot?"

"Sam wasn't keen on the pub, so we didn't end up going." She hummed Denim and Lace.

"He's a strange bloke."

"Pete or Sam?"

"Sam. There's nothing strange about Pete."

"But I'm sure you could find other words for him."

"I might." He dissected a leg from the chicken.

She looked at Bob and smiled. Since she had known him, even before they got together, he had rarely said a bad word about anyone. She liked this about him.

"You get to know him better?" he said.

"Pete or Sam?"

"I see you're in one of those playful moods."

"It was good to get out today. Darling, you were right."

"What's his story then?"

She took a sip of wine. "I don't exactly know. He likes cricket, you can't keep him quiet about it. But he's what Mum calls a Captain Ahab. Dark and mysterious. 'There goes Captain Ahab' she used to say when I was a kid . . . she said it about Charlie Roberts all the time."

"Robbo? He wasn't mysterious, he just didn't like your mother. She made him nervous. If that's all it takes, there's quite a list of Captain Ahabs around town."

"Shame about Robbo's wife. Pete says it's pretty serious. I feel sorry for him . . . all alone on the farm. At least his kids are boarding. I shouldn't say it, especially when he's down on his luck, but when we were at school there was a rumor that Robbo was seen rooting a goat. Kaz Phillips said that's why he was the first boy in class to get hair on his chin."

"Maybe your mum saw him do it."

She laughed. "She would have shot him if it was our goat."

"Well, if you girls weren't so stuck up, only wanting to date the city boys, good looking fellas like us wouldn't be forced to have our way with the livestock."

"Ah, now I understand. And what was your favorite livestock, Bob?"

"At school or now?"

She grinned. "Surprise me."

"Well, at school you start small, like Robbo did. A goat, sheep . . . merino if you can find one, lanolin's good for you. But now it's a different story. So, when you're tucked in bed, sound asleep like a princess, I like to sneak out with Betsy. That old mare of yours is always up for it."

She gulped her wine. "You leave Betsy out of this . . . I've had her since school . . . the poor sweet thing."

"So you think Sam is rooting the odd hoofed creature? A good looking fella like him should be able to do better than that."

"You must say it's a bit odd, going on a road trip with your mother."

"If it was your mum, yes."

"Don't you think it's strange they don't have a car? Public transport around this part of the State is pretty well non-existent. I mean, it was pure chance you stumbled on them out at Simpson's road."

"They seem to get around okay. And you can't help giving Lil a hand . . . even when she doesn't ask for it."

"Let's get them over for dinner soon," she said.

"See what I mean?"

She hummed Denim and Lace.

Bob cut a slit into the leg and poured gravy over the meat. "I had a chat with Doc today."

Her wine glass stopped halfway back to the table. "You sick?"

"Fit as a fiddle. But he was on a tea break, and we had a chat." Bob topped up her glass with the chardonnay. "I wanted to get an update on those tests of yours. To understand them."

She looked up at him and noticed he had yet to start eating.

"He didn't tell me though. Confidentiality and all. He seemed a bit on the evasive side. Not like Doc, normally."

She kept on eating. She wasn't going to spoil the mood.

"But I was more interested in the tests themselves. Understanding the plumbing side of it."

She raised her eyes. "Well, perhaps you should ask me about my plumbing . . . and not put him in an awkward position."

He stopped and adopted his wounded schoolboy look. "I've tried. But every time I mention it, you get cranky."

"Bob, I've had such a nice day—"

"Like you're getting cranky now."

"Why don't you start your chicken, it's going cold."

"You're just as evasive as Doc. You not hiding anything from me?"

She slammed the knife and fork down and the wine glass shifted and spilled some. "Can't you drop those bloody tests? I've told you, he needs to get them all back before the plumbing—as you so tenderly call my reproductive organs—can be truly sorted out."

They both were quiet for a bit.

She sighed. "You have an amazing ability to bring me down sometimes, Bob. An amazing ability."

He shifted the vegetables around on his plate. "It's good to know I'm amazing at something."

She watched him push his plate away and noticed he still hadn't taken a bite. The dog barked near the side of the house. The air-conditioner rattled. And little Jamie came over and sat on her knee.

* * *

Gordon fussed over the table for the third time. The cheese and pâté were cheap but the best the local store had in stock. He wished there was bread—the hard-crusted baguettes that he had practically lived on in Europe. He could do without the cheese but he wished he had bread. He liked the wine, a Coonawarra red, it was his last bottle and he had kept it for his birthday, but this was better than that—he had company and he usually didn't for his birthday. Last year Sally had invited him over for a drink and a meal at the pub, but he thanked her for it and kept on home. Sally had her family so he didn't want to intrude.

He moved over to the kitchenette and tasted the gurgling stew in the slow cooker. A bit salty but only a bit. The meat was soft and he peeled off some strands with the spoon and it was good now but would only get better. He went back to the table and wasn't sure about the candle—too eager, perhaps. He took it away. And put it back. And thought about taking it away again. The room light had no dimmer, it was too bright with it on, so the candle would be just right, if it wasn't too eager. Treat'm mean to keep'm keen. He had never lived by it, but thought there might be some truth to it.

Jesus, I am lonely.

The CD player was ready to go. Sade, The Best of, Smooth Operator, it was perfect but perhaps too eager, like the candle. It would have to be one or the other, so he went back to the table and took the candle away again but kept it handy just in case things moved faster than he guessed. The round table was small and the chairs were close, not opposite—he would sit closer to the kitchen, she on his right side, his good ear side. He turned the CD player on, Sade and the stew filling the room, and he thought about bringing the candle back but didn't. And he fussed over the table some more.

Just before seven, he went into the clean bathroom—he always kept it spotless, the new toilet roll, soap, the mirror without a blemish; a choice of hand or bath towel. Maroon. He put his hand to his mouth and detected a hint of stale something. He swigged the Listerine kept under the sink, gargled long at the back of his throat, spat and gargled again. He rinsed the sink down and wiped it dry and brought his hand to his mouth and nose. Cool mint fresh. Then to the bedroom with the never-used sheets, the maroon spread, silk or something like it, satin probably, the bed could be bigger, a standard double, he wasn't tall so in the small room it was more practical, gave him more walking space, more room for the telly. He didn't want to get ahead of himself, but tonight he wished it was bigger, a queen.

Loneliness could eat his insides away when it wanted; creep up on him if he didn't keep busy—like when the motel was empty, or when it was full and noisy, with couples or families with lots of kids. And especially at dinnertime, irrespective of the season.

It was 7.15, so she was technically late, but she might need some more time to get ready—makeup time, to hide Doc's handiwork, he hoped. He sat on the couch and listened to Sade and thought about taking a sip of the red but resisted. The stew filled the room, yellow bright from the strong ceiling light, and he got up again and set the candle back on the table and lit it this time, to make it look used.

His knee started to ache, a niggling reminder of his age. Age had left him a stain or two, and he hadn't found a way to scrub them clean. You know you're old when you watch a movie for the second time and can't remember what's going to happen. Age and loneliness seemed to come to his life as a couple.

When it was 7.30, he started to feel uneasy. He was sure she'd said seven, so she might have decided against it. He had been out before to make sure the wire door was unlocked. Twice. He had said the food could be eaten at any time—maybe fashionably late, then. But she might have changed her mind. The ooze on her face. The makeup couldn't be good for the spots. Might cause infection. Doc might not let her put it on. He thought of her hips loose against the cotton. He liked her smile and didn't care about the spots but she might not know it. He could have waited for a better time. He shouldn't have opened the bottle. His birthday bottle. He would have to drink it now, even if she didn't show.

Jesus, I'm lonely.

At 7.45 the toad croaked twice when he went outside. She was at the end room, Sally had said. She was tidy, Sally said as well. There was little to clean up—even the loo. He quiet stepped along the cement, but didn't make it to the end. Room 3 was lit inside. Room 3 was lit and had that muffled sound he had got to know over the years, a sound that bounced off the double brick walls but spilled easily through the window. The thin glass could never keep it from the landing. The moans were always loudest on the landing.

There was a sinking loneliness in his stomach. He liked to keep to himself at night, not stray outside when couples were boarding. He was a handsome boy, Sam. Strange eyed, but handsome. He must have pulled a bird from the pub, and why not? Good luck to him. But he wished he didn't have to hear it.

He quiet stepped to number 4. The room light was off. The telly screen didn't flicker. The curtains were open and he saw the bathroom light was off as well. She might be asleep. It was early but she might have fallen asleep. It would explain it.

He put his hand to the window to shield what little stray light there was. The bed looked made up. He thought about knocking but he didn't want to disturb next door.

Perhaps she had gone to the store.

No, it was Saturday and it closed at five. Six if you wanted petrol. There was only the pub. A bottle of wine, perhaps.

It made some sense. You meet someone new at the pub and get chatting and the time moves on, especially if there was some confusion about the dinner, that comment about eating it at any time. So he would walk on down to the pub and have a look. Just poke his head in the door—maybe to buy another bottle, though Pete kept only the cheap stuff. He would leave a message on the office door and be back before ten minutes.

He quiet stepped on the cement and stopped at the high pitch moans outside number 3 again. The room light was on, and the television too, and a thin slice of inside could be made out from the not quite drawn curtains. From where he stood, the insides looked like a scene painted on a thin tie. A bit of white wall, a bit of picture frame. When he moved his head, the tie moved too and the insides flashed across in a thin-striped wave.

He moved a step to the side, his head as well, so the stripe spanned further and a bit of the refrigerator came into view. A silver and white tie and the groans from somewhere else he couldn't see.

It was dark outside and the porch light was out. There was no moon. It was dark and they couldn't see him. Couldn't hear him because of the telly and their high-pitched moans. He moved more.

A stripe of bed came into view. A shoulder. Black hair. Black hair and eyes and olive chest skin flashing across the tie-stripe view. He moved a bit closer, the tie widening thicker, the black hair thrashing around, black eyes, mouth open. Tongue, red pink.

He looked back at the street but the moonless night hid him well.

And so he moved closer—though, unlike at number 4, he had no need to put his hand to the glass this time. The insides splayed open their view easy to him, the bed, and the moans, all open mouthed, and the rest of it all.

THREE

Billy and Sissy sat cross-legged on the ground. They were neither in the cleared circle proper, nor in the tall wheat. Rather, they sat at the edge, their knees sticking out, their heads in, which is where they stayed throughout the performance. Sarah played with a bunch of little red flowers that sprouted at her feet. She pulled the petals off and blew fine dust from their stems. Billy, though, couldn't stop watching the nightingale.

Rusty hadn't liked the singing. He had come with them as far as the crop but headed back home, low shouldered, as soon as they could hear the singer. It seemed like he wanted to put his paws over his ears, like when the New Year's fireworks went off at the pub, or lightning struck at the outhouse a couple of months back.

When they arrived the morning was still blue-brown. Sarah wanted to be there before the nightingale started, so she had dragged Billy out of bed when he was still sound asleep. But even before they had reached McCarthy's gate, they heard the wheat singing, and she felt cheated and started to run ahead into the crop.

The nightingale hadn't even noticed they were there. Sarah had waved up at him when they first sat down but it seemed his eyes looked through them, or were closed, which sometimes they were, especially when his arms rose and his voice was at its sweetest. And even when a song was finished, and his arms sank down, his head dropping to his chin, he still didn't seem to notice them, even though Sissy made some feigned coughs.

But before she had time to say something proper, a new song lifted up from the circle and Sam's rolling head and shut eyes moved to a sound as beautiful as the last.

At the end of the final song he moved his neck in a slow full circle, rubbed at his face and scalp, then began to leave, all without noticing they were there.

"Why do you sing like a girl, Mister?"

"Sissy, shoosh."

"You said he sung like a girl too."

Sam stopped near the furthest point of the circle and moved his neck around again, his back still facing them. "I don't sing like a girl."

"You sing great," Billy said.

Sam turned around and his dark eyes found them for the first time.

"I still think you sound like a girl, Mister."

"Sissy, shut up."

"Stand up," Sam said softly.

The girl stood at the edge of the wheat, then moved a step into the circle.

"Sing something."

She turned to gauge Billy's reaction but didn't wait for his approval. "Jesus loves me, by Sarah Anne McConachy." She stood with her back arched high and brought her arms up like the nightingale had.

> "Jesus loves me
> Yes I know,
> For the Bible tells me so,
> Little ones to Him belong,
> They are weak, but He is strong."

Sam lifted his hand, and she stopped.

"It goes longer, Mister."

"You know what you sound like?"

"An angel?"

"A girl."

She twisted to look down at Billy.

"Do I sound like that?" Sam said.

Billy, still seated low at the edge of the curtain of wheat, finally found his voice. "No, you don't."

"No." He looked down at Billy. "I don't." His eyes pierced. "Stand up."

Billy stood and brushed the chaff from his jeans, surprised he was able to move again.

"Sing something."

"He doesn't sing, Mister."

"Sing something."

"She's right. I'm not that good at singin'."

"Sing something."

He breathed in and brought his arms up. "Jesus loves me—"

"No more Jesus."

Billy looked into the wheat for a clue, then expanded his chest again and raised his arms,

> "Queensland is our home . . . we're the lucky ones
> Queensland is the only place to be
> From the Isa to the coast . . . we've such a lot to boast
> Queensland is the only place for me."

Sam nodded. "I sing only from here." He pointed at his high forehead. "But you sing from that little lump in your throat. You have something that I don't. You just need to sing from your head. The rest you have."

"But he doesn't like singin', Mister."

Sam looked at her like a packet of biscuits again.

Billy said, "Would you teach me, Mister?"

"He said he wouldn't, Billy. I told you."

"I've been told you have a horse."

"Mr. Ed."

"You ride him much?"

"Have to. Dad says he'll sell him for pet food if I don't."

"What about me, will you teach me to sing?" Sarah said.

Sam looked down at her. "No."

"Well, you're not teachin' Billy, then."

Sam looked at the boy. "You're ten, yes?"

"Just turned."

"It's not fair if you teach him and not me."

He kept at Billy. "You would practice?"

"Yes, Sir."

"You won't disappoint me?"

"Not sure. I don't think so."

"It's not fair!"

Sam gave her a quick glance. "You have time, little lady. All the time in the world."

"Mrs. Shipping says I sing like an angel." She stamped her feet. "Don't laugh Mister. . . . she really did."

The nightingale turned and moved out of the cleared circle into the wheat field lit orange by the early dawn. "I'll see you tomorrow then, Billy."

The girl kicked into the wheat chaff. "I ain't going to do your chores, Billy. And anyway, it's too early for stupid singin'. And I already sing like an angel and you don't."

But Billy didn't care about chores. He was going to learn to sing like the nightingale.

* * *

The toad croaked twice.

"Coo-ee, Gordon." The high pitch crow came from the office.

He sat at the table and continued to eat his Cornflakes.

The toad croaked again.

"Gordon, you in there?"

He poured some more milk into his bowl.

"You hiding from me, luv?"

The sun streamed in from the back window, cutting a bright slice across the table, warm against his neck. Gordon waited for the toad to croak her exit but it didn't come as the milk started to warm in the bright half of the table.

"I know you're in there, Gordon."

He stood up, put the carton back in the fridge; and waited for the toad to speak.

"I've got all day, luv."

Gordon stood and leant against the kitchen bench; the empty wine bottle, the cheese turned butter-yellow with beads of sweat on its surface, the dissolved stump of candle wax.

"Ain't I a payin' customer, Gordon?"

He saw the red mop of hair through the beaded entrance, the same color that had kept niggling at him all night, images that wouldn't leave, like a stone in a shoe. He pushed off from his leaning position and went through to her.

"There you are. You look very rugged unshaven, Gordon. Very masculine."

"What can I do for you, Lil?"

She looked into his eyes and he felt his breath catch.

"What about last niight, luv?"

"What about it?"

"Our dinner daate."

"At seven."

"Seven? Was it really seven, Gordon?"

He looked at her face. The spots had formed into yellow-brown cornflake crusts.

"Time must have got away from me, luv. But I came, Gordon. I came and found the back in 10 minutes sign on the door." She smiled at him. "That was a long fucking ten minutes, Gordon."

Who was this woman? "I wasn't feeling well."

She stared at him and said without the Queensland twang—now flat, deep throated, "Don't lie to me, Gordon. It annoys me."

He swallowed an invisible lump and his breath seemed wanting for a second.

She laughed. "A woman's got to get herself ready . . . with this face of mine it takes time."

"I don't think you've been honest with me, Lil." He shifted his gaze to the table. "With your supposed son and all. I didn't mean to pry, but when you didn't show last night I went out to knock on your door . . . and passed Sam's room . . ." He looked up but not into her eyes. "It's none of my business, Lil. You're an attractive woman." He wanted to look at her but didn't have the courage.

"Oh, now I understand, Gordon. Thank you for telling me the truth––a quality I admire."

He looked up and saw the smile that took up most of her face. He liked how she didn't hide the burnt crusts with makeup. He liked the confidence about her. And something else he couldn't define.

"I can trust you to keep our little secret to yourself, Gordon? This town of yours wouldn't understand."

Who would he tell? Sally, perhaps, but no one else. "Of course, Lil."

"You're a good man."

He rearranged the stationary on the desk. "Sally will be in around midday, to clean, if that suits you both."

"Lovely."

He looked down at the table again. "And if you feel like a home cooked meal . . . Sam of course is invited . . . I could make some extra any time. The pub food is okay, but for a change a home cooked meal is nice."

"That would be very pleasant, Gordon." She said this with a dialect that was somewhere between Queensland and a place more exotic. "I might just keep you to that. Tell me, how does a girl keep occupied around here, 'ey?"

"Well, there's plenty of work on the farms, most are on one . . . or looking after the family. Most have them."

"They marry young here, the silly things."

"I guess it's the boredom, Lil."

"Shamayim! We oldies know better, 'ey Gordon?"

"I guess so." He started to scribble his signature on each of the sheets for no good reason. A heavy sense of dread, that stayed with him throughout the night, the early wakening hours until the sun rose dry mouthed, came over him. He tilted his gaze to her, and she stood a great mop of red with a grin that seemed different than before. It came now from the eyes.

"You have the motel to keep you busy, luv."

"It's pretty slow. When there's a funeral we're usually full. During the footy season sometimes the lads stay on at the weekend. Domestic disputes give us the longest stayers. Not so long ago, we had one stay for nearly four months before his wife took him back. But this isn't a travelling route any more. Never really was."

"It found you, Gordon."

"My wife's idea more than mine."

"And she flew the coop?"

"She didn't find it as exciting as she thought."

"And left you alone, dear Gordon."

He sorted the papers into a different pile. "You're not looking to buy a motel by any chance, Lil?"

She cackled. "Very tempting, Gordon. Change the name to The Divorce and Death Arms. Shamayim! Where did you get Coral Waters? Don't tell me . . . keep it a mystery. But no, Gordon, I've never owned real estate in my life. Sam has wanted to on occasion, but not me. And I managed to talk him out of it."

"Very sensible, Lil."

There was silence for a bit.

"Well, I'm off. I might explore a while, take in the air before it gets too hot." She moved to the door. "And if it's okay with you, Gordon, when it comes time, Sam might not be able to make dinner."

And he felt a rush bright on his cheeks as the toad croaked twice her exit.

* * *

The road kept flat all the way, flanked by wheat chaff and eucalypt parts, leaves turned the color of the falling bark, twisted corrugated sheets, branches haphazard, tufts of grass with sticky seeds, everything dry, even though the rain had not long gone.

The country around was flat like the road and spread furrowed land that sprouted the occasional tree stuck down and out of place. Nothing moved at all—the warm, dry air, clouds faint and high and sparse. Everything was still.

Lil turned into the first dirt road, keeping to the side, away from the potholes that were carved deep in its center; the red dust a thin layer on her shoes. She looked out of place with her knee length white dress, her cornflake-crusted arms bare to the sun, her face hidden by the wide brim of her hat. She moved not as a person, but as a scarecrow on the blood red road.

When the sun had raised up a couple of hands, she went through an open gate and followed another dirt road at the same strolling pace. The path remained flat, green wheat fields on either side, the rising sun hot on her arms. Up ahead, the land lifted into a gentle slope and the sun reflected off the home that sat on it, a bright white. Directly above, a crow wheeled and swooped down near her, but she moved at the same pace without ducking her shoulders or moving her hands. The bird landed further on and sat at the road's edge, watching her come closer. But when she reached it she went past without changing her stride. And when she was well beyond, the crow lifted its black wings and took off along the path and sidled her head again, but she kept on going without flinching, eventually through another gate that lead to the homestead bright white in the sun.

Up close, the house was old and frayed, the white really a sun-faded yellow or light green, peeling off in blistered strips, the galvanized roof rusted in parts, lifting off in others. Around the place, the wide-eyebrow roof of the veranda leant with the tilt of the house, hunched over with the slope of the land.

Lil opened the back door that lead into the kitchen, took a mug from the cupboard, and drank three cups of water. It was cooler inside, the window shutters drawn to keep it that way, the air stale without a draft. She moved down the hall past old black and white portraits behind glass, family shots some, others of a young man in an army uniform—cavalry though the horse wasn't there—smaller ones with the same uniform and the Pyramids behind, and a fat cheeked baby with a lacy bonnet tied tight around the neck. She glanced at these old portraits for the barest of moments before entering a bedroom as dim as the hall.

The house sat still like the outside, and the heat managed not to break through, and the sun moved from its peak and started to fall lower in the sky. The land gave no sound at all. And she lay with her eyes closed but didn't sleep a second.

Outside, the crow hopped on the tufted lawn, fossicking for insects.

It was late afternoon when she heard the sound of a car coming through the gate. The car door open and shut. The back door swing and closed. The noise became harsher; the burp of the fridge, the sound of a plate or cup on the kitchen sink, a chair drawn out and sat on, the movement of shoes on lino.

Lil got off the bed, arched her neck to relieve the stiffened sinews of age, and walked down the hallway, past the family photographs, into the kitchen, and stood before the seated man, who looked up at her.

He saw the shape at the hall's entrance, and he squinted up at it. He had to look twice because you just don't expect to see a stranger like she was, your brain doesn't register it at first. But he looked again and he tried to process what he saw, to say something.

She beat him to it. "You must be Robbo, luv. I'm sorry to hear your wife is ill."

She stood lit with the sun from the open shutters, her breasts and wide hips flab white, her hairless mound, her arms and face and legs mottled, darker, her smile. And he watched a hand move up from her plump side; saw what it did; then the other hand, fingers; and witnessed what most men could never imagine, let alone ever hope to see.

* * *

"Who's that? Are you seriously asking that question, Lil?" Pete said.

"Deadly, sweetness."

"How long have you lived in Queensland?"

"Long enough."

Lil and Sam sat at the bar in the early evening amongst hunched regulars; the air heavy with the scent of XXXX and sweat.

Pete said, "Hey Mickey, she's askin' who's the bloke in the photo."

"You not from Queensland, Lil?"

She turned her head down the limb of the bar. "I am sitting here, aren't I, luv?"

"Sam, tell your mum who it is."

Sam looked at the photo but didn't reply.

"Where the fuck have you two been livin'?"

"Pete, I think you are teasing old Lil," she said.

"Tell her, Pete." The livid regular lifted his schooner like an appendage and the publican moved over to the framed photograph and tilted it horizontal but kept quiet.

"Is it a relative, luv?"

"Hear that, Pete. She's askin' is it a relative."

"Tell her he's your brother, Pete."

The publican turned to his parishioners. "Yeah, that's right, he's my brother."

"I think you really are teasing old Lil." She flashed something short of a smile.

Pete shook his head. "Jesus, Lil. What rock have you been livin' under. It's King Wally."

She studied the photograph that held pride of place in the center of the pub, just above the cash register. Where a picture of the Queen would have been in the old days—now replaced by a monarch of a different lineage. "He doesn't look like a king to me, luv."

"King of fuckin' Queensland. Best footy player in the history of the sport."

"Mal was better," someone said downstream.

"Mal was very good. But Wally was there when it mattered."

"True that, Pete."

"My old man said Churchill was the best he's seen," upstream said.

"Who the fuck was that?"

"That's what my old man says."

Downstream said, "How can Wally be your brother, Pete? We ain't related." Laughter drifted in the stale air.

"How good would it be if he was?"

"Nah, you'd get sick of hearing that's Wally's brother every time you came in a room."

"Think about who you'd meet in those rooms."

"Mickey's met Choppy Close."

"True, down at Cunnamulla. He came strolling in the pub like he was just one of the locals."

"You get his autograph, Mickey?"

"Better . . . a photograph . . . it's in the livin' room at home. I framed it."

"If you were Wally's brother you could meet Fatty and Mal and Alfie . . ."

"I'd love to meet Alfie."

"And Locky."

The bar signaled its approval in unison.

"And free tickets to Origin. Maybe sit on the bench."

"Mickey, now you are fuckin' dreamin'."

The faces of the hunched regulars glistened a lighter shade of ruddy brown, sepia as their schooners, the furniture, the walls.

"You goin' to eat at the bar, Lil?" Pete said.

"We might just do that. You have any vegetarian meals?"

"The chicken is good."

Sam looked up from his lemon, lime, and bitters but didn't speak.

Pete wiped down a glass. "You don't say much, do you Sam?"

Sam's dark eyes drifted back down to the slab of the bench.

"If you're still eager to play cricket, I'll have to put you 12th man. I told Shaz . . . we're all full up."

"That's a shame," Sam said, quiet and deadpan.

"But you'll get a game one day, someone's bound to be busy. Especially at harvesting time or school holidays."

"He has to carry the drinks if he's 12th man," someone said further away. Guffaws filled the low-lit space.

"You teasing my boy, now?" Lil said.

"Just havin' a laugh, Lil."

She smiled. "It looks like teasing to me, Pete."

"Looks can be deceivin'."

"Good one, Pete," the further away man said.

He grinned as he poured the XXXX on tap. "What you two havin' for dinner then?"

"Two salads," Sam said with his head still down.

"What do you want on it?"

He looked up at the publican. "We want nothing on it."

"It's hardly worth the cook to get off his bum for two salads."

"We don't want any meat on our salad. If there was . . . it wouldn't be a salad."

"Want dessert?"

"What about some fruit?" Lil said.

"We have fruit salad."

"Fresh?"

"Fresh out of a can."

"We'll pass," Sam said.

"It's not the fuckin' Hilton you know."

Sam looked up with dark eyes and kept staring at the publican.

"Well it fuckin' isn't."

Downstream said, "My father was pretty adamant Churchill was the best he's seen."

Pete said, "Your father wouldn't know what day it is. Who'd he play for?"

"Souths."

"Like Mal."

"Not Brisbane. South Sydney."

"Fuck off," Pete said.

The bar approved with slouched over laughter.

Lil took a sip from her drink. "Now, Pete, I'm sure chef can oblige this little salad whim of ours. And we might eat out back. It's such a lovely night." She eased her fat hip off the stool. "A lovely night, in the lovely tidy town of Goo-burn-burnin.'"

The bar fell silent for a while. Heads low to tipped up schooners.

Upstream said, "You know what. I'd like to meet Big Artie. What a champion he was."

Out back the air came off the land dry and tepid. Dusk fell on the beer garden and the cicadas sang, and the muffled chat of the regulars couldn't be heard from where they sat, alone, waiting for their vegetarian salad without the chicken.

Lil said, "There you go. You can be such a good boy when you want. I'm so proud of you, Sam." And she gave him a kiss on the cheek. "I know you don't like it here."

"It's all right."

"But I'm getting too old to move all the time."

"Then we'll stay a while."

"Really? It's fine by you?"

Sam looked out at the dry hidden land and never replied.

"I've got to tell you . . . you're still my hero, Sam." And she kissed him again.

* * *

Sharon had watched him move in and out of the kitchen, motion that seemed to lack any sense of purpose. Pointless.

She smiled at little Jamie who sat at the table, kicking his legs.

"You eating tonight, Bob?" She watched him look in a drawer for something. "Well, if you're eating, let me know. I've already had a bite."

She watched him close the drawer empty handed. Pointless. Little Jamie kept kicking his legs and smiling at her.

"I can heat up the chicken. That's if you're eating."

She saw Bob move out and down the hall and out of sight. And the room sat silent for a spell before the dog scraped at the wire door with its paw or nose or whatever.

She turned to the table and asked little Jamie whether he would like to draw—maybe a picture of Mummy. He liked drawing pictures of Mummy.

And she wiped down the bench again, rinsed the sink, washing the suds off the metal. The lemon and basil of the dishwashing liquid. The pointless dog outside that needed feeding.

She heard Bob come back from whatever he'd been doing, go to the fridge and take the milk, low fat, or fat free, whatever, and pour the cornflakes and sugar and milk into a bowl. And sit where little Jamie was sitting. Right on top of where he was sitting.

How dare he sit there?

She wished him away, but Bob never responded to her wishes, the sound of munching flakes loud.

How dare he?

"I might go out for a bit." And she saw a dab of cornflake at the corner of his mouth drop as he said it.

"I'm going to bed early, so come in quiet."

"You won't know I'm here."

She took the gloves off and laid them over the tap to dry. Some of the suds dropped and spoiled the clean, wet metal. She wiped the sink again and hung the towel to dry like the gloves. Switched the radio on to catch the news.

The Prime Minister said he would not rest until the terrorist threat was reduced. "In Australia we have values that other places may not share. It is these values that make us Australian, and our borders must be protected from those who don't share them. We decide who enters our land, and not a report generated on the other side of the planet without any responsibility for the consequences."

The coroner has yet to finalize his findings on the suspected suicide of ex-Australian Test Cricketer, Doug Janeway, who was found by his wife at home last Wednesday. Mr. Janeway played in two Test series in the late 60's, and captained Queensland to take the Sheffield Shield during the same period. He averaged 44 in first class cricket and was a handy leggie, said ABC cricket commenter, Henry Little. He was 72.

The fate of Tai Chi, a panda in the Queensland Zoo, remains in the hands of veterinarians . . .

Little Jamie had gone away. He always hated the news.

Sharon closed her eyes, rubbing at her neck, the side, the back, into her scalp.

The sound of the cornflakes and the radio broadcast. The sound of the moisturizer bottle squirting two dollops onto her palm.

The sound of dolor.

* * *

Bob sat at one tip of the U shaped bar, alone, as much as anyone could sit alone in Guburnburnin. The pub had settled boozed up into the evening. Bent over conversations in sepia surrounds. The XXXX kept him low on his stool and some of his worries at bay. Any more though, this beer-soaked courage might turn into something frightening. So he sat not touching the dregs in his schooner and kept his head down.

Pete interrupted his solitude. "What news with you, Bob?"

He lifted his glass off the table and examined the dregs. "The cotton crop should be fair."

"Robbo's havin' problems."

"Bollworm, I heard."

"Come on sudden, just in the last week. Teddy told him to hit 'em with pesticides way back, but he didn't listen."

"Robbo wants to go organic."

"Fuckin' stupid idea if you ask me," the publican said.

Bob tilted his glass and looked at the bubbles that made strings in the amber liquid. "It's good if you can pull it off. Let nature take care of the bollworm."

"Then why don't you do it? You've never been shy of chemicals."

He kept his stare at the remains of his schooner. "Maybe I'm just a lazy bastard."

Pete wiped down a glass. "You up for another?"

"I'll sit on this, thanks."

"It's not like you to have full strength, Bob."

"No, it's not like me."

"Shaz well, is she?"

"Last time I looked."

"You two have a blue?"

He took the schooner and quaffed what was left.

"Nothin' serious I hope?"

"I'll have one for the road, Pete." He watched the publican pour the XXXX.

The road home would be quiet, unsealed into flat country, little chance of an accident because there was little to hit. But he'd sleep it off in the car before heading off—not for safety though, rather the extra time away from the silence at home would do him good.

Pete returned sooner than he liked. "Shaz tell you about the cricket?"

He sipped into the head of the beer. "I'll tell you what, Pete. I'll continue to sit here and drink my beer if you stop the Shaz talk."

"Just makin' conversation." He wiped down the same glass. "You've put on a few pounds, I've noticed."

"Yes, Pete. I'm going bald and I've put on a few pounds." He examined the publican—tall and thin, a good head of hair, natural olive skin not from the sun, for he never saw it much, outside the cricket pitch. All in all, a good-looking bloke. So he understood the attraction that Sharon might have had, once upon a time.

"Too much of the good life, hey."

"Blissful." Bob lifted himself uneasily off the stool and staggered against the chair. "I think I'll play the pokies for a bit. Give you some of that jackpot back."

The six slot machines sat by themselves at the rear wall like a circus. Bob sat in front of one, took out some spare change from his pocket, and primed the pokie. Pineapples, strawberries, mangos, grapes and the elusive banana. The fresh fruit of Queensland spun around to a digital tune of something familiar, and he felt light and happy for the barest of seconds. The fruit salad gave nothing back, so he pressed again and more still, until his change had gone and he fed a twenty into the machine and finished three more schooners and another twenty before the fruit and the tune mixed up his head and he slumped dizzy for a bit.

"You alright, Bob?"

He looked at the publican and straightened his back but didn't reply.

"Why don't you stay at the Coral for the night?"

When he closed his eyes the room spun, and he felt his guts rising to his mouth.

"You should'a had something to eat. You don't hold your grog well, you never have. I'll give Gordon a call and let him know ya comin'."

He swayed on his stool, and the water brash tasted sour and just as he opened his eyes, his neck spurted amber cornflakes onto the machine and the wall and his shoes. The spinning room kept on, and he felt the back of his throat lift up and out and he spewed again.

Pete twisted around and shook his head. "Jesus Christ, Bob. You're a fuckin' useless girl sometimes."

But he knew this already.

* * *

The morning light was bright on the kitchen table. Scramble egg, bacon, hash browns, baked beans. Thick white toast on the side with marmalade. Brewed coffee.

"What did I do to deserve this?"

"Gives me an excuse to cook, Bob."

"You feed everyone like this at the Coral?"

"No."

"Then the question still stands."

Gordon poured the coffee that filled up the space with the scent of roasted beans. "Thought you might need some pampering."

Bob held the mug to his nose. His mouth desiccated. Tart.

"Staying overnight at the Divorce and Death Motel. Hope neither applies to you."

Bob sipped the coffee but didn't reply.

"Not that it's any of my business."

"I reckon this breakfast gives you a right." Bob cut the butter in thick slices and spread it over the toast. "Tell me something Gordon, you miss Helen?"

"I miss lots of things. But we had our time together."

"When Sharon and I first dated—five years ago—I used to look in the mirror every morning and ask why someone like her would go out with me?"

"It's a time old question. Maybe she looked in the same mirror?"

"You think?" He could hear the pleading in his voice.

"You're successful. Have the best crop in town. First irrigated. First with most things when it comes to that farm of yours."

"I'm not sure that matters so much."

"Might not." Gordon got up from the chair and took the tomato sauce from the cupboard.

"Did you ever look in the mirror, Gordy?"

He sat back down and spooned some bacon and beans onto his toast. "Probably. I mustn't have listened to the answer though. Never saw it coming. Woke up one morning, we were all full up—"

"Matt's funeral."

"Yep. Matt was dead. I was the pallbearer—the Dead Man's best man so to speak. Sally was away on her honeymoon, so Helen and I were doing the cleaning ourselves and the speeches at the funeral. I don't know about you, Bob, but I'm not great with speeches, I've got to practice, otherwise I'm all over the place. And so I wake up in the morning, come out here, and just where you're sitting, right where your toast is, was the Dear Gordon letter. Except it didn't start with Dear."

Both men sat and looked at their breakfast for a bit.

"You know there was a rumor." Bob lifted his gaze to Gordon. "Not that rumors mean much around here."

"About Matt and Helen?"

"Yep."

"Well, that particular rumor might have some legs to it." He cut a strip of bacon and wiped it with the tomato sauce.

They sat together in silence for a bit, the English breakfast fading slowly away. "Hey, Gord, I saw something interesting on the TV the other day. Scientists were studying a type of owl, can't remember the name, but they wanted to see how large their territory was, did they overlap with other territories, stuff like that. These owls are one of the few animals known to mate for life. They pair off, keep to one area, and then when the kids grow up they move away and the parents stay on in the same place. But they're nocturnal, so these scientists needed to put a tracking device on them. They managed to catch about four pairs that were in the same area." He swigged at his coffee. "Anyway, you know what they found? After about a week of tracking they noticed the females flying off every so often into an area beyond their territory. They stayed put, sometimes for an hour, until the male from that territory came to the same spot. They were rooting. About once a week the females went off into another territory and shagged. But the males always kept to their own territory. So these scientists went to South America to look at another bird that also mates for life. And they found exactly the same thing there."

"Helen's not a bird, Bob. Her brain's not the size of a pea."

"Maybe nature's nature. Maybe we haven't got any control over it."

The sun from the back window fell on the table and kept their food warm. They ate unhurried, drawing out the quiet time of the morning. For a while, nothing was heard but cutlery and the sound of their own chewing.

Then Gordon said, "This is a fucking hole of a place. Helen was right to leave. If you don't take action, if you don't have the guts to take action, to change things, you get yourself in a rut. She was right to run. I was the gutless fool."

"Seems to me she threw you in the deep end."

"I'm a grown man. I can swim."

Bob dug into the tepid eggs. "These from Cully's? They say you can't tell the difference between farm eggs and regular, but these are farm."

"Nope. Regular from the store."

"Funny, they taste richer. Must be the company."

Gordon laughed. "You really chose your spot last night—the bloody pub. Next time you want to drown your sorrows, knock on my door."

"Will I get breakfast like this?"

"Your turn to cook next."

"I might take you up on that. You were saying about taking action. I might be considering a bit of action myself. I've been chatting to ChinGas about selling the farm. It's early days . . . but I'd sure appreciate your thoughts on it."

"Let me tell you, if they found anything valuable under the Coral I'd take the money before you could finish your eggs."

"This was my grandfather's farm."

"Well, unless you're expecting him to come back to life and work it, I don't see how that comes into the calculation."

"My folks have moved to Brisbane, but Sharon's mum is still here."

"So that's another reason to sell."

Bob smiled. "She's as hard as nails, is Elsie."

"She stayed here once—they were renovating her bathroom I think. Jesus, Bob, I hope Sharon hasn't any of her mother in her."

He only hesitated slightly. "Fortunately, not."

"Listen, Bob, my advice on selling up isn't worth two cents. Your farm is the pride of the area. You've worked on it since you were a kid. If I cut you it wouldn't surprise me if cotton fell out of the wound. And yes, the world needs wheat and cotton, and you've given them plenty. But it's not going to be the end of the world if a small bit of Guburnburnin changes tack and produces some gas for a while."

"It might stuff up the land for others."

"It might. But it might not. And no offence, but cotton hasn't the best track record for looking after the land." He took a mouthful of coffee. "But I'm no farmer. If it was left to me, I'm afraid the whole world would starve."

The phone rang and Gordon handed it over. "It's Sharon."

Bob looked at the receiver and wished it away. But it didn't go anywhere. "Hi." His jaw jutted out as he listened. "Anyway, how did you know I was here?" His mouth inched further open then retreated back to reply. "Pete should keep out of my business . . . Well, I was going to phone after breakfast . . . and killed is a bit unlikely. But I'm sorry. . . When did Pete phone you?" He shook his head. "So if you knew last night . . . how could I be killed in an accident? . . . What from the pub to the Coral? . . . I don't care what your mother says."

Gordon swigged at his tepid coffee and smiled.

"I won't have lunch, Gordy has fed me like it was my last meal . . . That'd be nice. You need me to get anything? . . . Just a bit of a headache. . . . I'll tell him."

He handed the receiver back. "Sharon says thanks for looking after me. And has invited you over for dinner. She said it has to be soon . . . otherwise she'll tell people that the Coral is haunted."

"Might be good for business. A tourist attraction." He grinned and put down the phone. "You ever surf, Bob?"

"Don't have any balance . . . and it's a bit of a trek to the nearest beach."

"Shame. But I was thinking that my marriage was a bit like surfing. You get up on the board, try and stay on, then if you're lucky and you don't fall off you ride the wave for as long as you can. But eventually you have to fall. It's the only thing that's certain. Then you drag your board back. I never liked that part of surfing, nobody does, swimming back with the waves coming at you, sometimes dumping you down on the sand, or on the coral where I used to surf, doing all this just to get back to the same spot. And then do it all over again." He stood and started to stack the plates. "The key of course, is hopefully you'll get better the longer you practice." He grinned. "And don't get caught in a rip."

* * *

"Okay. Wally number one. Mal number two. And Big Artie number three. That's settled then." Pete pushed the XXXX over to upstream and took a swig of Johnnie Walker from a glass under the counter—hidden away, though everyone knew about it. "And no fuckin' Churchill."

"Good one, Pete."

The livid regulars laughed, and so did the stranger.

Upstream proffered, "Did anyone see that young Sydney bludger on the telly last night? She really gave it to him."

"I would have shot the fuckin' dog," downstream said.

"Why does he keep goin' on the show?"

"He gets money for it."

"The fuckin' dole and TV money. Not a bad life."

"They said in the papers that he was on drugs during the show."

"They probably gave them to him in the green room."

"You been on drugs before, Mickey."

"Never."

"What about you, Pete?"

"A little bit of weed."

"I heard a whisper they give him harder shit, as much as he wants. Only if he keeps coming back on the show."

"Fuck, she gave it to him last night. It must be good shit for him to come back and get bashed around . . . week after week."

"It's easy, people like him take what they can get, whenever it comes," the stranger said.

"Where you from, mate?"

The stranger turned back down and spoke to his drink. "West."

"Big area. Could you be more specific?"

"West Queensland."

"Does this place of yours have a name?"

"West of Charleville."

"Getting warmer, starts with . . ."

"Worrobobo."

Some of the bruised faces turned to face the man.

"Hear that fellas," Pete said, "Worrobobo. You've had a bit of fun there lately. I'm sure you know what I'm talkin' about."

The man kept his gaze at his schooner. "I prefer not to talk of it, if that's okay by you?"

"Be a sport. We don't get anyone interestin' comin' through these parts that often."

"Or ever," Mickey said.

"You know anyone who saw it happen?" Pete said.

The stranger lifted his gaze and scanned the U in a complete arc and the maroon faces followed his eyes as he did. "Everyone saw it. Everyone in the fuckin' town saw it."

"Well, can you be more specific?"

"What do you want, a photograph?" He took a swig from his schooner. "I left the place a few days after it happened. And I wasn't alone."

"Mustn't be many left. Worrobobo is a two horse town."

"Bigger than here."

"Three horses, then."

The livid faces laughed and the stranger staggered a bit on his stool and swigged the dregs of his glass.

"I'll shout you a schooner if you tell us what ya saw."

"No thanks. Not worth it."

"Drinks are on us for the evenin' if you tell," upstream said.

"You own this pub now, Mickey?"

"Come on, Pete. He's a celebrity."

Pete rubbed his chin and glared at the man. "How about it, then? Free drinks for the night."

"You got somethin' to eat with those drinks?"

"Jesus, mate. This story better be fuckin' good."

The stranger pushed his empty glass to the publican, and the livid eyes kept their gaze steady on him.

WORROBOBO

ONE

"You know, Sam, I really like it down here," Lil said. "Down by the river, quiet at night. Cozy almost."

"This isn't the Seine."

"You want to live back in Paris?"

"Non."

"I should think not." Lil stoked the wood stove, and the fire cackled cinder sparks onto the worn linoleum. "Baked beans and toast for dinner, Sam?"

"Are you asking or telling?"

"We could go up to the pub if you like."

"Beans will be fine."

"Let's stay cozy in our little west bank hamlet tonight . . . and if you're a good boy, I just might give you the pleasure of fucking me."

They had been in Worrobobo for a few months, a town with three paved roads that run parallel, connected with two short streets, unpaved, one going a bit further to stop ragged close to where the river bent away. Only a few shacks of houses sat down at this end of the dusty street, since they were the first to flood when the river ran high.

They were different, the citizens of Lower Worrobobo. They were unconnected to the town water supply, the large rain-water tanks rusted ochre at the flanks of the shacks. And they were not lamp lit at night, the path a black staggered route when no moon was out; the footpaths showing no separation from the dirt road, formed from years of silt that settled down after the floods came. The people of Lower Worrobobo were not quite vagrants, but sometimes came very close to it.

Sam kept his eyes on the television, an old black and white that sat on the kitchen table. He adjusted the antenna and the picture sharpened a touch.

"I notice you're going through one of your colorful phases at the moment, Sam."

"Quite."

"I'm not trying to interfere . . ."

He turned his gaze from the screen to her.

"Far from me to interfere, but Worrobobo might not be the best place to enter this colorful phase of yours." She peeled open a can of Heinz Beanz. "This look of yours is more for a city . . . Paris, say. But Worrobobo, I'm not so sure."

"Then let them eat cake."

Lil bent over and kissed him open-mouthed. "As to your fancy . . . it's just a suggestion." She wiped at her upper lip. "That moustache of yours will give me a rash if I'm not careful."

"Then be careful."

She looked over to the television. "God, they play this game of yours so late?"

"It's in Perth."

"Where's that?"

"On the other side of the country . . . there's a time difference."

"Well, it seems like the game just never ends."

"Five days."

"Unbelievable, Sam." She stirred the beans in the small pot on the stove. "And where are we at, in this exciting spectacle?"

"Day five, one hour to go."

"Thank the Heavens." She grinned at this. "And who will be the victor?"

"Nobody."

"Excuse me?"

"Nobody . . . it's going to be a draw."

The beans started to bubble.

"You must be joking, Sam. Five days for a draw?"

He adjusted the antenna again and didn't reply.

"I don't remember seeing this game of yours in Paris. Or America."

"Quite."

"Another one of your colorful phrases. 'Quite.' A very theatrical turn of phrase for you, Sam."

"Quite."

"Butter or margarine on your toast, Sam?"

"Butter."

"And your hair in that pony tail . . . very theatrical."

"Quite."

"But for Worrobobo . . . maybe a bit too much." She scraped the butter on the toast, burnt at the edges like the linoleum. "You seem to be reliving your Carlo years, Sam. At least the outside persona. And of course, at your early morning outings."

Sam turned his gaze to her for a second, then back to the players.

"I hope you weren't hiding that from me."

"I stopped hiding anything from you long ago."

"But you don't always tell me everything, Sam."

"Likewise."

"Oh, don't be a baby. You hear everything from me. Sometimes I think you don't *want* to know everything, but that's too bad, Sam." She bent over and kissed him on the cheek. "Because that's how it's always been . . . and always will be."

Sam adjusted the antenna. The picture was fuzzy again.

"But I would have liked you to tell me about your morning excursions. Not that I would dream of interfering."

He turned his gaze back to her but didn't reply.

"Kylie is a sweet thing," she said.

He curved back to the play. "Not quite ripe."

"No, she isn't experienced. But it's nice for me to have a friend so young."

"Friend?"

"Lover would be too strong a word for it, Sam."

"Maybe not for her."

"I admit she's quite smitten with me. A schoolgirl crush."

"Who's the schoolgirl, you or she?"

Lil went over and kissed him open-mouthed, slipping her hand down to his crotch. "But my baby is so faithful to me."

"Quite."

"It's touching, Sam." She kissed him gently on his cheek. "It really is."

He adjusted the antenna and the field of players transformed into gray horizontal stripes before settling again.

Lil said, "It might be good for you to have a dalliance every so often. People will talk."

"I don't have the energy."

"But you have the energy for this silly game of yours." She poured the beans over the toast and put the plate in front of him. "Here, baby, just the way you like them."

The ad-break came and Sam cut his dinner into mouth-sized triangles. He grinned. "No bacon flavor in the sauce this time."

"No, and thank you for this. It's nice of you to be considerate when you shop . . . at least on this occasion."

"The bacon added some flavor."

"Please, Sam, why do you say such things when you know how I'll respond?"

"Quite."

She watched him in the little kitchen seasoned with tomato and beans. "Tell me, Sam, that shirt of yours, where did you dream that up."

"It's Hawaiian."

"It's like a bowl of fruit. And those pink buttons . . ."

He tabled his cutlery and preened his handlebar moustache. "Why don't you go for a wander, Lil . . . I'm sure there's someone in this town you haven't tried yet."

"No, Sam. Tonight it's just you and me together. I made that promise and I intend to keep it."

And he adjusted the antenna again.

*　*　*

Sam moved up the street, the early morning sun low in the sky but still warm. The corrugated iron of the houses glistened, chickens moved wherever, pecking into the un-kept grass, around rusted detritus, the creaking sound of a wire door shutting, some washing hanging from a cord wound across the branches of a tree.

Lower Worrobobo was calm at this time of the day. Almost peaceful.

He had been down by the river before the sun had risen, following the bank away from town. It had been a dry spring and the river was low and he walked along the baked earth until a collapsed embankment blocked his way, about two hundred yards from where he started.

The eucalypts tilted along the rise and he sang his nightingale croon in the sunken edge of the stream and the orange sun rose and lit him as he did. He stayed there exactly an hour—a full performance, broken only by a lull of shallow breaths, the movement of fauna—before rising up again with his arms that seemed to hold on to the heavens as he sang.

The riverbank was hard and flat, and it wasn't until he reached back to the street that his crocodile-skin boots, which curved up to a sharp point, became stained with the earth. As he hiked the dusty incline, Upper Worrobobo seemed to twitch more than its sleeping cousin down near the river; barefooted toddlers chased a mangy dog; a porch radio played country and western, its owner washing an aging Corolla in the drying sun.

When he arrived at Athol's Store the few customers turned their heads and followed his steps with their eyes.

He heard a snigger.

Athol himself followed him with more than his eyes, coming out from behind his counter. "Hey, you. You're a real fancy pants, aren't you fella?"

Sam picked up a melon and brought it to his nose.

"A queer one . . . if you know what I mean."

The melon was not ripe. He placed it back and brought another to his face.

"You *eat* the fruit . . . it's not perfume." The man stopped a few feet from Sam. "And I noticed a whiff as you came in. Are you wearing that Sheila's eau de cologne again?"

Sam placed the melon back down.

"Listen, mate, there are folks around here that are becoming real wary of you." Athol turned to a woman who had stopped further along the aisle to listen. "You might as well know, the cops have been notified."

Sam turned his deadpan gaze from the fruit to the man.

"That's right. I thought that might get your attention."

Sam turned back to the fruit and pinched one so hard the skin broke. He brought his finger to his mouth and slowly licked the juice.

"We have kids around here . . . and we like to protect them from *queer*" —he pronounced this in a high girly voice, "—ones like you."

The woman upstream fidgeted in her basket, feigning an interest away from the scene.

But Athol kept on. "That young blonde sister of yours might be cute . . . but she can't sweet talk away our feelings for a fancy pants like you."

Sam went over to the tomatoes and put a few in his bag, the woman shying away as he passed.

"Fucking poofter," Athol said, then walked back to the checkout till.

It was warm in the store, and the scent of ripened fruit filled the space. The scent of soap and dog biscuits in the adjacent aisle. Fertilizer further on. Sam took his time and filled his bag in the hushed place, careful with all of his selections, just as he had been with the fruit.

In time, he went up to the till, where the storeowner stood waiting.

Sam put his bag on the counter.

And when Athol took the first item out, Sam touched his hand, drew him near with his stare, and kissed him open mouthed, long and deep with his tongue. And when he was done, he whispered into the man's ear, so softly that the nearby woman, who had lingered in the store beyond her normal shopping time, couldn't register a word.

And when he was done with his whispering, he picked up the bag of goods and left the store into the heat of the day, without paying; leaving Athol to stare blankly at the swinging door, like he was waiting for a show to begin just as the curtain rises.

* * *

In the afternoon of the same lazy Saturday, the streets of Worrobobo started to squirm, slow at first, but soon building to a tumult. Men, women, and children moved quick stepped, some running, carrying empty sacks, old shopping trolleys, children pulling go-carts, adults too, all in the direction of Athol's Store.

In Lower Worrobobo the movement was even more frenetic, and the second wave met the first returning in the middle of the dusty street—a hurried discourse in the heat of the day.

"Take the ute, pet."

"Can't get near the place."

"Hey, Becky . . . you're only allowed to take bags in."

"I gotta bring the frozen stuff home before it melts."

"I ain't got enough room in the freezer, luv."

"Tell Bobby to stop eatin' those lollies and get that cart of his and meet me out front of Athol's."

"Can you get me some pots . . . ours are falling to bits. And a toaster if they're still around."

"Doubt much of the expensive stuff is left . . . but I'll have a squiz."

"Christmas has sure come early this year."

"And birthdays and New Year's Eve and bloody Boxing Day all in one."

A dance of heavy labored laughter went in and out of Athol's Store. Ice-cream painted kids skipped outside, dogs licked at discarded bits that melted on the ground, and horns bellowed from wedged-in cars that had come to a standstill in the main road out front.

Christmas Day may have arrived a month early in Worrobobo, but Father Christmas was missing.

"Athol's shut up shop for good, Macka told me."

"Someone says he's sick."

"Gotta be, to give all this away."

"God bless him, though."

"What about his missus . . . it don't make no sense."

"Don't question, just get in there before there's only bones left to pick at."

A police car flashed red and blue down the road, but the wedged-in cars had nowhere to go. Two men carried a sack of potatoes and said there were more out back. Some complained that no family could eat that much, it would sure to spoil, but they went on carrying all they could lift.

The hot tumult kept on at the same furious pace until, just as the sun was making its final descent of dusk, little Bobby pointed up at the store roof. Others stopped and looked as well, and little Bobby giggled and asked what the man was doing with no clothes on.

"Jesus," someone said.

"Get the kids away."

"Get the constable." And someone did.

The galvanized roof was blistering hot, but the storeowner's feet seemed not to care. Athol walked along the precipice to and fro, a haphazard wander as the citizens of Worrobobo started to collect below him.

The constable shoved his way through the crowd and stopped. "What you doin' up there, Athol?"

But Athol kept on his restless wander. His eyes wandered too but at nothing that seemed fixed in space. And when a crow flew down by his head and seemed to clip his face with its wing, the watching crowd shrieked. But the naked man never flinched, just kept his wandering-eyed stare, as if it never happened.

Someone brought a ladder from the store, and they began to assemble it and held it under where Athol was standing.

And little Bobby asked what was in the naked man's hand.

"What you got there, Athol?" the constable said, calm as he could.

Someone said it was a corkscrew but little Bobby had better eyes and knew it wasn't. "What you got that can-opener for, Mister?"

A shudder came from below and a woman started to scream. The ladder was held and the constable raced up, but it tilted to the side and he fell to the ground.

"Jesus, someone get up to him."

And they dragged little Bobby away, though he kept twisting his head to look, and so did the other kids, and the dogs licked at the ice-creams that were dropped and forgotten about. The townsfolk scrambled to put the ladder up as some of the women began to wail, their desperate pleas unheard, and the constable raced up again, seemingly an eternity before he managed to stand unsteady on the roof, with the heat of the iron rising to his face, and he grabbed the naked man's arm, swaying a bit as he did.

And Athol stood, not straight but with his legs separated apart, looking down at himself, at his blood-ruddy hands pulling open his sac, and the meat of his testicles that he had splayed open, unwrapped, for all the citizens of Worrobobo to see.

* * *

Outside of the kitchen window, Lower Worrobobo kept on its erratic movement. Inside, though, the dark room held its order, Sam putting another Cheezel to his mouth, pausing in mid chew to adjust the TV antenna.

It was more than an hour before *Big Brother* would finish, and Sam stayed at the table, disregarding the huddle that had formed out front, that kicked into the earth of the street, with stooped heads, muttering thoughts aloud, trying as one to make sense of what they had seen.

And Sam and Lil ate in for dinner—pasta with fresh tomato and basil collected in the morning at Athol's store for no payment. For Lil thought it best they eat, on this particular night, alone. She sighed. She would miss Worrobobo.

* * *

The constable walked from Athol's instead of taking the van. The late afternoon breeze smelled of rain and the gray clouds that held it strained yellow light on the town like a sieve.

When he began his descent the asphalt melted into bluestone gravel and by the Sampson's house turned into corrugated red-brown earth. He stopped at a tree where a little white cross with sun-bleached plastic flowers was tied to the base of the trunk, marking the spot where Freddy Sampson and his girl had rolled their car on muck-up day ten years or more back. After the accident the gravel was laid ready to pave, but the flood came soon after that, and the money was used to extend the bus station instead. R I P was painted in little black letters down the long stem of the cross, in what seemed to him an unsteady hand, and he wondered if it was done by Freddy's younger brother who would have been less than ten at the time. And he wondered what the family felt as they drove into their home every day and saw the cross before entering the drive.

He heard the go-cart before he saw it, the feigned siren, ee orr ee orr, like a high pitched donkey, spitting up dust as it came down behind him.

"You're a police officer now, Bobby?"

The boy turned the steering wheel tilting the cart off its inside wheels and around to face the cross.

"I can be your deputy, hey, constable?"

"I need all the help I can get."

"Can I get a badge?"

"I'll see what I can come up with."

The boy looked at his holster. "And can I have a closer look at that gun?"

"You don't really want to look at that now, do you, Bobby?" Though he thought it dumb to say.

"You ever shot anyone?"

"Never."

"You musta shot a cow or something. My pop shot Scamp when he went off somewhere he shouldn't have. He said he was a workin' dog, and if he didn't work then he couldn't feed it. And if he couldn't feed it, it be kinda to kill it."

"Well, perhaps he was right."

"What happened to Athol, constable?" The boy stared up at him in a matter of fact way.

"He was sick, son."

"I've seen it done on lambs at Pop's."

The image of the metal wheel turning slowly into Athol's skin, tangling hair, the blood and dangling meat, kept on at him. "Try and forget about it, son."

The boy turned the wheel back and lifted the cart to face down the incline of the road. "Dad says he's been cursed . . . like when the Abos' point the bone. You ever seen someone with the bone pointed at them?"

"No." The image of the splayed scrotum kept on. "But he's just sick, son. It happens to some people. Try and forget about it . . . and I might see if I can find that badge for you."

"Okay. You know where I live . . . down at twenty-three . . . it has Santa and the reindeers out front. It gets lit so you can see our place easy at night." The boy lent forward in his chair and dragged the dirt with his feet propelling the cart down, ee oorring as he went.

The clouds had settled low above him now, and he thought it might have been wiser to take the van. When it started to spit, he took longer strides, steam rising off the still warm earth, and he walked up to the door just before the rain fell heavy. But he didn't have to wait outside because she stood at the wire door like she was waiting for him to come.

"Come on in and get dry, officer."

It was dark inside for the windows were small and the gray outside barely lit up the place. The ceiling was low, he could touch it if he wanted, and the rain drummed on the iron roof and spilled down over them.

"Let's go into the kitchen, it's much more friendly in there."

He had heard she was well liked in town, by the men at least. There were rumors. And it was said Athol liked her too. She was a pretty young thing, and he knew how pretty young things could cause a stir in Worrobobo when they first set up camp.

"Sit down here and I'll make us some tea."

"That's kind of you, but don't bother about me."

"Don't be silly, officer. I would offer you something stronger but we don't have alcohol in the place and you probably wouldn't accept it anyway."

She smiled at him and he thought he understood why the men liked her so much. She had an exotic way with her. Exotic for Worrobobo.

He said, "You have an interesting accent. You weren't born in Australia?"

"If you can guess where, I'll be impressed."

"Give me time, but I might need more than one attempt."

"Take three." She laughed and he watched her blue eyes fall over him with the drumming rain.

"Your brother isn't here?"

"Alas, no. He's out foraging for food."

"I was particularly hoping to talk with him."

"Well, he hasn't long gone. But you're welcome to wait."

He watched her boil the water in an open lid pot. "You don't see these old wood stoves much anymore."

"We like it. And it smells so lovely."

He looked around the Spartan surrounds—a few plates and cups on the sideboard, no papers or magazines or books, just a TV on a faux timber laminated table, with three different chairs. It was as if they had just moved in, yet he knew they had been in Worrobobo for three months or more.

"Canada?"

She laughed. "No. I spent time there but not for long. I don't like the cold weather." Steam rose from the iron pot. "Now, what has my older brother been up to?"

"Country towns have their own special problems, Miss."

"Call me Lil."

"And this country town is no different, Lil. It seems the folks around here have taken a disliking to your brother, and believe he's a—" He paused to try and find the right word, "—a danger to people." He watched the bubbles grow in the pot. "Now there is no evidence that I can see of any danger, but evidence doesn't mean much once they get talking, rumors become facts, and before you know it—"

"Something unpleasant happens." She sighed. "I've warned him . . . dress down . . . he mainly keeps to himself though . . . I really can't see how people could believe he's a danger to anyone."

"Well, a person's sexual preference is their business . . . and legal in Queensland well over a decade now."

"What a progressive land we're living in," she said.

He looked at her but she seemed to be earnest as best as he could tell.

"Sweden?"

"Sweden. I don't believe I've ever been."

"You look like one of the singers in ABBA. I loved that band." And he thought she was just as cute.

"That's two guesses," she said.

"Anyway, a man's sexual preference is his business, but there was a witness to something between your brother and Athol."

"That unfortunate man."

"Yes. There was an incident on the same day . . . nothing illegal that I can make out . . . that has led people to . . ." He paused again.

"Yes, officer?"

"To want blood."

He watched her pour the water into two mugs and dunk a teabag into them.

"I hope you take it black." The air rose tea-flavored in the dank space. "So that poor man, Athol, has said something about my brother?"

"Unfortunately, Athol hasn't been able to say anything."

"He's not dead?"

"No, no. But he's not able to be interviewed at the present time."

She sighed and sipped her tea. "The poor man."

"And perhaps it isn't safe for your brother to be out by himself at the moment."

"Oh, don't worry about him, officer. He can look after himself."

The tea was too hot for him to drink and he put the cup on the buckled laminate. "I wonder, and I'm certainly not forcing you, but could you tell me something about your brother . . . that might help me understand his behavior?"

"We like to move around, call us nomads if you like."

"Are you working?"

"No, our needs are simple, as you can see. We've saved a bit of money, but Sam doesn't work much these days. I look after him, and we seem to manage okay."

"Russia?"

"That was your last guess. Let's keep it a mystery, but be sure to pop in if you think you've worked it out."

He let some of the tea cool at the edge of the cup and sipped it. "Do you mind telling me how long you intend to stay in Worrobobo?"

"I suspect not as long as I would like."

The rain eased off a bit and the light seemed brighter in the room. "Perhaps I should go and look for your brother. But if he returns, before I find him, I wonder whether you could phone the station."

"Unfortunately, we don't have the phone on. But seriously, officer, Sam can look after himself. Trust me on this." And she drank more of her tea.

When he left the shanty house the road was fashioned into pools of brown rain. Brown water came in a stream of sorts down the lowest edge of the road, eventually to spill into the river, brown as well.

Lower Worrobobo never seemed to be clean, even after a downpour.

It was a dirty place in all seasons.

TWO

The bus station was larger than someone passing through the town would have expected, but Worrobobo sat near a four-way junction that sent narrow highways into each compass point of the State. So the untidy hamlet became a forced meeting place of strangers, who rested while waiting for their connect to arrive.

Stephen slumped back on one of the benches with his feet on his knapsack. He was tired and his right knee ached from sitting for so long in the one cramped space, and he wasn't looking forward to the final 400-kilometer leg of his journey. He had walked around the town but found nothing of interest—the entire town seemed subdued, and the only store was closed and looked abandoned. So he came back into the almost comfortable air-conditioned space, at least compared to the relentless heat outside.

He sipped his vending machine coffee, now lukewarm, and eyed another that dangled junk food, but thought the better of it. He had kept his weight down, lean to his liking, his sweaty trade made it easy, and a spell off the grog hadn't hurt either. He might start back when he got to Brisbane but wasn't sure—the dry months of shearing had made him feel surprisingly good.

"You have far to travel?" The pretty young blonde sat down in front of him.

"Brissy," he said.

"Brissy. I've never been." She put out her hand. "I'm Lil."

Stephen shook her hand and studied her for as long as he thought proper. She was a bombshell, and he felt the waiting time might go a bit quicker now.

"What about you?" he asked.

"Haven't really decided . . . except to leave Worrobobo."

"Take pot luck, hey?"

She smiled at him with her blue dolls eyes. "I've always been lucky."

"I can see that."

"And what about you?" she asked.

"Lucky? No, I've been lots of things, but lucky isn't one of them."

"Not even at love?"

"Not especially."

She looked him over. "A good looking boy like you? That surprises me."

He smiled and he felt a delightful ease well up and he hoped his bus might be delayed for a bit.

The waiting room started to swell, a line now forming in front of the vending machine. Some had to sit on their luggage, or rest on the floor.

"Why you leaving?" he asked.

"We've had a bit of excitement here a couple of days ago. The town isn't quite what is was." He watched her turn around but wasn't sure what she was looking for. "And the main store is closed, and the closest is in the next town, and I don't have a car." She smiled at him. "But enough of my problems . . . let's talk about you. I like your olive skin. Are you married?"

The delightful ease bulged into another form. "No. Never have been."

"Children?"

"None." He grinned. "How am I doing so far?"

"So far . . . top marks." She twisted around again and he watched her long legs snake as she did. A flash of her thighs, then she turned back to him. "And you are travelling alone, it seems?"

"All alone." He watched her eyes that wandered over him, and he felt like a car in a not so fancy showroom—second hand with not many kilometers on the clock.

She turned again, and Stephen watched a gray ponytail man with a giant moustache enter the bus station. Beside him, an older plump woman with flaming red hair held on to his arm. The room seemed to hush a bit, and Stephen noticed the chatter move in the direction of the mustachioed man. And the bombshell nodded in the man's direction, and some connection was plain to see.

"One final question, which might seem a bit odd. Do you play cricket?"

He laughed. "Years ago."

And she smiled and her eyes went up and over him one more time.

Stephen watched as the room's eyes stayed with the gray ponytail man. He might be a movie star, from his getup and all, but Stephen didn't recognize him. Maybe the redhead was his aunt. Or an older sister. He doubted they were lovers.

"That guy seems to be getting some attention," Stephen said.

She shifted her legs, and her short skirt inched up as she did. "Yes, I'm afraid so." She leant toward him. "That bit of trouble we had the other day . . . the town seems to think him responsible." She sighed. "But it's too gruesome to talk about. I'm surprised you haven't heard."

"I've been shearing at the back of Woop Woop, no TV, just sheep from the time I wake, to the time I go down. I even count them to sleep. Then it's lamb for breakfast."

She smiled at him. "I do like your olive skin."

"I like your skin, too."

"And your hair . . . it would look nice slicked back I think. Some oil perhaps."

She twisted around and nodded, and the gray ponytail man seemed to nod back, but Stephen wasn't too sure.

"Well, that's settled then," she said. "We like each other."

Her thighs opened not so slightly, and he saw under her skirt and his delightful ease bulged some more. "Why don't you freshen up in the rest room and meet me out front in five minutes?"

"I guess I'm luckier than I thought," he said. "Must be my thirtieth birthday present come a day early."

"Happy birthday." She smiled in a strange way and he felt strange as well, but he lifted himself off the bench, his knapsack in hand, and went into the restroom as she asked.

The room was warmer than the waiting area and stunk of shit and piss. Stephen washed his face and took his toilet bag out and thought about shaving but decided against it. He rolled some deodorant under his arms. Brushed his teeth.

And when he looked up he saw the gray ponytail man standing behind him. He hadn't heard him come in. Older close up, his aged freckled face painted with makeup, his handlebar moustache curling at the tips; a smell of cologne amongst the excrement.

"May I ask whether you're a bowler or batsman?" the ponytail asked.

* * *

The women's restroom didn't smell of lavender either.

Beryl looked at herself in the mirror and brushed her mop of red hair with her fingers. It needed a trim but it always looked like it did, even when it'd just had one. She staggered a bit at the edge of the basin, splashing the tap water on her arms that had reddened from too much sun. And picked at the sore on her arm.

She turned around to see she was alone, tilted her hip flask high, and stole a few sips that warmed her throat. She had planned to sleep the rest of the trip until her newfound friend entered the scene.

And she felt light and happy and she sipped at her flask some more.

He was a handsome man. A bit of a dandy, but that might be fun. But he had character, with that moustache of his, and the rest of the get up. And it wasn't as if she expected it to last. Just a bit of fun, and she tilted the metal flask high to her mouth. Whatever happened, she won't be bored. Boredom sucked.

The door swung open and she stuffed the flask back in her handbag and fumbled to find her makeup case. The light was bright, with a bank of fluorescent bulbs just above where she stood, so the little red crusts splotched proud on her face. She brushed the powder that softened them some, though it clung to the crusts like frosting.

Beryl lifted her hand to her mouth and smelt her breath. She must like this man, for she never usually bothered to hide her habit. And she searched for a mint in her bag.

"No need for that, dear."

She looked up and saw the pretty blonde woman in the reflection of the mirror, standing behind her.

"You see . . . I'm not that fussy."

And she watched the blonde raise her hand to her shoulder, and it felt warm like the whisky.

* * *

The bus waiting room was like a zoo, and some of the travelers spilled outside, preferring the heat to the mob indoors.

The room fidgeted a bit when the constable entered. Little Bobby had told him he saw the man with the big moustache come down to the bus station just a while back. It didn't need elaborate detective work to find someone in Worrobobo. The town usually did it for you.

The constable wandered through the labyrinth of suitcases, and the crowd kept to its fidget as he passed, but there was no sign of the man. There was only the restroom remaining and he entered and the faces all turned to him restless as well. He looked under the partition of the cubicles and saw some legs, and he waited for the door to open but it wasn't the man. So he went back out again.

"Looking for someone, sweetness." A redheaded woman sat on the bench and looked up at him.

"A man, mid to late forties, with an old fashioned moustache."

She cackled. "Like a circus ringmaster?"

"Something like that."

"We did see him, didn't we, Sam?"

The constable looked at the man sitting next to her, but he didn't seem interested.

"I thought to myself, when he came in, there must be a circus in town." And she laughed again. "We chatted for a bit. He seemed niice, didn't he Sam?"

But the dark haired man kept his disinterest plain to see.

"And what did you talk about?"

"Let me think. Sam, you might be able to help? This son of mine, detective, is in another world sometimes." She grinned up at him. "He kept on about that silly game of cricket. I don't understand it myself. The fascination of it all. And the time it takes . . . Shamayim!" She cackled. "But what's this about? Perhaps something to do with that excitement a few days ago. Tell me detective, how is that man doing? A naaasty thing for people to see . . . especially in such a quiet little town. Very naaasty."

He focused on the crusty-faced woman with too much make-up. "He is not doing well, madam."

"Did you hear that, Sam?" She sighed. "Of course he isn't."

"Do you mind telling me if the gentleman with the moustache told you where he was going?"

"Absolutely not, detective."

"Senior constable, madam."

"You hear that, Sam? Senior constable. This must be important!"

He watched her sway on her chair and the reek of alcohol drifted up to him.

"Madam, do you have any information that might be helpful?"

"As a matter of fact I do. I think he said he was going to the park to practice his giggly."

"Giggly?"

"Googly," the younger dark man called Sam said.

GUBURNBURNIN

ONE

The midmorning sun streamed into the kitchen on little Jamie's face.

Sharon wiped down the sink until the stainless gleamed in the sun. "You're a good boy." She didn't usually talk to him out loud.

Little Jamie smiled and kept on with his drawing.

"Let me see this picture of yours." She moved over to the table and put her arm around him. "How lovely, Jamie. Is that mummy?"

Little Jamie nodded.

"And Daddy?"

He nodded again.

"And Grandma . . . and you, I see you over there."

He beamed up to her.

She went over to the fridge and took out the meat for the evening meal. She liked it to thaw slowly—too fast in the microwave and it didn't seem to cook near as well.

"Would you like chops for dinner?" She opened the vegetable drawer. "And carrots . . . helps you see better . . . and cauliflower . . . puts hairs on your chest." She took out the vegetables. "That's what Grandpa said when he was alive. I wish you had known your Grandpa . . . he would have loved you, Jamie."

He sat smiling and swung his legs under the table and kept on with his drawing.

"Grandma can be a bit mean sometimes, I know. She has a good heart . . . but she's just a bit mean. Hard might be a better word. Grandpa was never hard. He was as gentle as a lamb."

Sharon went over and sat down next to Jamie.

"Come and sit on my knee and I'll tell you about him."

And the pit of her stomach warmed up as he did.

"When I was young, a bit older than you, he and I would go into his shed. He said it was our place . . . and Grandma was not allowed in *our* place." She held him tighter. "He would take out the cigarettes that he hid behind the wood pile and he would smoke and tell me stories of what he did when he was a boy. Naughty things, mostly . . . and I would laugh and beg him to tell me more. And Grandma would call out to come in for lunch or dinner and sometimes we didn't and she had to come out and knock on the door. Don't enter our special place I would scream out . . . and Grandpa would wink at me and put out his cigarette and tell her we'd be out when we'd finished our work. We never did any work, Jamie . . . Grandpa would take a hammer and bang it on the wood to pretend . . . but we never did any work in our special place." She rocked him to and fro, and the pit of her stomach kept warm as she did. "Draw me another picture, Jamie. Anything you like."

She lifted him off her knee and he went back to his work and she to hers.

"What will we do today? I must phone Grandma later, or I'll be in trouble—can't have her come knocking at the door. We can watch TV . . . I taped my silly shows . . . Daddy will be home a bit later than usual, so it's just you and me and that scruffy dog of yours . . . I'm a cat person . . . Your father likes dogs but he doesn't look after them, of course . . . *we* do all that, don't we."

She looked out the kitchen window at the scruffy dog that sat in the shade of the tree.

Little Jamie held up his picture.

"Let's see what you have drawn for mummy. Oh, Jamie, that's so lovely. We're in the park playing cricket. That's me with the bat . . . I'm not very good, you know . . . and that must be Daddy holding my hand . . ."

Little Jamie looked up and shook his head.

"Grandma?"

He shook his head.

"Who is it then, Jamie?" She noticed the hair, colored with black crayon. "Is that uncle Sam?"

He nodded.

"You like uncle Sam, then?"

He kept on coloring and swung his legs. "Yes I do, Mummy. I like him very much."

Jamie rarely spoke. But when he did, it was always important.

* * *

Behind Billy, a curtain of wheat hung yellow-gold. In front—the color of brown sugar; the morning air still fresh with the smell of cereal.

This was his third lesson in as many days. He was told he didn't have to come so early, but he wanted to hear the nightingale sing before he practiced. He was good at copying—drawings, basketball, chopping wood—so he thought he might be as good with copying singing. But the lessons weren't going as he thought they would.

"Release your breath when you sing. Don't hold it," Sam said.

He went through the vocalizio—'aaaaaaaa,' up and down, up and down.

"Billy, don't strain your voice. Never!"

Sam never raised his voice, except to warn him about straining. Billy thought this caring in a funny way.

Sam pointed to Billy's throat. "This is what you have that I don't. It's precious. It's everything." He sighed. "You must look after it. If it hurts when you sing, we must stop. Bring it down. *Stai calmo*, Billy. *Stai calmo*."

He found it strange when Sam talked in his foreign way, but he seemed to understand what he meant.

'E' up and down, up and down.

Billy did it, careful not to strain.

"*Poco vibrato*, Billy. Let it come if it must, but don't force the vibrato . . ."

Keep his voice from warbling, unless it decided to. He did 'eeeee' again, the scales the only sound coming from this vast field of wheat.

"Rest now."

He dropped his hands and kicked at the ground of the cleared circle. "This is crazy, how the crop doesn't grow here. It's like in that movie . . . you know, where it was made from aliens." He looked at Sam, who didn't seem interested, but he went on anyway. "I'm not sure I believe in space ships and stuff like that. What do you think, Mister?"

Sam kept staring away from him.

"Our teacher says she doesn't know either . . . but it might be true. Not on Mars, she says there are no aliens on Mars. But other planets further away. What do you think?"

"I think you should rest your voice."

Billy kicked into the dirt again and did as he was told. He was tired from the early start, but if he could sing like the nightingale he would come again the next day and the next. For as long as it took.

They stood still in the clearing, the smell of fresh Weet-Bix all around them. Soon he sang the falsetto 'ooh to ahh', up and down, up and down.

"Somewhere in the middle of the throat. Let it come from there."

Up and down. Billy's hands rose and fell with the falsetto and the sun came warmer on his face, lighting more of their little stage.

"*Stai calmo*, Billy. *Stai calmo*."

Up and down. Up and down. Staying calm.

***

"I want to do some tests on you, Lil."

"You look worried, luv."

"You tell me you don't drink."

"Never touch the stuff."

"And you never have?"

"Oh, maybe in another life." She laughed. "Give me the worst. I can take it."

"Your liver is enlarged."

"Well, who would have guessed?"

"You've never had hepatitis, or your skin turn yellow, even for a short time?"

"Not that I can recall."

"These bruises on you, how long have you been getting them?"

"This old skin of mine, too much sun I think." She grinned at him as if she didn't have a care in the world.

"And your blood pressure is high."

"You can fix it though?"

"Yes, I can fix it."

"And this liver thing of mine, luv?"

He made some notes. "Let's get some of these tests done first. I'll take the blood now, but you'll need to go down to the Base hospital at Banga to get an ultrasound. It's a bit of a trek."

"I'll find someone to help me with that, don't you worry about that."

"I'm sure you will, Lil."

He smiled at her and she at him and he tightened the tourniquet around her arm.

"Every time I come here you hurt me," she said.

"It's an occupational hazard, I'm afraid."

"Don't worry about that either . . . I like to be hurt sometimes."

How strange this woman was. He inserted the needle.

"Mmmm . . . you're making me all tingly, luv."

He felt his hand shake.

"Take your time . . ."

The tube filled red, and he unclipped the strap and withdrew the needle. "Press on your arm, Lil."

A bleb of blood trickled from the puncture site. He watched her take a finger, wipe along its ruddy course, and bring it to her mouth.

"It has such a unique taste, don't you think. Like gun metal."

He looked at her but didn't reply.

She sucked her finger some more, sliding it gently in and out between her lips. "Yes, like the taste of a revolver in your mouth." She laughed. "They should make an ice-cream flavor from it. I'll have a scoop of vanilla and a scoop of blood?" She cackled even louder. "Or one scoop of blood and one of cunt, please. What do you think, luv?"

He kept his gaze but had no idea what to say.

"Oh, I see I shock you, don't I?"

He found his voice. "A bit."

She laughed. "I like your honesty. As a matter of fact, I like the honesty of all the people around here. What a strange land is this state of Queensland. But terribly honest."

He smiled with her again—the image of the vulgar dessert melting a tad.

"You more than anyone would be in a position to know the strangeness of the place," Lil said. "Doctors are second only to priests as keepers of secrets."

"I guess I've lived here most of my life. So it's not so strange to me."

"Well, I can say with a long life of travel behind me, this land of the Queen's is like nothing else I've known. It's like everyone is waiting to catch a bus. Very patiently. Just waiting. Some indoors. Some outside in the sun."

He smiled. "Perhaps we all go through that at some point in our lives."

"Yes, luv." Her voice softened. "But in most places the bus eventually arrives." She laughed. "Cunt flavored ice-cream. Shamayim! You see why I don't drink . . . could you imagine the result? The same goes for my boy, Sam. In fact, doubly so for him. We both don't touch a drop for the very . . . same . . . reason."

"For your health, Lil?"

"Oh no, luv. For everyone else's!"

And she reached out and held on to his arm and laughed and laughed.

* * *

The table was covered with white lace; bone china with roses and daisies and gold lips.

Bob said, "We only get out our Royal Doulton for royalty, Gordon. So be impressed."

"That's not true, honey," Sharon said. "We had it out when mum was over the other week."

"That's what I said."

"Very funny." Sharon brought the lamb already cut into thick pink slices. "Who's looking after the Coral, Gordon?"

"I put out the no vacancy sign. Anyway, mid-week is usually quiet."

"Unless some stray drunks come from the pub," she said.

"Touché, honey bun." Bob winked at Gordon. "You got me back for that quip about dear old queen mum."

"You should know, Gordon, my mother has been very good to Bob."

"Should he know that?"

Bob's voice had an edge to it she didn't remember seeing before. "I think you should slow down on the wine, honey. At least before you eat."

"You sound like Pete, now. I preferred it when you sounded like your mother."

"I like how you have decorated the living room, Sharon," Gordon said.

"You don't think the curtains are too much?"

"Absolutely not."

"Matches the Royal Doulton," Bob said.

"Well, it's like being in spring all year round. At least that was my plan."

"This wine is something, Gordon. You've got to come around more often."

"Yes, Gordon. Don't be such a hermit."

"Tell me, honey bun, in what way has your mother been good to me? Gordon wants to know."

Sharon brought over a bowl of peas. "She accepted you right from the start, didn't she?"

"Why shouldn't she? Do I have two heads?"

"You soon will if you keep on gulping that wine down. Is that your third or fourth glass?"

"I am being a bit of a pig. Sorry, Gordy."

Gordon smiled. "Drink as much as you like, just don't throw up on my shoes."

"Wasn't that funny," Sharon said. "Pete was so annoyed."

"Oh, I'm sure he's had worse," Gordon said.

Sharon brought the roast vegetables to the table. Pumpkin, potatoes and cauliflower. "The white sauce is for the cauli." She unwrapped her apron and her spring dress puffed out as she did.

"You look gorgeous tonight, honey bun."

"That might just be the wine talking . . . but thank you."

"Really, smashing." Bob sipped more of the red. "So mother accepted what about me?"

"Gordon, do you take gravy?"

"Please."

"Tell Gordon what mother was so good to accept about me."

"I'm sure he's too bored to hear anything more about my mother."

"Then tell me, honey bun."

"I blame you, Gordon, you shouldn't have brought such a good wine. Just a cask of plonk next time will do."

"Well, if it wasn't my two heads . . . perhaps you're referring to my age?"

"Take another slice, Gordon."

"Yes please, Gordon. Take as much as you like. I might have just the red for dinner."

Little Jamie made his first appearance and he sat in the empty chair at the end of the table and smiled up at Sharon.

And they all sat down together.

"Tell me, Gordon. Bob says you're thinking of selling the Coral."

"One can only dream," he said.

"And would you stay in town?"

"Sharon, can you seriously ask that question?" Bob said.

"Well, honey, it's expensive in the city. There are advantages out here."

"I would like to move somewhere near the ocean."

"Maybe Cairns?" Bob said.

"Oh, it's far too hot in the summer, honey. What about Noosa?"

"Expensive."

"I was thinking maybe somewhere overseas."

"Good on you, Gordy."

Gordon probably missed it, but Sharon could hear the slur in Bob's voice. "Now you're making me jealous, Gordon."

"We could do the same, honey bun. Sell out to the gas people and move on."

"Maybe when mum has passed on."

"God, I swear I'll beat her into the grave."

"She's old . . . and I've all she's got."

"Gordon, what about shacking up with Sharon's mum. She's loaded . . . and she likes a drink. Didn't you get to know her that time she stayed at the Coral?"

"Can we move the conversation away from my mother for a bit. Or Gordon will never come back. Will you?"

"I'd come back for a dinner like this any time."

Sharon smiled and so did little Jamie.

"Where overseas?" she asked.

"Maybe Italy."

Bob gulped his wine. "Then I'm coming with you. Hold up, here's an idea, what about Sharon and her mother buy the Coral, and you and I go off to Italy."

"Very romantic, honey."

"I'm not going to be the woman though, Gordy. If you know what I mean."

"Yes, you can't stay on those old arthritic knees of yours for too long, can you, honey?"

"Touché again, honey bun. You *are* in good form tonight."

"Eat your dinner before it goes cold."

"Yes, honey bun. If I'm a good boy will I get some dessert?"

"Not if you spill any more wine on the lace."

"Oh my God, the lace!"

"Gordon, don't think my husband is a drunkard. In fact, it's quite out of character for him."

"Yes, quite out of character. How do you like the new me?"

"It's best to humor him." She reached over and touched Bob's hand. "You are wonderful, darling. Isn't he Gordon?"

"Wonderful."

"You keep flattering me, Gordy, and I *will* be the girl."

Sharon smiled and patted his hand. "There's a good boy. Eat your dinner. More lamb, Gordon?"

"Well, if you won't tell old Gordy what your mother accepted about me, perhaps you could tell him about something else he doesn't know about."

"I might have some more pumpkin, Sharon."

Bob topped up his glass. "You see, Gordy, Sharon and I have tried for some time to have a third addition to the family. Surprisingly, it doesn't appear to be any problem with *me*." He swigged the red. "Sharon's had lots of tests, down at the Base, but for the life of me I can't seem to find out the results."

"Have some more gravy."

"Yes, the tests were done weeks ago. Maybe a month. But the results seem to have gone astray."

Little Jamie looked up at Sharon and showed her the picture he was drawing. She almost said something about it but bit her tongue.

"I can't seem to get the results off Doc, though, Gordy. Which is unusual for him. He crossed the street once to tell me Sharon's map of Australia . . . that birthmark of hers . . . was nothing to worry about. But clearly these tests seem none of my business." He drank more wine. "But maybe you would like to know the results, old man . . . what do you say?"

The room fell silent for a bit, with all but Bob gazing at the Royal Doulton.

"You see, Gordy," he said presently, "I'm a bit flummoxed. A nice word . . . flummoxed. It's one of your mother's, honey bun. But I am a bit. If the tests are all okay, then why doesn't Sharon want me to know?" He cut into his meat and continued his ruminant way. "One possibility is she was hoping for a bad result. A problem not fixable . . . so I could just give up on the plan, what was originally *our* plan . . . and just forget all about it." He skewered a chunk of lamb on his fork. "But why not just lie? 'It's bad news, honey, I don't have any eggs . . .' and take the pill behind my back. That's what I'd do, Gordy."

Still no response, from either of them.

He chewed into the meat. "Damn good lamb this." He wiped his mouth and took another swill of the red. "And on the other hand, if the results *are* bad, really not fixable, which is uncommon with IVF and all, I've read about it . . . why would she not want me to know? Perhaps she feels she's failed me. But Gordy old boy, she knows I adore her . . . who in this town could possibly think that Sharon could fail *me?* The opposite, yes . . . of course. 'Sharon's just packed up and left . . . we knew that was on the cards,' they'd say. 'I'm surprised she's lasted so damn long.'" He wiped his mouth. "On the other hand, if it is bad news and fixable . . . IVF is hard stuff Gordy, daily injections, lying waiting to see if those little implanted embryos hatch, it's not for the faint hearted, so I've read. Petra Donaldson went through it, you know Petra, ruined their relationship she said. So I could perfectly understand if Sharon is having second thoughts about it. I really would understand!"

He stopped.

Gordon stared at him with a hint of a smile.

Sharon kept her gaze at the cauliflower.

And little Jamie no longer sat at the table.

"So, Gordy, do you see why I'm so flummoxed?" He took his wine glass and finished it. "Oh well, just my silly thoughts. Silly old Bob. Too much wine again. Quick, put down the plastic before the carpet gets soiled." He took up another chunk of meat. "But I must say this lamb is delicious, honey bun. Really top stuff."

* * *

The wire door let the quiet warm leak into the sunroom—a space not so sunny since the old timber shutters were always kept closed at this time of year, barricading the room from the corrugated heat outside.

She had left him more than an hour ago.

Robbo flicked the page over and stared at the writing without the words assembling into anything meaningful. And so he turned back to where he had first begun.

Among Australia's key cotton pests is the global insect nemesis of agriculture, Helicoverpa armigera. More commonly known as bollworm, the larvae of this beast munch on precious crops causing damage estimated at greater than US$2 billion worldwide each year. The bollworm's weapon is simple: it rapidly evolves resistance to insecticide sprays.

The grandfather clock that ticked too loudly for such an isolated place, far away from any public road, far away from the neighbors, showed she had left him an hour and twenty minutes ago, precisely.

Tick-tock. Tick-tock.

To tackle the problem, in the mid-1990s Australian cotton breeders began incorporating Bt insect resistance genes in their varieties, leading to plants that produce a substance that is toxic to the bollworm.

The sound of something living leaked into the shaded room from outside. Maybe footsteps in the dirt. He stood and walked over to look through a space where one of the timber shutters had buckled into a thin slice—no more than a keyhole into the bright outside.

The sun stung his eyes, but the view of the path from the gate was clear as the sky, and no visitor could be seen. Maybe a fox, but it was a bit early for them. Anyway, it didn't matter, since there was nothing around the place to worry about—unless the foxes had got a taste for cotton.

Robbo went to the kitchen table and sat back down.

Tick-tock. Tick-tock.

Since introducing it over a decade ago, there has been an 80% reduction in the use of chemical pesticides previously required to control bollworms. But a recent study indicates that harmful crop pests are becoming resistant to the genetically-modified crops.

Tick-tock. Tick-tock.

It would take an hour to get to Banga Hospital, longer if he had to stop at the store for grapes. No more flowers. Molly didn't appreciate them as much as before.

And flowers didn't seem appropriate today.

Tick-tock. Tick-tock.

In Australia, cotton growers must plant non-Bt "refuges," to provide a home for non-resistant pests to breed – because, when a resistant insect mates with a non-resistant partner, the resulting offspring is non-resistant.

Tick-tock. Tick-tock.

Molly wasn't getting any better, and Doc suggested she go to Brisbane, but he couldn't promise that it'd make any difference, so she preferred to stay closer to home. Doc said he had contacted the specialist and everything was being done according to the book. But, it seemed to Robbo, the book had only a few pages left to it.

He went back to his own book and the grandfather clock kept its steady pace in the background.

The Australian strategy also attacks the hibernation tactic of bollworms. Growers must cultivate the soil under Bt cotton to kill any resistant pupae during the winter.

It had now been one hour and twenty-five minutes, precisely, since Lil had left him.

Tick-tock. Tick-tock.

Maybe he could take some apples from the pantry instead of stopping for the grapes. It'd give him more time. Just in case.

He stood and went over to the wire door and opened it and went out into the still air, becoming wrapped in the blanket of the day. He walked the flat path to the gate and the view of the plains opened up to him and he could see as far as the true horizon, and the dirt road that fell straight down, branching twice, three times if you wanted to go around the dam, before reaching the tar road that led to Guburnburnin—visible to him, but out of earshot.

There was no one in sight.

Even if she went the long way home, she'd already be back by now.

He sucked in the air and walked back to the house, the sun hot on his neck.

When he sat inside, his eyes took time to accustom to the dim room and the page slowly brightened in front of him.

The bollworm was an ugly fucker.

Tick-tock. Tick-tock.

Molly liked apples. If he left now he could be back before sundown. That's if he didn't stay the whole visiting hours. Anyway, she'd be tired, so best not to stay too long.

Tick-tock. Tick-tock.

Would she come back in the dark? The place was easy to find. He'd keep the front porch light on for her just in case. The old homestead was like a lighthouse at night. Don't forget to turn the porch light off, Robbo—Molly was scared the light drew too much attention to them at night. Out there all alone. The kids away at school. Molly had seen *Psycho* too many times.

Tick-tock. Tick-tock.

But she had never come at night before. At dusk, but not at night.

He felt a churning in his stomach. Like bollworms wriggling in his guts.

Robbo turned back the page and started again.

Among Australia's key cotton pests is the global insect nemesis . . .

Tick-tock. Tick-tock.

Maybe he would give Molly a call at the hospital. See how she's doing. Not now, though—it was her rest period. Maybe at visiting hours. Smack on 5.30. How is the nausea? Any vomiting today? How is the pain?

Tick-tock. Tick-tock.

Yeah, I don't think it's serious. Some stomach bug, he'd say. I'll be fine. I agree—best not to give it to you, darling. Best not to risk anything. But I'll see you first thing tomorrow. After sorting the dam out. That bloody pump. Anyway, no matter what, I'll be over tomorrow night.

Tick-tock. Tick-tock.

Because she never came at night.

Tick-tock.

* * *

"I don't drink, Gordon."

"It's a fine Coonawarra, Lil."

The table was set for two. No Sade. No candle.

"I haven't touched a drop in such a long time. It doesn't seem to agree with me."

"Then I'll keep dry myself."

"Dear Gordon, always the gentleman."

The early meal seemed more appropriate. Just like an old aunt visiting. Or an elderly parent.

"I appreciate the invitation, Gordon. With what you saw . . . my behavior the other night was not . . . respectful." She laughed. "There's a word I don't use much . . . respect."

"Don't think anything of it, Lil."

"Oh, I usually don't, luv, but every so often it's deserved. It is delicious lamb, so tender. This slow cooking of yours is really something."

He went over to the CD player and Sade decided to sing, but not too loud.

I gave you all the love I got . . . I gave you more than I could give . . . I gave you love.

"Such lovely music, Gordon. You're quite the romantic. I bet you're a poet."

He laughed and felt a rush on his cheeks. "Not me, Lil. But I admit to reading some on occasion. Wordsworth is behind you on the shelf."

Sade kept on in the lamb-scented space . . . *this is no ordinary love . . . no ordinary love.*

"What a strange thing she sings about." Her twang seemed to dissolve away for a bit. "What's ordinary love, I wonder?"

He wished the candle was lit, but there was too much light. "I can't say that I know, Lil." He watched her eyes scan the bright kitchenette.

"I can't say I know either." She said it without any mirth—like she was mildly surprised by the answer.

He wished he had drunk before she arrived, and he thought about opening the red anyway. "It's none of my business, Lil, but Sam . . . are you very close?"

She lifted her eyes from the bowl of fruit and snapped back into a thick drawl. "Liike peas in a pod, Gordon. Liike peas in a pod."

Sade kept singing about no ordinary love and he thought about switching her off.

"But we respect . . . there's that word again . . . *respect* our different needs . . . if you know what I mean, handsome Gordon."

He felt the rush, hot on his skin again. "I'm not sure what Wordsworth would say about that."

"What a funny thing to say. But I take your point." Her twang fell away again and it seemed to him he was talking to two different women.

"Maybe you could read to me some of this Wordsworth of yours later, Gordon." She looked around the room. "What a cozy place. And you have interesting little trinkets around the house."

"From my travels."

"Ah, you travel? This makes sense to me."

She kept her eyes on him, and he felt like an insect in a jar. He felt like he should lift his wings. Or touch the glass with his antennae. And he described the trinkets to her, their places of origin, and some stories connected with them.

"I lived on a rooftop in Athens for six months when I was twenty," he said.

"Where is this place, Athens?"

He looked at her, and for a brief moment she was in the jar. "Greece, Lil."

"Ah, Athena," said in her strange tongue with no hint of the XXXX drawl.

"You've been there, Lil?"

"Long ago." She nodded her head. "But it was the place to be, back then." She smiled. "And Sam loved it. The desert dries his nose he says. Always picking at it. But Athena, with the sea, and . . ."

"The desert?"

"He became obsessed with it for a time . . . khohl!" He watched her wriggle—a comfortable squirm. This woman oozed comfort. "Lilit . . . let's stay here a while, he said to me. Away from the . . . khohl." She laughed. "How could I say no, luv! Of course, we stay away from the desert place now, but in those days it wasn't so easy to get away." She looked up at him. "I see I'm talking too much, luv. What is it about this tidy town that makes me think of old times, 'ey? It's you, Gordon, that I'm much more interested in, right here in the present. You can't turn back time. Trust me, handsome Gordon, you simply must trust me on this."

"But if you could . . . what would you do?"

"Shamayim! That would be such a long, long time ago . . . and you know something, handsome Gordon . . . I'm not sure I would have done anything different." She stared at him. "And what about you?"

"Well, I guess I'd not have married. Or married someone else."

"Interesting . . . we might have something in common there, sweet Gordon."

"And not have bought the Coral." He sighed. "And—"

"And, and, and, Gordon . . . this is what happens when you dwell on the past."

Sade moved to smooth operator, and the room dimmed as dusk fell. By the time Wordsworth appeared the candle was lit.

"You say this is his best poem," she said. "About daffodils?"

"And about being alone with them." He lifted his wings to display their full pattern.

"Alone with daffodils. How very, very strange. A night of no ordinary love and solitude with flowers . . . who would have thought . . . in the land of the Queens." She turned the pages over and read to herself, her lips moving without the sound. "If you don't mind, I might borrow this little book for my boy . . . see what he makes of it. Sam can be very . . . artistic on occasions." She crowed up a laugh. "It's one of our more obvious differences."

He wanted to spend some time outside of the jar but couldn't find a way out.

"Goodness, Gordon! Look at the time, we've been here for hours." She stood and grinned at him and some of the crusts on her face started to ooze through her makeup. "I must say this has been a de-liightful evening."

She moved over and kissed him on the cheek like an aunt. Or an aged parent.

"You've got my juices flowing, handsome Gordon." And she went through the beaded door as if she had just popped in to deliver the mail. "No need to see me out, luv."

And by the time she had gone back to her room, he had opened the red and poured his glass to the brim.

* * *

"Class be quiet! You are like a pack of galahs." The teacher stood out front behind the white board that took up most of the wall.

"We have two galahs at home, Mrs. Shipping."

"That's nice Sarah McConachy. Now try not to behave like one."

"They're cockatoos, Sissy . . . not galahs," Billy said from further up the back.

She turned her head to him. "They are too!"

"Galahs are pink . . . not yellow," he whispered, not so softly.

"Mrs. Shipping, can galahs be yella?"

She watched the eyes look up at her. The little ones at the front more keen than the year sixes at the back. She loved country classes, but the span of ages tired her more than she wanted.

"Try and find out at home and let the class know tomorrow, Sarah. But for now, it's singing we need to concentrate on. We have the Christmas concert coming up and need to practice. And we need to choose a person to sing the solo parts." She smiled as Sarah McConachy sat up straight like a soldier. "One of the older children, Sarah."

She watched the little girl slump down and grumble something under her breath.

"Are there any volunteers?"

The eyes at the back pointed every way except to the front.

"My brother is takin' singin' lessons, Mrs. Shipping."

"Shoosh, Sissy." Again a not-so-soft a whisper.

"Billy, is that true?"

The boy grimaced at his sister, who turned back and stuck out her tongue. "Yes, but I don't sing songs yet."

"That's true too, Miss. It's so boring . . . that's why I don't do it."

"Well, Billy. How about giving the class a demonstration?"

She smiled as the boy grimaced at his sister again. But he stood all the same. Billy was a good boy.

"Come out here to the front."

The boy moved up the narrow aisle and tugged at his sister's hair on the way past.

"Ouch! Mrs. Shipping!"

The class of galahs squawked up.

She regained control. "Billy is very kind and brave to share his singing with us. Whenever you want to start, we are ready to listen" She glared at the class. "In silence."

The boy breathed in deeply, raising his arms up as if he was ready to catch a large beach ball, and started to sing simple vocal exercises: 'A' up and down, 'E' up and down, moving to the falsetto 'ooh to ahh.' But the sound had a purity . . . she had never encountered anything like it. It seemed to effortlessly fill the room and gave the impression it could have filled an auditorium with no more strain. The motion through the ranges was seamless and under absolute control. It was . . . the sound alone simply filled her with joy.

When he finished the class kept silent until Sarah Anne McConachy broke it. "See, I told you it was borin'."

But no one laughed.

It was moments like these that Mrs. Harriet Shipping lived for. She went over and touched the boy's shoulder. "Well, Billy, I must say that was something special. And class, I think you'll all agree . . . we have found our solo performer."

And Sarah Anne McConachy huffed up something and sulked for the rest of the day.

* * *

"If I tell you something, Mister, promise not to get mad?"

The lesson had finished and Sam had just parted the yellow wheat to exit.

Billy didn't wait for a response for it usually didn't come. "You know how we had that deal not to sing for anyone else?"

Sam turned but didn't respond.

"Well, Sissy told Mrs. Shipping about my lessons . . . and she made me sing in front of the whole class . . . and she must of liked it . . . because I have to be a solo . . . in the Christmas concert." He held his breath.

"You are not ready."

"I told her that, but she wouldn't listen."

"Tell her again."

"She's my teacher . . . I got to do what she says."

He watched Sam look down at the trodden chaff.

"What songs?"

"Well, I have to sing lots with the class, but one just myself." He took out the slip of paper and handed it to him.

Sam studied it and laughed. Billy didn't know he could.

"This is impossible."

"But I got to."

"She's mad."

"I got to, Mister! Even if I stop the lessons, I just got to."

"You speak Italian?"

He shook his head.

"*Lascia ch'io pianga,*" Sam said in that funny way of his. "You understand this?"

"I got to."

"Let me cry."

"Don't cry, Mister."

Sam laughed again and Billy felt strange when he did.

"When is this concert of yours?"

"Last week of school. Mrs. Shipping said we had four weeks."

"Mrs. Shipping is a fool."

"She said it's her favorite . . . and nobody 'cept me could sing it."

"An idiot."

"She said she's been teaching twenty years, and I'm the first she's ever asked."

Billy looked up at a crow that turned an arc down low to them and he ducked, though the bird was a fair distance away when he did. Sam didn't move an inch.

"I was wonderin', Mister, could you teach it to me?"

"Yes, of course. But I'm not going to."

Billy kicked into the chaff.

"Even Nicola wouldn't be able . . . so I leave the impossible to Mrs. Shipping."

Billy kept his eyes to the ground and kicked at nothing in particular. "Can I keep practicing with you then?"

"Yes."

"Thanks." He did more kicking. "And . . . if you ain't doin' anything . . . would you come and hear me sing at the Christmas concert?"

The crow turned again but kept its course higher in the sky.

Sam turned and parted through the curtain of wheat. "See you in the morning."

* * *

Sam had to wait for the wheat harvest before he was asked to play his first game of cricket. They were down a few, and even Teddy had to chip in.

Sam was a bowler, but they lost the toss and were sent in to bat. Marri was on top of the ladder, and their quick bowler was something else. So by lunch, most of the Guburnburnin Hooters were out, yet he was still waiting his turn.

"You should have been put in before me, Sam," Sharon said.

"How do you know? You haven't seen me bat before?"

They sat on the picnic blanket away from the others. She knew he was playing so she'd made an effort for lunch—Chicken Cacciatore, her mother's special recipe, with extra oregano.

"Well, if you're not better than me, you've got to get another interest," she said.

"Like what?"

"How about stamp collecting?"

He looked at her and she poked him in the ribs.

"There must be something else you do well besides this silly game. Sitting out in the sun, waiting to play all day."

"Why do you play then?"

She dissected the chicken with her plastic fork. "It gives me something else to do in this God forsaken place."

He looked at her with those dark eyes of his. "You think God has forgotten this town of yours."

"Why wouldn't he?"

He looked up into the cloudless sky. "We can only hope."

She laughed. "You're something else, Sam. I really don't know what to make of you." Jesus, he was good looking though. "Where you from, Sam. I mean originally?"

"Cairns."

"The big smoke." She laughed. "Well, bigger than here." She tilted her head to the sky, then adjusted her hat so it shaded her face some more. "It must be nice to live by the ocean. I dream of it sometime."

"Then move there."

"Oh, us country girls seem to be stuck out here. It's a curse, I'm sure." She watched him eat his chicken. "Bob's third generation. I'm third generation." She laughed again. "Actually, the whole fucking town is third generation."

"Then stay."

"What would we do if we moved to the ocean? Give me some ideas."

He took a chicken leg and nibbled at the wet meat. "Find some . . . *passione*."

"Ooh, say that again."

"*Passione.*"

She felt a rush but he seemed not to notice the effect the word had on her. "I used to have a soft-drink at school called that. Sickly sweet, but I loved it." She giggled. "Anyway, get a *passione*. Like this silly game?"

"No. Like stamp collecting."

"Oh, you're a comedian, Sam." She put more chicken on his plate. A dab of coleslaw. "I know I've asked you before . . . but do you have a girl back home?"

"Did you ask me?"

"You forgot. On purpose, I suspect."

"No."

"Well, that makes sense. Travelling with your . . ."

"Mother."

"Not that there's anything wrong with that."

"Quite." He turned to her. "You are barren, aren't you?"

She felt sick in the stomach. "I beg your pardon?"

"You are sterile."

A panic set in. "Who have you been talking to?"

He picked up a chicken wing and sucked the skin away, and the juices went down his chin.

"Has my fucking husband been talking to you?"

"No."

"How do you know about this?"

He put the remains of the wing on his plate. "Why does it matter?"

She didn't reply.

"It doesn't matter, you know. Being sterile. It doesn't matter one bit." He said it like he was reading a train timetable. Without a hint of *passione*.

Sharon went back to her chicken, and when she eventually decided to speak, it was about the weather.

It was soon after lunch when he got his turn to bat.

"This is your big chance . . . don't stuff it up," Pete shouted as he walked out to the center. And Pete grinned at Sharon, who wished him away, like she usually did.

"Go get'em, Sam," she sang out, and the heads of the Hooters turned as one toward her. But she didn't care at all.

The Marri fast bowler came back from his spell. Their captain tossed him the ball and told him to be quick with the tail. Sam marked the centre stump with his shoe. He seemed nervous to her, and that struck her as cute.

When the first ball came down, Sam lifted his bat and let it fly past off stump. With the second delivery, he clipped it between third man and point for four.

"Whoo hoo," Sharon screamed and the Hooters clapped and the sun baked down on the dirt pitch and them all. Sharon stole a look at Pete, who looked more than interested in the play than usual.

The Marri quick rubbed the ball into his red-stained groin, and as he approached the wicket he seemed to be running a bit quicker this time. The ball lifted from the centre of the pitch and she saw Sam watch it fly past his ear. When the keeper caught it, he walked a few yards down the pitch and patted down the dirt with his bat.

The Hooters clapped and Sharon felt proud and Pete went to shout something but didn't. And at the end of the over, Sam had scored another boundary, and the Marri quick nodded to him, and the Hooters shouted up some more encouragement.

But in the first ball of the next over, Teddy swung and missed—his off stump rattling away from his pads. And so the team was all out.

And for the rest of the day, Sam didn't get a bowl, even though the Marri Marauders were two for a hundred and eighty by the close of play.

* * *

"What have you been saying, Bob?"

"What, honey bun?"

"Was it at the pub?"

"I have no idea what you mean?"

"When you were pissed? Was it before or after you vomited on Pete's floor that you decided to talk about my fucking plumbing?"

"Calm down."

"Or was it to Lil? When you drove on the many journeys for her doctors' appointments, did you mention it then? I want to fucking know!"

"I don't know what you're talking about."

He hadn't even had a chance to remove his hat before she turned on him. And even while haranguing him, she kept looking at the empty chair at the table, which was very strange.

She sat down on the chair next to the empty one and started to cry.

"My fucking plumbing is no one's business!"

Bob stood where it had all started but didn't feign to move. He wasn't sure where the land mines in this conversation were.

She stared at the empty chair again. "Do you understand, Bob?"

"No, honey bun." He felt hate and he couldn't shake it away. "I don't understand. It's not *just* your business."

"It's not fucking yours, let me tell you that!"

He went over to the wall and put his hat on the hook.

She sat and cried some more, and he heard the dog bark out the side of the house.

"I'm going to have a shower," he said, "then head off to the pub for dinner."

And he watched her move her lips at the empty chair and thought it strange but didn't really give a shit.

* * *

The high beam lit up the road the color of slate; the plains a halo of bottle green. Bob slowed to fifty as he entered the town and pulled over to the petrol bowser because Mickey's light was still on in the store.

He got out and filled the tank, and Mickey waved at him through the window and registered the amount on his account. He went over to the glass door. Mickey flicked a switch under the desk and the door unlatched.

"Do you mind if I get some nibbles, Mickey?"

"Never one to turn down a customer."

Bob took a basket and went down the dim aisle; the place only lit by the light at the cash register.

He packed a basket with a block of white chocolate, family size, a bag of mixed nuts and sultanas, salt and vinegar Thins, also family size, and a bunch of bananas.

"You got the munchies, Bob?"

"I'm having a party. Want to come?"

"I've got to finish these lousy accounts. But it looks like you're a pretty classy caterer."

"You know me. All class."

Mickey added the goods to his account, and Bob got back into the Statesman Deville and moved away down the road, past the pub and out of town. He lent over and opened the packet of Thins. The radio crackled an old Air Supply hit, and he kept on at a steady pace, just below the 100 speed limit, and the green plains began to undulate a bit as he went further away from the town.

By the time he hit Banga, he had finished the chips and two bananas. The main street was sparsely lit with the same old electric lights that first went in before he was a kid. He parked the car outside the hotel and opened the family chocolate block. Sharon said dark chocolate was good for you, so it was the only flavor found in the house. He took a couple of rows of the white block, bit into it, and watched the door of the Banga Hotel swing open. The pub looked pretty full, though normal for Saturday trade. His farm was an hour and a half from here, but he was third generation, and even though the town had new folks brought in for the coal-seam gas, he would be sure to know at least a handful of them inside.

So he decided not to go in. He wasn't feeling social.

The chips and chocolate had made him thirsty, and he felt stupid he hadn't bought some Coke at Mickey's. Family size too. So he went out of the car, opened the boot, pulled out the four-liter water container, and skulled a lot. It tasted of warm plastic, and he skulled some more, closed the boot, took the container back in the car, and headed off down the road, steady, just under 50.

Along the same stretch he passed the hospital, the windows a soft glow in some of the wards. Which one held Robbo's missus? It wouldn't be so bad to lie in one of those beds, as long as you were pain free, with no responsibility, just waiting around for the inevitable that would come to us all one day. He felt sorry for Robbo more than his wife, which he felt bad about, but that's how he felt.

He passed the new motel that was doing a good trade, he'd heard—coal-seam again—and he thought about stopping for the night but he didn't feel tired. So he kept on driving, further west and out of the town, just below the speed limit. Hall and Oates sung in the car, clear because the local radio station broadcasted from Banga. *Watch out boy she'll chew you up . . . oh-oh here she comes . . . she's a man-eater.* And he took another slice of Milky Bar, as the road rose and fell with the undulations of the land.

He imagined what it would be like to lie in the hospital bed again. Warm under a couple of blankets. Propped up on a pillow so he could see the TV better. Flicking the stations because he had the control. With no worries about the farm and all that was flying around him. Why would you be worried if you knew your time was almost over? Maybe it would get lonely. Maybe it wouldn't.

At midnight the land flattened, the halo of bottle-green replaced with soft shades of chocolate. A land not made for much, though people gave it their best shot. At the T-intersection he had to make a choice, south toward New South Wales, or north further into the State. He was a Queenslander, born and bred, so he turned right and headed north. The reception from Sunny Day FM was long gone, and only the ABC could be found on the radio. Country and Western replaced the hits of the 80's. Johnny Cash, Lee Kernaghan, Kasey Chambers. *Barricades and brick walls won't keep me from you . . . well I'll be damned if you're not my man before the sun goes down.*

And the news. *The Queensland road death toll had its lowest drop in percentage terms in more than three decades. While the road toll was at its lowest in total numbers, authorities say it is disappointing the decrease in number from the previous year was not more significant. In a related incident, a seven-year-old girl was killed in a possible hit and run accident in the outer suburbs of Brisbane this morning. The child was playing at the edge of the road and was struck by a passing taxi. Observers said the taxi moved 20 meters beyond the accident before returning to the scene. The child's family was seen in a distressed state while waiting for the ambulance, and the girl was pronounced dead on arrival. A neighbor had this comment - "We are terribly upset for the family and little Tamsin. God rest her soul."*

The taxi driver is said to be in shock and was not available for comment.

Benny McDonald has been suspended from the Brisbane Broncos for six weeks after being found in possession of an ecstasy tablet at a nightclub in Fortitude Valley. While training has yet to hit full steam with the Broncos still in preseason, the five-eight said he had let his team, family and fans down, and accepted the punishment. The NRL has instituted a drug rehabilitation and education program for Benny.

Tai Chi, a 28-year-old panda of the Queensland Zoo, was found dead in his enclosure yesterday evening, after a long battle with cancer. Veterinarians say he had not responded to the chemotherapy as they had hoped.

Hollywood mourns the death of screen star Peter Matheson who died in what is suspected to be an AIDS related illness in Beverly Hills in the early hours of the morning, US time. Matheson, a onetime Academy Award nominee, had a long career in film and television. His brother and sister were at his bedside at the time of his death, and flowers were seen on his footprints in Hollywood Boulevard. He was 87.

Bob turned the radio off. The high beam kept his course clear and straight and for over an hour he hadn't passed more than a few trucks. If he had bought the Coke, he wouldn't have felt so tired, but he hadn't so he did. He pulled over to the side of the road, as far from the asphalt as he could get, and tilted back the front seat all the way. And he slept restless, with a niggling ache in the low of his back, before the morning sun rose to wake him.

* * *

"Mum, I told you I don't know where he is," Sharon said.

Elsie grimaced, her hands clasped together on her lap. In front, a floral teapot with matching cups and saucers sat on a round teak coffee table like flowers sprouting out of soil. "That's not like Bob. Your father, yes, but not Bob."

"What?"

"Your father ran away. Twice in fact."

"Before I was born?"

"No dear, you were at school. Boarding. Don't look at me like that, Sharon. There's a lot you don't know about that man."

Little Jamie sat next to Elsie on the bottlebrush lounge—it always made their meetings more tranquil. It was a stinking hot day. The porch windows were open and what feeble breeze came through the fly screens didn't give them any respite.

"Jesus, mum, can you put the aircon on?"

"Don't take the Lord's name in vain, Sharon. Anyway, the westerly should cool things down before too long." She poured the tea and put an Iced VoVo on each of the saucers. "You worshipped your father, but he had his faults, you know. Men out here get fidgety. Always have. When he came to his senses, he came back with his tail between his legs. They usually do." She nibbled into the pink and maroon biscuit. "But I repeat, I always figured Bob was cast from a different mould. Maybe you should contact Hec."

"That's all I need, get the police involved. The whole town would know about it before I got off the phone."

"You make your bed, you lie in it."

"What's that supposed to mean?"

Sharon watched her mother take another nibble of the VoVo as little Jamie moved away from her with a frown.

"I think you're too hard on Bob," Elsie said.

"Well, talk about the pot calling the kettle—"

"It's just my opinion, take it or leave it." She sipped the Earl Grey. "The tea's a bit weak, we should have drawn it longer."

"I know I'm too hard on him, Mum. So I don't need you to confirm it."

"He's a good man. Weak as this tea, but that's not a disadvantage. I wish your father had been more like him."

"Dad *was* like him."

Elsie laughed. "Oh. A case of marrying your father is it? That explains a lot."

Little Jamie jumped off the lounge and sat on Sharon's knee. He snuggled into her and she felt calm but only for a second or so. They both sat in the sticky heat, and the westerly that her mother had promised had yet to show itself.

"You look thinner to me, Sharon. Have another VoVo." She took two more out of the biscuit tin, one for herself. "You tried to phone him, I gather?"

"His phone is switched off. He didn't take the charger, so he's probably saving the battery . . . for emergencies." She sighed. "I sent him a text. Actually two. But I've had no reply."

"Oh yes. What did you write?"

"Please phone me."

"Practical, I guess."

"And 'We need to talk'."

"Much the same as the first."

"Well, what would you suggest?"

"Do you love him?"

Sharon dipped the VoVo into her tea and watched coconut bits float to the surface. "Sometimes."

"Then maybe tell him?"

"Sometimes not."

"For goodness sake, Sharon, what fairyland are you living in? You could do a lot worse than Bob. And have done. Pete Stephens was a real catch."

"Mum, we went out for less than a month."

"How you put up with someone like him, even for a month, was and still is beyond me."

"Mistakes, Mum. We all make them."

"Well that was a doozy." She sipped her tea. "Not that there's anything wrong with a publican, in principle. But Pete has been a no-hoper since he was a kid. Even your father raised his eyebrows with that choice. And he wasn't one to raise his eyebrows at his little precious very often." She dipped her biscuit like her daughter. "And I think that might be part of the problem."

Sharon sighed in the still heat of the room. "Mum, I wonder why I come here so much."

"Well, it's just my opinion." Elsie snapped the VoVo with the front of her false teeth. "But you got away with far too much from your father. I had to do all the discipline. And if you really want to know my opinion—you probably *don't*, but while you're in my house I guess I've got a right to voice it—you get away with far too much from Bob." She sucked into the pink coconut icing and took a sip from her cup. "He's as weak as this tea."

* * *

Sharon walked out to the back verandah and watched little Jamie run between the peach trees that separated the Gutree property from their own. When she was a child, her mother had got into a battle with old Mrs. Gutree over one of her dogs, always shitting on her garden and not its own. If she wanted a dog she'd get one herself, Elsie said. So, in the heat of it all, her mother had the trees planted, their branches trained into a V, so she couldn't see the Gutrees or their blasted dogs from the verandah—which was always occupied in wait for the westerly. She could see the trees were well laden with fruit, some of the peaches had fallen already, and she made a note to get some of the harvesters to come over before they started to rot—though Elsie preferred them to ripen on the tree, as God intended, and use the overripe ones for jam.

She went down the verandah steps and the sun struck down on her and she walked over to the shed and went inside. It was cooler there, her father had put double insulation in the ceiling and walls, and the space smelled of warm timber oil. She closed the door and stood in the dark for a bit, taking in the smell of her childhood, before flicking the light switch on. The tools were just as Dad had left them, all on their proper hooks, and she lifted one of the saws that had rusted, since they weren't cared for like before. Which was fair enough.

She thought about calling little Jamie in but decided against it.

Sharon looked at the wooden sign that hung in pride of place on the inside of the door, DADS SHED carved into the block, the etched letters painted black, though some of the paint had peeled off by now. She had made the sign in Woodwork in the first year of high school. Not many of the girls did woodwork, most chose Home Economics, and her father was so proud he bought her some extra tools to mark the occasion, though she never remembered using them much. She made him a bottle opener as well.

She turned around and saw it hanging on a nail near where the fridge used to be, which was always well stocked with XXXX. Elsie didn't have any use for the fridge and said it was a place for spiders to live, so she'd chucked it a while back. Which was fair enough. No point in running the electricity if she didn't need it.

She smiled as she remembered her father burping on purpose then blaming her for the smell. But she liked him doing it and would egg him on and was even allowed a sip of beer herself, way back as far as she could remember, and when she got to eighteen they used to share a bottle in the shed, just the two of them, when she needed some advice, which she usually feigned, just so she could spend some time with him alone. *What do you think of me going to Brisbane for nursing?* She had no intention of doing it but thought he might have an interesting opinion. *What about joining the army?* He used to laugh at this and said she wouldn't last a week. *Johnny keeps asking me out, do you think I should say yes*, which her father thought was a good idea, just to shut Johnny up for a spell.

The air was cool and so quiet she could hear herself breathing. She brushed a cobweb from the painted sign and took a deep breath before switching the light off—and smiled, as she caught a whiff of beer and stale breath from behind her, just before she opened the door and the bright sun entered the space.

Outside, she looked around for little Jamie, but he wasn't playing near the peaches or on the verandah either. He'd probably gone back inside to sit with Gran while she knitted herself a sweater—one that she'd never get to use because it was always so hot in this God forsaken place of theirs, where the westerly never came.

She checked her phone again for messages but none were registered. So she went back inside to get little Jamie and head off, just in case Bob had moved on from his fidgety ways, and had come back home with his tail between his legs, like her mother had said her father used to do.

* * *

Bob adjusted the venetians, and the afternoon sun tilted away from his face. His rest would have to be short, the sweltering heat building in the Statesman, and he rubbed his stubble and felt the need of a shower even more than before. He imagined water falling on his face, tepid, from a rainwater tank heated just from the sun. As a kid he wasn't allowed to use the rainwater for washing, he'd get spanked if he got caught. But when he thought he could get away with it—always in the middle of the day when nobody could escape the heat, inside or out—he would sneak out, lie under the tap, and let the water fall. He thought this was what heaven would feel like, if he were good enough to get in.

Bob massaged the back of his neck. The water kept falling but the sticky heat never strayed far. Deodorant would have been sensible, a toothbrush, his electric shaver. He reached over to the half empty packet of nuts, the only food remaining, and ate a handful.

He felt the Statesman shudder as a truck went by.

But he had water and petrol and the car was in good shape. The books in perfect order. A couple of credit cards all paid off. So things weren't too bad.

It'd be better if it wasn't so damn hot.

He could have gone east and then up the coast, or down. Down would be better. Buy a pair of swimmers and wash in the surf. He wasn't a good swimmer, but it would be something to plunge into the water, pop back in the Statesman still wet, windows down to let the ocean breeze in, cooling his skin with that strange smell, not the salt from sweat but fresh, tepid, like the rainwater. But instead he chose a northwest route, driving deeper into the furnace of the land. He laughed.

Northwest in summer, what would Gordy say? Why not head to Ayres Rock instead? If you want heat, then do it right.

And he thought about the bacon and eggs, tasting free range even though they weren't, and he took another handful of nuts and tried to sleep but couldn't.

He pressed into the back of his neck and felt a knot of muscle pinch as he did. He got a lot of muscle pains. *Bob. I know about this,* Elsie had said, *fibromyalgia Doc calls it, you should go and see him.* So he did and Doc laughed and said Elsie was a bit off on her diagnosis. Doc said it pleased him though, nice to know the community still had a use for his skills, and sent him for physio and it got better, as he said it would.

The Statesman rattled as another truck passed.

He reached forward and switched the radio on.

This country shouldn't support people like him.

I agree entirely, Madam.

He swears at the interviewer, what a mouth he has. And I don't see what the point of getting high is all the time. I simply don't.

Boredom. Or that's his claim.

Well when I get bored, I don't abuse my body.

I hear you.

I don't wander the streets.

Ditto.

I don't shout over the fence at my neighbors. As much as I might like to, sometimes.

I think you've knocked it on the head, there, Madam. We might think of shouting out at the world but we have a better—

Upbringing.

Listeners, I think this lady wants my job. What do you think, Clyde?

Oh, Phillip, who could replace you?

Clyde is nodding his head, listeners.

Don't be silly, no one could replace you.

I think you might. But we've got to go to the news . . . and when we're back, I'll open something new for discussion. We choose who comes into our country . . .

You should choose Phillip.

[Laughs] *You are too kind, though Clyde is shaking his head about that. But, after the news, I want you listeners to say what type of person we want. Give our Prime Minister a little help. You know he listens. So we will take calls now. And maybe also open the lines about what you think of the new show on telly. I got to laugh, the biggest fatty versus the thinnest skinny. Is that what it's called, Clyde? That's it. Last night, and what a show it was, the fatty— I'm sorry I can't remember his name—the fatty had won the cooking contest, which you out there all predicted he would, the skinny won the interior decorating contest, ditto, but the tie-breaker was a real line ball. If you haven't seen it, I won't spoil it for you, but they sent them both to a bar, and the first to pick up someone won the contest. Don't worry, they're repeating it tonight. But you just have to see it. So while we're at the news, Clyde is going to take calls . . . who do we want in our country Australia . . . and who is your favorite to win . . . the fatty or skinny?*

Bob tilted the seat upright, and the heat of the sun struck down on his face. He twisted his neck and heard something creak, leant over, and took a swig of water, tasting even more of plastic. He turned the key and eased the car back onto the road. And he kept on going straight, until after an hour or so, he turned into the single lane highway that headed due east.

* * *

The Bjelke-Petersen Community Hall was dressed with red and green streamers, red and green balloons, *Have a Merry Christmas* in red and green letters. The electric fans, running full bore, clicked overhead on parents, grandparents, friends of the family, all fanning themselves with their concert programs. The choir had just finished the last carol, *Away in a Manger*, and Mrs. Shipping turned away from the piano keys and smiled at her sweating audience.

"Those of you who know me well, know that I have a great love of classical music. And indeed, some of my most treasured moments are simply sitting in my little lounge room, listening to my collection of CDs. One of my favorite pieces . . . no, my *favorite* piece . . . is by George Frederic Händel. *Lascia ch'io pianga* or Let me weep." She smiled. "And let me say I have wept when listening to it on many occasions."

The audience flapped their programs.

"So today, we close the school concert with a special performance of this—not the entire piece, but the first half—by one of our choir members. Billy McConachy has been practicing only for a short time, but I must say we are all very proud of him." She looked down at his parents who beamed up at the stage. "He will be accompanied by the Australian Brandenburg Orchestra. But how, you ask, will we get them all into this little hall of ours?" Some of the audience laughed, politely. "Fortunately, they all fit onto this CD." She nodded to one of the children who manned the player at the edge of the stage. "And so, without further ado, give an encouraging applause for Billy McConachy and . . . *Lascia ch'io pianga*."

The boy walked onto the stage and the fanning audience clapped, politely. Mrs. Shipping raised her finger, waiting for the applause to cease, before giving the signal to start. Billy lifted his arms up to his side, breathed in deeply, and nodded to her. She dropped her finger and he began to sing precisely when the music began.

Lascia ch'io pianga . . . mia cruda sorte . . .

His eyes were always closed, as his high-pitched aria filled the little hall, with the fans slowing to a halt and the audience smiling as one. Even Sarah Anne McConachy, who sat on her father's knee in the front row, kept her grin throughout. Mrs. Shipping watched the boy's arms rise and fall, missing the occasional word, but his voice remaining pure, and she nodded as he hit the high notes nearly always on the mark.

When he finished, he opened his eyes and the audience clapped, enthusiastically. Some even stood.

Mrs. Shipping went over to Billy and placed her hand on his shoulder. "You must understand how difficult this is. Not just the piece itself, to sing in Italian, not understanding the meaning but being able to produce such a beautiful sound."

The fanning resumed. The audience nodded, and Billy smiled at them all. In the front, Sarah Anne McConachy put her hand up and some of the children started to giggle.

"Miss, why don't you ask the nightingale to sing it? He understands the words, I bet he does."

She watched the girl turn on her father's knee and look up to the back of the hall. Billy pulled a face at his sister and shook his head.

"Well he does, doesn't he?"

Some of the parents turned as well, but Mrs. Shipping couldn't work out whom the girl was referring to.

"It's him, Miss." The girl pointed at a good-looking, raven-haired man in the last row who seemed not to register much, if his eyes meant anything.

Billy croaked, "Sissy!"

"Well, he does sing in Italian. We heard him." Mrs. Shipping lifted her arm up to the man in welcome. "If there's someone here who shares a love of classical music, I'm sure we'd all be very grateful." She looked for some inkling of a response from the dark haired stranger but he seemed uninterested, though it was hard to tell. "We would *certainly* be grateful."

Some of the Dads started a slow handclap, and the audience laughed as they did.

With most of the hall turned to him, Mrs. Shipping watched the man stand and thought he was going to move out the back door but he didn't. Instead, he came out the front as the slow clap softened.

Billy looked at her with worried eyes. "Miss, he doesn't sing in front of others."

The man made the first step up.

"Wonderful, please come on the stage."

"Miss!" The boy looked like he was going to cry, and she watched him turn to the man and say something she couldn't hear.

"I don't want to embarrass you, but I understand this man has been Billy's singing coach . . . and, well, you've just witnessed what a splendid job he's done."

The audience applauded again.

"In fact, I've been wanting to meet you formally." She laughed." And I guess this is as formal as you could want."

The man nodded and may have smiled, though again, she wasn't too sure. But he was a good-looking fella. Maybe he could give her a hand with the choir next year. It would be nice to get some help.

"Okay, if we could all hush a moment . . . children put your fingers to those lips and seal them." She held her finger up and looked at him. "Whenever you're ready."

The good-looking man nodded, and when the Australian Brandenburg Orchestra started so did he.

Oh, my . . .

Harriet Shipping had travelled more than most around these parts. She had been to many of the great opera theatres—the Met, La Scala, Vienna. She'd heard Sutherland and Pavarotti at Carnegie Hall, right up the front she was, and always made the trip down to Sydney when something special came through. And the acoustics of the Community Hall were fair at best, the clicking of the fans, the heat that never made an escape, the scraping of metal chairs against the timber floor. But when she was asked by the local district teachers' association at her retirement dinner some twenty years later, what her greatest single musical experience was, she had no trouble in answering them.

It was the five and a half minutes in that echoing, sweltering, clicking hall when the nightingale sang.

* * *

"It's him," she whispered.

Mickey kept scanning Doris's groceries but turned to see the oily-haired regular—Sam, that was his name—enter the store.

"The nightingale," she said.

"The who?"

She leant over to him. "The singer. He's foreign. An Eyetie, I think."

Mickey shook his head. "You been sniffin' diesel again, Doris?"

She threw him a face and turned to watch Sam move down the aisle. "Harriet Shipping says he's classical trained. Somewhere flashy, Europe probably."

"He's from Cairns, Doris."

"Rubbish. You haven't heard him sing. I have, and I'm telling you for a fact, no one from Cairns sings like he does."

Mickey shook his head and scanned a bottle of detergent.

Doris leant over again and whispered, "Slower, Mickey." She turned around and raised her voice. "Oh, goodness, I forgot the sweet'n sour. Arthur loves my sweet'n sour pork on Thursdays. I'll be back."

He watched her prance down the aisle and brush past Sam. He thought for a second she might have gone for the grope.

Sam kept on with his shopping and didn't respond even with eye contact.

"The sauces are in the other aisle, Doris," Mickey said.

She feigned a surprise and moved away into the next aisle. Mickey watched her peering at Sam through the tins on the shelves and eventually tailing him back to the register.

Doris smiled at Sam who stood waiting in line with a basket full of groceries. "Sorry, dear. Forgot the sweet'n sour." She handed it to Mickey and turned completely around to face her prey. "That was a wonderful performance you gave us." She looked into his basket. "Oh, pasta. My Arthur loves pasta. I guess you know how to prepare it better than most, though. What sauce do you recommend?"

Mickey kept his gaze at the oily-haired man and wondered how he could possibly avoid speaking this time.

"Tomato," Sam said.

"Fresh, of course?"

He nodded.

Doris turned again to Mickey with a grin. "Home-made pasta sauce, how could it be anything else." Then twisted back to Sam. "We did meet after the school concert, but only very briefly. Mrs. Jones, remember? I asked whether you'd be interested in giving a rendition of something for the CWA."

Mickey watched Sam's face transform into someone with a toothache. "Country Women's Association," Mickey said.

"The Banga branch. We hire the movie theatre every month and have a little soirée to raise money for the Flying Doctor Service. And let me say, we've had some wonderful speakers over the years."

"Really, Doris?"

"Yes, Mickey. Senator Flo spoke twice while she was a sitting member of parliament."

"Sorry I missed it."

"That event was for members only."

He kept scanning the goods, slow as instructed.

"I think we might be able to fill our little theatre if you could grace us with something similar to last week. Because, young man, I think it's fair to say, you are the talk of the town."

"One hour," Sam said.

"A one hour show, how marvelous!"

Micky would have bet a million against that.

"Mrs. O'Reilly, she's our current president, will be so excited." She lifted her hands as if in prayer. "We need to get some posters out. I will personally take charge of that. Mickey, pass me that pen and pad." Which he did. "On the poster, it would be nice to have a little information. I'd like to keep your name as 'The Nightingale'—of course, at your own discretion. But it's who you're known as, around these parts." She looked at Sam who nodded. "And maybe some places you've performed . . . yes, I think that would make a splash."

Sam looked at her blankly.

"Well, were there any places we might know of? Maybe the last major venue?"

"Madrith," he said. It had a foreign twist to it..

"I apologize, I don't know where that is."

"España."

"Oh, Madrid. Wonderful!" She looked over to Mickey and nodded. "Cairns, hey?"

Mickey kept on with the groceries and shook his head.

"From Spain to Banga, a one hour performance of the Nightingale!" She softened her excitement a bit. "I'm embarrassed to bring this up, but I'm also in the CWA choir." She said the name in a whisper. "We mainly do private performances, nothing fancy, at the hospital sometimes, nursing homes, certainly nothing like you would ever be used to . . . but I was wondering whether you might like—"

"No."

Mickey laughed.

"I perfectly understand, dear. I perfectly understand."

And Doris snatched the sweet'n sour sauce from her basket and turned to Mickey. "I don't want that now."

* * *

"Billy, you are straining!" Sam closed his eyes. "*Stai calmo, stai calmo.*"

'Aaaaaa' up and down, up and down.

'Eeeeee' up and down, up and down.

Scales in the wheat fields.

Sam lifted his hand. "*Riposati.*"

Take a rest, right. "I don't have to be back because school is finished up."

Sam didn't reply.

"So if you want me to stay longer, I can practice some songs."

"You aren't ready."

Billy kicked into the wheat chaff. "Mrs. Shipping—"

Sam raised his hand.

"Well, when will I be?"

"I want to go riding with you."

"What's that got to do with singin'?"

"You have a horse, and I have one I could borrow."

"Riding's borin'. Take Sissy, she always wants to go."

"I want to ride with *you.*"

Billy kicked into the ground again. "Maybe . . . if you let me do some songs."

"Listen, Billy. You have something that I'll never have." He pointed to his throat. "That is everything."

"But scales are borin'. And Mrs. Shipping—"

Sam raised his hand.

But Billy kept on this time. "I was goin' to say Mrs. Shipping says it's a contract. We do it at school. If we promise to do somethin' then she promises, too. So, I mean, *we* could do a contract. You with your ridin' and me with my singin'."

"To sing a song you need one thing." Sam pointed to his skull.

"I know, I know. You told me a thousand times."

"You don't have that. It takes years."

"I know. But it's a contract. And nothin' to do with singin'."

Overhead a crow circled high above them. Billy usually liked crows—his father said they kept the mice down. And Sissy was scared of them, so that was a bonus. But this one seemed always to be hanging around, and had swooped down more than once at him, usually on his way to practice. It must have a nest around.

He watched Sam stare straight at him, which was sort of unusual. It made him feel funny.

"Okay," Sam said. "But you still have to do the same time on your scales. The songs will have to be extra. After the riding."

"Deal."

"But you must understand, Billy. I take contracts very seriously."

"Me too. I always keep'em. Just ask Mrs. Shipping!"

* * *

Billy couldn't sleep. His window was opened to the westerly, but there was no breeze to be had, and the fan at the foot of his bed didn't do much but push the still hot air from one spot of his room to another. He lay without a sheet, without a shirt, just boxers to cover himself so Sissy wouldn't be able to bellow out his nakedness if she wandered by his door, even though he could hear her snoring. Doc had said her tonsils might have to come out if they didn't shrink some. He loved her, but he wished they'd make the decision to pull'em so he could get some sleep.

He rolled into another position. It wasn't too late because his folks were talking in the lounge room, the telly turned down low, and he could make out what they were saying, even through the whirr of the useless fan.

"Are you happy about Billy's lessons, Judy?"

"You heard him sing. It was marvelous."

"Every morning, though?"

"He's on holidays now. And to be honest with you, I wouldn't care if he wasn't. Did you hear what his teacher said? The best voice she's ever trained."

"Yeah, I was proud of him too. But, I don't like that he kept it from us."

"He was probably embarrassed. Like in that movie, Billy Elliot."

"That kid was a fag you know."

"Not then. Only later."

"Exactly."

"Oh, don't be so bloody stupid. He's just a little boy." He heard his mother move to the kitchen. "Mrs. Shipping said he would be a shoe-in for a music scholarship at one of the posh Brisbane schools."

"I don't want him boarding."

His mother came back closer, and her voice raised a tad. "Listen, Ed. This is a great opportunity for Billy, and I don't need you discouraging him."

"But there's something funny about that fella."

Her voice trailed off and he heard the fridge door burp. "Do you want the last of the Sara Lee for dessert?"

"Sure, thanks. And that hair of his. Like an aging rocker."

"He's artistic. Something we haven't been used to around this town."

"Why would a famous singer come and stay at the Coral?"

"Maybe to get away from the spotlight for a while."

Billy heard the microwave bip. It was too hot for pie or he might have made an appearance.

His mother's voice softened. "Why don't we invite him over for dinner? Get to know him better. Would that help settle you?"

"Maybe."

"Do you know how much those scholarships are worth?"

"I've got an idea."

Her harshness now returned. "Well, unless you're planning on winning the lottery . . . or selling the farm . . ."

"I told you *that's* not going to happen."

"Then be grateful for the blessing that has come our way. For once in our bloody lives."

Billy rolled over and put the pillow over his ears because he never liked it when his folks fought, especially if it was over him. And even though this jumbled the chatter, he could still hear his sister snoring.

* * *

Sally knocked on the door of number 3, waited a moment, said "Housekeeping," and knocked again. When no sound came from within, she turned the key and entered the room, taking her cleaning kit with her.

Inside, a dank smell of cum festered in the heat. Again. She wished he would keep the window open, but he never seemed to. So she left the door open and turned the ceiling fan on.

God knows who he was fucking all the time. She thought about asking Gordy, but knew it would irritate him—the motel owner's code of silence. She wondered if there were any prostitutes in the district, and laughed at this. What a shit job that'd be.

Maybe it was a bloke. He never seemed to take any notice of her, if he came back when she was cleaning. She didn't know if there were any fags around town. And you couldn't keep that a secret. Maybe he was rooting one of the pickers.

She stripped the bed-sheets, threw them on the floor, and opened the cupboard where she kept a couple of spares—that's if they weren't pinched. They'd lose at least one set every six months or so. How Gordy managed to make a quid from this place was beyond her.

She took a clean sheet and stared at the small suitcase that was never open. It was old, but seemed to be made of good quality leather—solid, with thick cream stitching that hadn't even frayed. Why had Gordy made a point of asking her not to touch it? She had pulled a face at him and he brushed her away—the customer was always right, or something of that sort. As if she'd be interested in the lodger's spare undies.

Anyway, he kept it locked. She had tried it before.

Sally made the bed. She picked up the dirty sheet and dropped it on the plastic chair sitting outside the door. It was a stinking hot day, and she wished she'd come earlier, but he rarely left before eleven. Jimmy Doyle said he saw him bowling down at the cricket field by himself. In this heat, he must be mad. She peeked next door and the old woman didn't seem to be around, either. At least she'd get both rooms done together. Be home for lunch.

She went into the room and looked at the strange case again. Went over and pressed the button.

It clicked open.

She closed it again. If it was so damn important why couldn't he bother locking the thing? She shut the cupboard door and started on the bathroom. In fifteen minutes she was done, and she went back outside, wiping the sweat away from her face, and looked through next door's window to confirm his mother hadn't returned. Thank God for small mercies.

Sally went back to get her cleaning kit, and, before leaving, pulled the curtain across like she always did. But instead of moving on to number 4, she closed the door and switched the light on, which wasn't usual at all. She went over and opened the cupboard, and unlocked the suitcase—the lid burping open.

And took a peek inside.

* * *

As he entered the pub, the regulars of the brown surrounds acknowledged him, and he sat at the bar.

Pete came up to him wiping down a glass. "Haven't seen you here a while, Robbo. How's the missus?"

"Not flash."

"You on your way or just coming home from the hospital?"

"Home, I guess." If the truth be told, he didn't really know. He turned and scanned the place. "It's quiet tonight."

"It's quiet most nights."

"Anyone out back?"

"We don't open the Bistro mid-week. You lookin' for a feed?"

He didn't know that either. "Maybe."

"I'd recommend the chili con carne. I got a batch heated up."

"The chili strong?"

"Nah. Makes you fart though."

"Maybe I'll hold off a bit."

Pete poured a schooner of XXXX and slid it in front of him. "On the house, Robbo."

He nodded.

"I'm real sorry about your Missus. I guess you're here to get away from it for a spell . . . so I won't harp. But I'm real sorry."

He nodded again.

"Unless you want to talk about it."

He took a mouthful of beer. "I might have to get the kids home from school."

"It's that bad, hey?"

"It's not fair to her, keepin' them away."

"Hard on them bein' there, though."

"They got a lot of livin' left. So whether it's hard on them or not. . . it don't matter."

The door swung open, and he twisted his neck sharp to see who entered.

"You waiting for someone, Robbo?"

He went back to his schooner. "Just sittin'."

Pete nodded to the newcomer and kept on rubbing his glass. "Those kids of yours, Robbo. Both boarding, that's got to add up . . . the hospital bills and all."

"Insurance covers most of it. Not much option for the school, though. Molly wants the best for them, which is fair enough."

"I guess." Pete took a sip from his neat Scotch hidden under the bar. "Did you hear the whisper goin' around? Bob's done a runner."

He lifted his head and stared at the publican. It was about the last thing he'd expected.

"I know. I couldn't believe it meself. Talk about a bloke punching above his weight. Actually, Shaz said to say hello."

He nodded. "I might pop in and see how she's going."

The publican grinned. "I thought about the same."

"Still sweet on her, hey?"

"Nah. That was ages ago. More fish in the sea."

"You catch one yet?"

"Too much fuckin' work, with the pub and all. Anyway, you got the best sort in town."

"Fair enough." He kept his eyes on the amber glass.

He had visited Molly in the early afternoon. She was dozing when he came in, propped up on three pillows, her breath harsher, like one of the hands who had Cotton Lung until Doc diagnosed it and sent him packing. Her skin seemed different too, a lighter shade, waxy, and he put the bananas down in a bowl—they had extra potassium, which he'd thought might be good when you're sick. He sat next to her and read the *Woman's Weekly*, just the pictures, before her breathing changed, and her head turned, beaming with that *I'm all right* smile of hers, even though he knew she wasn't.

Molly told him her neighbor had gone home for Christmas, would be back on Boxing Day. They had organized her drips and pain pump so she could manage them at home. She laughed that the woman, Jeanie, when the relatives got too fussy, would bump up the dose of morphine in her little pump, which would make her drowsy and keep them quiet for a bit.

I'm lucky I don't have family like that, Molly said, and she held his hand when she said it, smiling, and they talked about her coming home in the same way. She thought that might be a great idea, the girls could tend to the lamb. Robbo was a disaster in the kitchen, and she could shell the peas, for fresh peas were mandatory at the homestead on Christmas Day.

"Tell me, Pete," he said suddenly, "the red-head that's new in town. She come in here much?"

The publican wiped another glass. "Lil? Yeah. And her son too. The *nightingale* they call him. Jesus Christ."

"You expecting them tonight?"

"No idea. They're no boozers. They usually just come for dinner." Pete waved at departing trade. "And you know something? I think Gordy might be sweet on her. He comes in every so often askin' her whereabouts. Poor bastard."

"He's a good bloke, Gordy. It'd be a real loss if he closed the Coral."

"Yeah. And *his* missus did the running. Gordy and Shaz left at the altar. Can you fucking figure it?"

"Who knows what goes on behind closed doors?"

Pete went to tend to the others, and Robbo sat with his XXXX alone for a while. If he had a second schooner he wouldn't risk it to Banga.

The cops had been testing for booze of late, just before the eastern entrance to the town. And there was no other way in.

What a selfish prick he was.

It was three schooners before he ordered the chili con carne. By that time the threat of farting no longer worried him so much. He had spoken to Molly on the mobile and said the Ag-inspector had come later than he should have, so he couldn't make it that evening. She understood. She was good like that. And she was interested how the bollworm was going. Even in the state she was in, still interested in that ugly little grub. Jesus. He spoke outside, of course. And if the saloon doors swung open he muted the phone. Had to turn it off once and call back. Bad reception on the hill. It was renowned for it.

Yeah, what a fucking selfish prick he was.

"How's the con carne?" Pete asked.

"Not bad. Maybe one more to wash it down."

It was eight-thirty and the place had quieted somewhat. One of the pokies sang 'Yes we have no bananas' in a digital remix. Over and over, until he couldn't get the tune from his head.

What the fuck was he doing here?

But he knew too well the answer—behind closed doors and all that.

"How's the cricket team, Pete?"

"Strugglin'."

"I hear that new fella isn't bad."

"The nightingale. He'll have to prove himself. And I might just make him wait."

He looked a question at the publican.

"Well, he's so fucking eager. And Teddy was supposed to be in the team, so he's pissed off with me. And the nightingale eats a fuckin' salad with a glass of fuckin' water!"

"Fair enough."

"Besides, makin' him sit out gives Shaz the shits . . . and I like to watch her *squirm*." Pete said the word like he was gutting a fish. "Keep that to yourself, Robbo."

He noticed the publican's words were slurred and wondered how long his liver would last before packing it in. His father's certainly didn't go the distance.

"I'm a cunt," Pete said, "you don't have to say it."

He swigged at his beer. "We all are, Pete. Some more than others. But we're all from the same mould."

"You becoming a philosopha, Robbo?"

He grinned. "Nah. Just another cunt."

* * *

Gordon wasn't sure whether to open the white or not. The candle was in place, some Bach to start off with, softly played. Soy-braised chicken, slow cooked with apple cider vinegar, some boiled rice, and homemade Christmas cake for dessert.

He took the bottle that had been chilled in the freezer—since he only thought about opening it a short while back. She didn't drink, and she wasn't the type to be coerced into anything. No, the alcohol was for him. Dutch courage. And the Riesling would go well with the chicken.

He twisted the screw cap and poured himself a tall glass. He hadn't eaten lunch, so one would do the trick. He switched on Bach and read some Wordsworth. And wandered lonely with the daffodils for a spell.

When the toad croaked, he skulled the dregs and danced over to the beaded doorway.

"Coo-ee, Gordon!"

"Coo-ee, Lil!"

She entered the room with a wide grin, her makeup no longer clumped to the healed sores on her face. "Bach in the land of Queens. How charming."

"Come in and get cozy, Lil." He kissed her on the cheek, but near to her mouth, and felt some of the hair of her fine moustache on his lips.

And his cock ached out of the blue.

Gordon watched her sit on the lounge and wave her head to Bach as she did.

"What is it about this music that's strange. Oh, I don't know . . . I'm getting just too old, handsome Gordon." She took the CD cover from the player. "Bach sonatas for violin and harpsichord. Where was I the first time I heard this? It wasn't long ago. Sam would know of course." She kept bobbing her head to the music. "Oh, Gordon. This will ruin my night . . . let me get him."

She popped off the lounge and left without a glance.

Gordon went over to the fridge, opened it, and poured himself another glass of Riesling. By the time Sam and Lil returned together he had quaffed half of it.

They stood in the little lounge room, Lil waving her head to the music, Sam in his bus-waiting stance. Gordon took another swig of wine.

"Well, Sam?"

"Could be anywhere."

"It was in Carlo's time, wasn't it?"

"No."

"Oh, shit. It was!"

"Lilit, I've said this many times . . . I do believe you are perpetually tone deaf. It has to be a curse. Maybe just to irritate me."

"Gordon, what does the information say about when it was written?"

He swayed over to the player and studied the CD cover. "The six sonatas were composed between 1717 and 1723, when Bach served as Kapellmeister for Prince Leopold August in Cöthen."

"1723 Samil."

"Don't be fucking ridiculous. Do you even know where Cöthen is?"

"Sam, don't be rude in front of Gordon."

"Carlo never knew of Bach."

She waved her head to the music as if Sam wasn't there. Or Gordon.

"If I had to guess, I would say New York," Sam said.

"That recent?"

"Yes. But I am impressed you knew who composed it."

He watched her smile, her head still conducting the sonata. "Gordon, Sam thinks I'm—"

"A heathen?" Gordon said.

She laughed up a crow-call. "Heathen . . . no, he wouldn't call me that."

Gordon watched Sam smile. He wasn't sure, but he thought it was the first time he had seen him do it.

"Lacking culture." She laughed again. "I gave him a surprise with that poetry book of yours, though."

"You didn't understand a word of it," Sam said.

"You can be hurtful sometimes." But she said it with her eyes closed and her head swaying to the harpsichord and violin, without a hint of reproach.

"May I go now?"

"Would you like to stay for dinner, Sam?" Gordon said.

"No, he wouldn't. Particularly after being so horrible to me." Her eyes were still closed as she floated with the music.

Sam turned away without any emotion.

And Lil, with her eyes still closed, twisted to the direction of the departing man. "Oh, and Sam. You'll be home when I get back, won't you, dear." She smiled and her head bobbed with the quickened violin.

And Sam exited without bothering with a reply.

Chicken and soy filled the candle-lit space. The bottle of Riesling more than half empty. And Bach had moved to his Brandenburg concertos.

"Even if I wanted, I couldn't drink," Lil said. "That doctor of yours is worried about my liver. More tests. I'm exhausted by it all." She smiled. "But believe me, it has never been good for my head. Sam says I am a different person when I drink. So we made a rule. And rules should *not* be broken."

Gordon's head swam, and he hoped the feeling would last, hangover or no hangover. But the morning felt far away, and he grinned again at Lil, her face flushed, yellow candle-lit, and she grinned back at him.

"I remember when Sam made the rule. My goodness he was angry." She laughed. "I got into a little altercation with the owner of an eatery." Her face moved closer to the candle and her eyes danced and the flame tilted with her breath. "Well, it was more than *little*, I think you would say. Afterwards, we had to make ourselves scarce. But oh, Sam was upset. Not with my performance, which he did admit later to be impressed with. But you see he liked the place, the whole town. And he can be such a baby when he doesn't get his own way."

The Brandenburg Concerto No. 3 finished and Gordon stood to change the CD. He felt Lil's eyes follow him and he swayed a touch before making it to the player.

"What are we going to do with you, handsome Gordon?"

She said it in that strange way of hers, all accent suddenly gone, and he felt like he was in the glass jar again. He put Concerto No. 4 on and came back, flapping his wings. "What ever you want, Lil."

She breathed in, and the candle flickered yellow light across the table. "Of course, Gordon. That's the way it always is."

She didn't smile like he expected she would. He lifted his wings and felt them scrape against the wall of the glass.

Her voice stayed in her newsreader speak. "That cleaner of yours . . ."

"Sally?"

"Sally, yes. I think she's broken our agreement."

"I'm not sure what you mean, Lil."

"With our suitcases."

He felt his heart race and lifted his head to see if there were any breathing holes in the lid.

"It's not your fault, Gordon. You are not to blame yourself."

"If it's true, let me talk to her."

The flame lit up her eyes. "Are you fond of her?"

"She's a good kid. Always helpful. And I've never had any complaints."

"She's not the first . . . and won't be the last. There's something about those cases of ours that attracts an interest. Sam has his own ideas, which I must say, are gaining more credibility as time goes on."

"Nothing was missing?"

"No no no. We wouldn't be having this type of conversation if there was."

"She's a good kid, really."

"Let's forget about it. I don't know why I brought it up. Well, yes I do know why. I think I'm becoming fond of you, dear Gordon."

He kept his eyes low. "Well, you know my feelings, Lil."

"So, my question stands. What are we going to do with you, 'ey?"

He lifted his glass and swirled his wine in the fashion of an emptying toilet. "My answer's the same. Whatever you like."

* * *

"Let's hold off on the maid," Lil said.

Sam looked over at her bent away form, naked on top of the covers. "Why?"

"She's needed."

"Oh? Have you fucked her?"

"Sam, you are increasingly becoming infantile. I swear, I'll wake up one day and you'll be shitting your pants."

"We have our rules."

She rolled over and laid her head on his chest, rubbing into his skin. "You know what came up over dinner? That restaurant in Chartres. Remember it? The source of our drinking rule?"

"It'll be hard to forget. That bird pestered us for years after."

"Until we went sailing. I liked that journey. It was an adventure."

"You didn't at the time. You were sick for most of it."

"Was I? I don't remember."

He turned his gaze to her mop of red hair.

"Well, I don't! I can't be expected to remember every little thing, can I?" She laughed. "But Chartres, that I remember."

Sam smiled.

"What was its name? Don't tell me . . . it's on the tip of my tongue."

"*La mare aux canards*."

"The Duck Pond, that's it. What a sweet little place it was. I wonder if it's still there?"

"It closed down the day after."

"Well, yes, I know that. But, little episodes of that nature can be good for business, after a few generations."

Sam smiled again. "Anyway, what about the maid?"

"Look, that man needs all the help he can get. It's not easy—"

"What has that got to do with it?"

"Don't be so difficult. Rules are rules, I know. But . . ."

"It's Christmas," Sam said.
"Very funny, Sam. Very funny." Though she didn't laugh.
But Sam did.

THE DUCK POND 1862

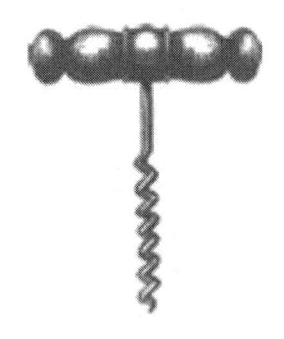

ONE

"I'm sorry, but it's Christmas Day, Mademoiselle. With the pilgrimage to the Cathedral, we're fully booked."

"What about that little table over there?"

"That's reserved."

"For whom?"

"Mon Père."

"I thought your father was dead?"

"I think he's referring to the priest, Lilit," Samil said.

She kept her gaze at the maître d'. "Well, when do you expect him?"

"He has much to attend to, as you could imagine."

"So that's settled then. We will sit there, and when he arrives . . . he arrives."

The waiter sighed. "It's a tradition of *La mare aux canards* that we reserve a table for our family priest on this holy day. It would be disrespectful—"

"If such a table was not used in his absence." And Lilit moved over to the little table and sat on the chair.

Samil smiled. "It would be less complicated if you let her sit, believe me."

The maître d' puffed up his cheeks, and wished himself away from the place as Samil went over and sat with her.

"What a wonderful table by the river . . . and with the snow falling. Was this a good idea or not, Samil?"

The little restaurant kept itself warm with a large fire that abutted the kitchen. Coats and cloaks heavy with melted snow hung along one wall, scarves too, all tattered, for the pilgrims weren't well off, or didn't seem to be. A chatter amongst creamy sauces, flushed with claret; all snug in this little candle-lit hamlet of a space.

"I have no intention of leaving when his father arrives," Lilit said.

"This is Christmas, Lilit."

"I'm aware."

Samil smiled, but he didn't make eye contact. Rather he kept his gaze at the view. The narrow river outside, no more than a stream, with its stone bridge arched like a half moon, was lit by two gas lamps, and the snow could be seen as it passed their flame, and closer, slanting against the window glass.

"I would like to see them try and move us," she said. "I really would."

The maître d' came over to the table, still puffing up his cheeks. "I would recommend the veal, since it's all we have."

Samil nodded.

"Velouté, béchamel, or sauce tomate?"

Lilit looked at Samil who took charge. "I'll have béchamel. My sister, tomate."

"Vin?"

Lilit smiled. "A large carafe."

"Haven't you had enough?" Samil said.

"A large carafe!"

He nodded to the maître d', who tilted his head to the side, puffed up his cheeks again, and went off to some other place.

Lilit looked around at the tables squashed into the little eatery. "Isn't . . . this . . . lovely."

"Are you being sarcastic?"

"Yes."

"It was your idea," Samil said.

"Well, we needed to get out. I was bored."

"Then go and fuck someone."

"What about Mon Père?"

"If it makes you happy."

She turned her head to the pilgrims. "I don't like this town, you know that."

Samil waited a bit. "I like the food here."

"The meat with all these sauces . . . how do you think that makes me feel?"

"And I like that it's not Paris."

"Is that the best you have?"

"And I like my work."

"Parfum?"

"Yes, parfum. I made a new scent today."

"I know. I can smell it, and it stinks."

"To you, Lilit, everything stinks." He said it deadpan, without a hint of frustration.

The door opened and a blast of cold air smacked the little eatery in the face. When it closed, a tiny priest hugged himself at the entrance, patting away snowflakes from his coat.

"Ah, Mon Père has arrived," Lilit said. "Now this *will* be interesting."

There was a conference at the doorway and the priest looked over to their table and the maître d' kept puffing out his cheeks like a fish. Some of the pilgrims stood and went over to shake the young man's hand. For he was young, newly ordained, and he was looking forward to his first Christmas dinner at La mare aux canards. The maître d', on the other hand, wished it was August.

Lilit stood, and the tiny room turned their gaze as if she was lit on a stage. "Mon Père, over here!"

Samil kept his eyes on the falling snow.

The priest removed his coat, hat, and scarf, and handed them to the puffy-cheeked attendant.

Lilit beamed as he found his way to their reserved table. "Father. What a strange name for such a young boy. Please sit with us."

The maître d' fluttered around the table not knowing what to do, since he knew the veal béchamel and tomate was well into its preparation.

"Sit, Father. You're making me feel uncomfortable," Lilit said.

And the young priest sat with them, but not on the chair that faced the river, which he had been told would be his and that he had been so much looking forward to. And when he did sit, the little table seemed cramped, even before the meals had arrived.

"Tell me about your day, Father," Lilit said.

The young priest smelt the alcohol on her breath and turned to the maître d' with a plea to escape. But he had inexplicably disappeared.

"Did you go to Notre Dame?"

"Yes, of course, Mademoiselle."

"Tell me about it. Tell me everything."

The maître d' appeared from nowhere with a large carafe of Bordeaux, which was actually the smallest he could find.

"Three glasses, Monsieur!" Lilit said.

The waiter puffed up his cheeks and went to scavenge another glass.

"Don't be shy now, Father."

"Well, I attended three Masses at Our Lady of Chartres."

"Nice."

The priest glanced over to Samil who still seemed more interested in the view.

"Tell me about her."

"Excuse me?"

"Tell me about the Notre Dame of Chartres."

"The Virgin Mary?"

"Yes."

Samil turned to Lilit and said something in a strange foreign tongue that somehow unsettled the priest.

"Nonsense. I want to hear!" she said, and some of the pilgrims turned their heads as she did.

The waiter came back with a glass and poured all three a small quantity of the wine.

"Are you a believer, Mademoiselle?"

"Oh, Mon Père, more than you can imagine."

"Then you have seen the *Sancta Camisa*, Our Lady's tunic?"

"I must say I have."

"And?"

"A fine tunic it is." She took her glass and emptied it in one gulp. "And well preserved, for its age."

The waiter came back to the table with both veal dishes on a tray. "The chef has made these as a special order." He raised his eyebrows at

Son Père. "We trust you can enjoy and depart . . . as soon as it's convenient to you."

Lilit stared at the maître d'. "You are starting to annoy me, Monsieur." And she said it in a different accent, as if she was another person all of a sudden.

The waiter puffed up his cheeks to maximum expansion and twisted an escape, and the priest lent back in his chair that faced the chattering pilgrims and smiled. "I feel you may not be the believer you say you are, Mademoiselle."

The first Lilit made a return. "Now what makes you say that, Father? The tunic?" She poured herself another glass. "Do I believe it was Our Lady's? I must say I don't—"

"Know," Samil said.

"Care!"

The priest stood up, and the tables around him acknowledged his plight. He raised his voice as if in sermon. "On this day, Mademoiselle, I find that quite blasphemous. And while the Anti-sacrilege Act has been revoked many years ago—for at one time such a comment would have led to your immediate arrest—I strongly object—"

"Samil, comfort Mon Père, please. He looks like he's going to burst a vessel."

The waiter entered the rumpus carrying a plate of foie gras and placed it in front of the priest. "It's our last, Père. We saved it for you."

The priest looked at the plate and faltered a bit, muttering something about Louis-Philippe's error on revoking the law, before sitting back down to the relief of the flapping-cheeked maître d'.

"Well. Let's not talk about religion," Lilit said, softening her voice. "It's such a touchy subject. Samil, you are very quiet tonight." She leant over to the priest who tilted away from her volatile breath. "Actually, he's always very quiet." And quaffed her red. "Where were we? Tunic . . . blasphemous . . ."

"Eat, Lilit," Samil said.

And she obeyed him because she was actually quite hungry.

The room of pilgrims kept on with their chatter as the three started to eat in the smoky surrounds. And the little eatery sat all bunkered in, the inclement weather holding no encouragement to do otherwise, and no table looked likely to present itself any time soon.

Lilit took another swig of her glass. "I don't think much of this wine."

"One couldn't tell," Samil said.

"It's the blight, Mademoiselle" the little Père said. "We're even finding it hard to get the sacramental vin."

"Ah, yes, times are hard." She took another swig and screwed up her face. "Tell me about this sacramental wine of yours."

"Lilit!" Sam kept staring at the window but his voice seemed to quake in the place. Indeed, it was reported by some of the pilgrims on the following day there might have been an earth tremor. But the subsequent events held more import, so there was not much discussion of it. Something that was not told by anyone was, exactly at the same moment, a raven landed on the outside ledge of the window, and perched, seeming to ignore the snow falling down on it, as if it was noon on a clear summer's day.

"Alright, alright. Enough of your anger, Samil," Lilit said. "What's your meal like?"

"It's fine."

And the low-lit chatter started up again around them.

Lilit quaffed her glass. "Mine is fine as well. Sauce tomata. How novel."

Samil took a mouthful of the meat and seemingly ignored the comment.

"You see, Mon Père, my brother has a greater choice of diet than I do."

The priest dissected another slice of pâté. "You have a weak stomach, Mademoiselle?" He twisted his head in the direction of Samil, who had let up a groan, like he was the one with the weak innards.

"These local sauces, Father. You can't boil a kid in its mother's milk."

The priest looked at Lilit as if she was a circus performer, though not a human one. "You are a Jew, Mademoiselle?"

"It's probably more fair to say I am a woman of tradition. Aren't I, Samil?"

They both turned to Samil, who kept his stare at the raven.

"This all makes sense to me, Mademoiselle."

Samil lifted his hand to attract the maître d' as the raven started to peck at the window glass.

The priest wiped his mouth with his serviette. "It's perhaps not my role to say . . . but perhaps, on this day, I might be permitted . . . The Almighty can be the judge of that."

Samil now twisted away from the snow and the river and the raven, but the waiter was nowhere to be found.

"If you are feeling guilt, Mademoiselle, about the killing of Our Savior, then perhaps you will seek repentance and avoid damnation."

Samil heaved a sigh and turned his stare back through the window, where the raven kept on striking the glass.

Lilit said calmly, "Are you enjoying your liver, mon père?"

The priest ignored her question and turned himself to look for the maître d'.

"This is a special dish born from an old tradition," she said.

The priest turned back to her. "I'm really not interested, Mademoiselle."

"It's like butter, isn't it? Creamy. But of course, well, I've made that point already, haven't I." She smiled at Samil's turned away head. "Anyway, the key to good foie gras is the force-feeding of the duck. Sesame or olive oil. Schmaltz if you have it."

The raven pecked at the window, and the glass splintered just a little. Some of the pilgrims turned their head at the strange tapping noise that came from the snow.

"I prefer schmaltz myself. As you might imagine."

The priest lifted his head back, in an odd way, extending his neck to look in wonder at the timber ceiling, as if at the celestial sky. All open mouthed.

"But you just have to get that schmaltz into the duck as quick as you can."

And the priest's open-mouthed neck swelled and contracted like a squeezed sausage.

"As . . . quick . . . as you can." The accent had once again disappeared.

And the splinter in the glass expanded into a radial lightning storm as the raven kept on with its violent pecking.

The priest's eyes bulged like something was pushing on them from inside his brain, and his gullet kept on pulsating, and his swollen belly started to push the little table away.

"Force all of that lovely schmaltz into the greedy duck's stomach."

Nearby some of the pilgrims turned and stared. Some cried out in panic. A few, rising away from their plates, crossed themselves.

And the priest's exposed belly, which had ballooned to such a size that it tipped the table onto the floor, its taught skin now an opalescent ivory, started to split like an overripe melon. And before anyone could take a breath, the young mon père's guts flayed wide open, a mulch of uncooked sausages and tripe, spewing globs of yellow chicken fat that rained down on the maître d' and the pilgrims and the little window that looked out to the river—lamp-lit—with the Cathedral of Our Lady of Chartres, in view of it all.

HO HO HO

ONE

Robbo sat in the kitchen with the timber shades tilted to allow the late afternoon sun to brighten the room. The table was littered with remnants of cake and little cut sandwiches, cucumber and egg and salami—new Italian stuff, Mickey had said, though it seemed a bit too spicy for the Guburnburnins, who had kept to the cake and instant coffee and XXXX.

The girls were now asleep in the cooler part of the house. It had been a long night, even though they had slept in the car on the way home. A long night slumped on chairs that weren't meant to be slept on. Molly had smiled and told them to go home. She had woken in the night and smiled and stroked their hair and said not to worry, to get some rest and come back in the morning. They didn't leave of course, they didn't even want to, not until just before dawn, or was it already light, and then Mickey had come to the rescue as he always did.

Fuck, if it were tomorrow, what then? Robbo couldn't have handled it if it was Christmas Day.

Teacake and sponge and apple pie with cinnamon. Jill Pettigrew brought cream, but most did without, and the girls were watching their figures, not that they had much to watch, they were slim like Molly, even before she wasted she was always slim. Not like their father, for whom stocky was the kindest description, short and big boned.

But they were from their mother's stock. And thank God for that. He was an ugly fucker.

Robbo squeezed his arm to make sure he was real. It sort of hurt, not as much as it should because the scratch drew blood. But it hurt, and he inched higher in his chair and the sun streamed down on his face and over the bits of leftover cake.

And the tick of the clock.

Tommy Richards had said it would be a bumper harvest this year. He had huddled in the conversation with him and Mickey and Phil from next door, all holding finger-sized slices of sponge on little paper plates. They all had said it. Not smiling or nothing like that, which would have been bad taste. But they were sure. And Robbo had told them, despite the bollworm, it would be good on his land too. They had said fuck the bollworm, though the language brought disapproving stares from the girls. They were of an age to give more than that, in the school yard with their mates, but the girls looked over and pulled faces, maybe out of respect for Molly, who didn't like to swear when they were present. Molly could swear with the best of them, but not with the girls around.

Robbo stared at the scratch on his arm. He licked his finger and rubbed over it like a paintbrush. It stung just a tad and he felt real again. He reached over and took one of the salami sandwiches. It was spicy, a bit too much for his taste. He liked plain food—meat and three veg. Lamb.

Molly did roast lamb on Christmas Day, not turkey or ham or prawns or chicken. It had to be lamb. God knows why. Fuck, he should have bought lamb, what was the time? Mickey would be around of course, Christmas Eve being a bumper trade day. He needed potato and carrot and cauli and sprouts—the girls didn't like sprouts but Molly did—and pumpkin and gravy. Fresh peas from the garden. He wasn't sure how to make the gravy. Mickey would be open but not for too much longer.

And he wouldn't bother waking the girls. They needed their sleep.

But later, when they woke, they could help him prepare for tomorrow. Even if they didn't want to, they could help.

For Christmas Day was about family, and they all needed to pitch in.

* * *

On Christmas Day in Guburnburnin there were no stockings under a glowing fireplace, no hearths of roasted chestnuts, no snowmen with carrots for noses. There was no white at all. On this particular day, the sky was cloudless and had been for more than a week. And by ten in the morning it was thirty-six degrees centigrade in the shade.

Lil grinned. "Well, isn't this niice."

"A fabulous spread, Sharon," Gordon said.

The table was laden with a lace cloth. A turkey, thinly sliced, baked pumpkin and potatoes, a bowl of green peas with mint sauce. Cherries and peaches and plums and nectarines.

Elsie said, "Pass the apple sauce, dear. A good turkey is not the same without it."

"There is gravy if you want. I made it earlier." And Sharon moved off to get it. "Eat your meat, Jamie," she said, though to herself.

And like a good little boy he did.

"Sharon says you're quite the cricketer, Sam," Gordon said.

"I do like the sport."

"I usually don't get to watch the Boxing Day test, too much work at the Coral. But they sure get a crowd down there."

"Well, if you ask me, those Victorians would watch a fly going up the wall if they put a fence around it," Elsie said. "And what about the poor families of the team. The men having to leave their children to chase a silly ball around a paddock for five days in the holidays."

"You tell'em, luv." Lil said. "In all my years I've never seen such a stupid game."

Sharon watched Sam eat his turkey, deadpan. He didn't seem to take the bait.

"Have you ever played any sport, Lil?" Gordon said.

Sam shone a hint of a smile as he chewed.

"Have I? Goodness, let me think a moment."

"Maybe when you were a kid?"

"Lil as a child," Sam said with a mouthful of lunch. "What an interesting image."

"No, not as a child."

"Quite," Sam said.

Her forehead wrinkled, as if she was passing a stool.

"The answer is no," Sam said.

And the table laughed with the smell of baked pumpkin and potatoes and apple sauce all around.

"Lil, why don't you come and play cricket with us," Sharon asked. "You couldn't be worse than me."

"Sam did, on a few occasions, get me to help him practice. But I kept missing the ball and he got frustrated and, well, we had a little disagreement. And you can probably guess what happened."

"Did you take your bat and ball and go home, Lil?" Gordon grinned.

"Something like that, luv. And oh . . . was Sam annoyed, 'ey!" She cackled. "So I don't play with him anymore."

"Good for you, Lil," Elsie said.

Sharon watched her mother laugh and felt relieved. Elsie was the elephant in the room, and she couldn't face any drama today. She nodded as Jamie ate another piece of turkey, carefully cut into little triangular pieces.

"What I would be more interested in knowing," Elsie said, "is how you're going with that young prodigy of yours, Sam."

"Exactly what I would like to hear," Lil said. "He never wants to discuss it at home."

"Billy has a good voice," Sam said.

"Just good?"

"Very good."

"Well, that's more information that I've been able to get from him, luv." Lil turned to Sharon. "We must get your mother over more often."

"Mum would make a good interrogator."

"Oh, fiddlesticks. Anyway, do you think Billy McConachy will become a famous singer? We've had many opera stars in Australia, but all women."

"Any from Queensland, mum?"

"Unfortunately not, so it's about time. Could you imagine . . . from Guburnburnin."

"So, Sam, answer dear Elsie."

"It's too early to tell. But . . ." He looked up at Lil. "I'm working on it."

"Oh, you are, are you?" Lil said in a strange voice.

Sharon watched the mother and son exchange glances. It was the same play of faces she traded with Elsie, which somehow made her feel quite at ease. It was nice to share the family angst around for a bit. Even on Christmas Day.

"Did you hear," Gordon said, "Robbo's wife died yesterday. The whole family was with her."

Elsie shook her head. "My goodness, what a Christmas present for the children."

"I've never met her," Sharon said. "Bob and I were invited to the wedding, but it was right in the middle of harvest and we had to renege. But I've only heard good things about her. Robbo is another good man, Lil."

"Is he, luv?"

She handed around the napkins. "Yes. And I feel so bad that I've never even met . . . Molly, isn't it. I guess you'll be full up at the Coral, Gordy."

"Yes, at the old Death and Divorce . . ." He faltered and looked at Lil and Sam. "You'll have some neighbors for a bit. A week or more, I'm guessing."

Lil looked up at Sharon as she took her serviette. "So, where *is* this man of yours hiding, luv?"

And the room fell silent for a spell.

"He's done a runner," Elsie said at last.

And there it was. "How wonderfully put, mum. More apple sauce, Sam?" She didn't wait for an answer but dropped a dollop onto the side of his plate.

"Sit down, Sharon" Elsie said. "You're like a blowfly buzzing around the place."

So she sat like an obedient daughter, and little Jamie climbed up on her knee and spooned some turkey and peas into his mouth.

"Why did he run away, luv?"

"Good question, Lil," Elsie said.

Sharon poured some of the gravy on the white meat. "Mum thinks it's because I'm a bitch."

"Sharon! It's Christmas Day."

"He'll be back," Gordon said.

"And I never used that word. I just said you're hard on him sometimes."

"It's the same thing."

"Have you heard from him, luv?"

"Not a word for two weeks."

"I hope he's all right," Lil said. "Maybe the authorities should be contacted?"

Elsie made a face at the table. "That's exactly what I said. But she didn't want the town to know . . . as if you could keep a secret around here."

"As a matter of fact I have talked to them," Sharon said. "They said they would pass the word around. But he had his ID with him, so if anything happened, like an accident, I would have been contacted by now."

"People just don't disappear without a trace," Gordon said.

She watched Sam look up at his mother and raise an eyebrow. How odd.

"Of course they don't," Lil said. "He's perfectly safe, I'm sure of it."

"But will he come back?"

"Oh, luv, I'm not the one to answer that. I guess nobody is . . . except him. But I know good men." She laughed. "And there's not that many of them. Of course, we have two sitting at the table now." She reached out and touched both Sam and Gordon's arm, who sat on either side of her. "But if Bob was here, we would have the pleasure of being with *three* good men. And how spoilt I would feel then!"

Sharon watched the table nod to themselves as she held little Jamie closer in her arms.

"It's a bit late for it, but shouldn't we say Grace?" Elsie said.

Sharon watched Sam stop in mid-chew.

"Grace, luv?"

"Grace, Lil. Would you care to take the reins?"

Sharon kept her eyes on Sam, who kept his mouth still. It was difficult to read his face, but there was something strange in his manner. Something between wary and eager, maybe.

"You know," he said, "I would really like to hear you say Grace, Mother."

Lil ignored him and turned to Elsie. "Tell me about this Grace of yours, luv."

And in the yard, the dog stopped licking itself and barked at a crow that landed near his water bowl.

"It's a simple prayer of thanks, Lil . . . to our Lord for giving us this, our daily bread. But as long as it's from the heart, whatever you say will be just fine."

"From the heart, Mother," Sam said, still with an odd face.

"Mum, maybe not everyone shares the same—"

"Sharon, if I'm not mistaken we're celebrating Christmas Day."

"Or a good excuse to break bread with friends, Elsie," Gordon said.

"I see we have some resistance so don't—"

Lil raised an arm. "No, No. Elsie is absolutely correct. If this is a tradition of the table, who am I to cause a fuss, 'ey? Sam and I are guests . . . and we are grateful for your hospitality."

"Grateful," Sam said, deadpan.

"My son and I disagree on tradition sometimes. So . . . you want a prayer thanking . . . our . . . Lord."

"Look at the size of that crow," Sharon said.

And they all turned to look at the bird perched on the ledge of the kitchen window.

"Sing a song of sixpence, a pocket full of rye. Four and twenty blackbirds, baked in a pie."

"Gordy, that would be some pie if twenty four of birds like that were stuffed in a pastry. One would be plenty."

"When the pie was opened, the birds began to sing."

"But what about the poor maid who gets her nose pecked off?" Sharon said. "I was scared stiff of crows because of that horrid nursery rhyme." Sharon laughed and held little Jamie tighter, then lifted her hand and shook it at the window. "Go on, shoo!"

But the crow didn't move a feather.

And outside, the dog had moved to the other side of the house and was licking furiously at his testicles.

"Mother, could you pass the gravy," Sam said.

Lil did as she was told.

"It looks like we're not going to get Grace, doesn't it," Elsie said.

Lil looked up at the ceiling. "What is a nice way of starting . . . Dear Lord . . ."

Everyone turned from the crow and lowered their heads. All except Sam who kept his eyes at the window.

"It's been a while since we have spoken," Lil said, "and so I really don't know where to start. This old brain of mine just doesn't seem to remember exactly when it was." She laughed. "But let's agree it's been a while."

Sharon peeked at the elephant in the room, who had her eyes closed and was nodding her trunk.

"I've been asked by this good table to say a little something in the way of . . . thanking you."

Sharon looked at Sam whose face seemed frozen of any expression. He had stopped eating, but had kept his knife and fork in hand. Like they were weapons.

"This table wishes to say thank you for providing the food on the table . . . which is . . . very . . . nice. And yes . . . the bird we are eating is one of your creatures, Lord . . . but that is the way of the world . . . and has been for a very long time."

The elephant nodded again.

"So, thank you, luv."

The table lifted their faces, wide eyed, as Lil sat with an expression that seemed pleased.

And Sam started to eat again.

"Well, Lil, what an interesting prayer that was."

"You said from the heart, mum," Sharon said.

"You really don't understand me sometimes, young lady. I thought it *was* very nice."

"Thank you, dearest Elsie."

"And what did you think of your mother's prayer, Sam?" Elsie asked.

"Very wise," he said with a mouth full of turkey.

"Maybe, Lil, you would like to join me at Christmas Mass in Banga this evening?"

Lil, with a piece of pumpkin on her fork, looked up and grinned. "Oh, Elsie, that would be . . . now what's that expression of yours, Sam?"

"Pushing the envelope?"

And she sang a high-pitched cackle.

"Let's open the wine," Gordon said.

And the crow lifted its wings and flew off into the heat of the cloudless sky.

But not too far away.

* * *

They trotted up the dirt path that cut the wheat field of McCarthy's farm down the middle. It was getting late, and the heat had started to settle, as the sun crept low to color the land a golden pink.

Billy had finished his singing practice before they headed out, which was unusual, since the contract said it should happen the other way around. And Sam was a stickler of habit, so he thought it odd. But he was happy to ride in the cooler evening. And besides, it was easier on Mr. Ed.

Billy was feeling good about himself. Sam seemed more pleased with his singing, as far as he could tell. He hadn't stopped him at all in Lusha key-panga, which was a first, and he promised that he could start another song that Mrs. Shipping was keen for him to sing. Sam never seemed to care for Mrs. Shipping's opinion on singing, but Billy still met with her every Wednesday at the Community Hall, even though it was still holidays, where she played him her favorite classical CDs. Sometimes they even sang together. *And* she brought cake.

When they rode, they usually followed the dirt path around the property, and headed back home in a half an hour or so. It seemed a lot of effort for such a short outing, but Mr. Ed still managed to sweat, so he wasn't complaining. Anyway, it meant he got to ride the gray gelding every day, which was kind of a contract with his father—though, strangely, his father didn't seem too keen on the idea.

Mum liked Sam though. Dad thought it was because of his good looks—Sissy had heard them talking one night when she couldn't sleep because it was too hot. Sissy's room was next to theirs, so she always had some gossip to tell, even though he thought she made most of it up. But when Sam had come over for dinner last week his mother was as happy as a lark. She had her brochures about some schools in Brissy, which Billy didn't really care for. And Dad said he didn't have to board if he didn't want to. Sissy said they had fought about it later, and he thought she probably was telling the truth about that, at least, given what he'd heard himself a couple of weeks back. But his mother really got on well with Sam, wanting to know all about his performances in places she called more posh than town.

Dad seemed more interested whether Sam had a girl—and when he said no, he even asked whether he'd been married before, but Mum pulled a face and they stopped talking about it. She was the boss of the house, except if Dad shouted, which he didn't do very often. And this didn't seem important enough to shout about, so they all finished their roast, and Sissy kept asking stupid questions about what food would make her sing best, hinting that she wanted to have some singing lessons as well. But Sam didn't want to know about it, and in the end she stormed off and sulked in her room, until the ice-cream cake came out for dessert.

Today Billy trailed behind Sam's black mare, and the wheat kept golden pink on both sides. Sam's horse was a real beauty, though he still didn't know who he had borrowed it from, or where it was kept. Sam didn't want to talk on it, so that was that, and he didn't really care, though he was keen to have a ride. But his father said he wasn't allowed. So that, also, was that.

The black mare turned into a scrappy path that had been fashioned not long ago, since the ground was soft and without a weed. Maybe it was something to do with irrigation, because it was too thin to get a harvester up.

"Why we goin' this way?"

Sam didn't turn around, so Billy followed, and Mr. Ed's ears went to a point since, he too, was a creature of habit. They rode in single file along the chocolate path until they came to a little clearing no larger than a tennis court. In the middle, an old gum had been fashioned into an equestrian jump, not high, though Sissy's Black Beauty—a stupid name for the pony since it was brown—wouldn't be able to make it.

Billy kept Mr. Ed at the entrance of the clearing and watched Sam arc his mare around and over the jump, clearing it by a meter or more, before trotting back to them.

"Your turn."

"Mr. Ed's too old to jump. Dad says it's his knees."

"The contract, remember?"

He looked at the jump, which was really quite low. He had jumped him a while back, about a year ago at Sissy's Pony Club in Banga, and he didn't think this was much higher. Mr. Ed's ears had flopped down, and he wasn't in too much of a sweat, so he gave him a pat and trotted around the same way as Sam, bringing the gelding to a gallop and made the jump easy as.

"Good boy, Mr. Ed." And he gave him another pat.

Sam sat high on his black mare and nodded. Above, a crow flew over them, low to the land.

"It's good for a horse to jump," Sam said. "It's natural. So let's keep this our secret. Anyhow, it's part of the contract."

And Billy gave the old gray another pat and they moved back single file down the freshly laid path instead of doing any more jumps. Because when the light was low the snakes were hard to see. And Mr. Ed was always skittish around snakes.

* * *

"How bad, Doc?"

"Well, Lil, I've spoken to the specialist, and he wants to do a liver biopsy. But it's pretty clear, from your bloods and ultrasound and your physical that your liver is in bad shape. Cirrhosis can be unpredictable . . . you can die from your liver not working, or from other problems like bleeding from the esophagus. We can give you a drug to try and reduce that. And there's always the possibility of a liver transplant."

"So . . . unpredictable and death sums it up."

"Let's wait for the biopsy. I've got this list of medications and foods you'll need to keep away from. And of course, no alcohol. The cause is not clear—"

"It's no interest for me, the cause, luv. But have I time to sort out some things?"

"It's unpredictable . . . but probably, yes. And the biopsy will give us a better idea."

"Don't worry about that, luv. Give me that list, and you better put me on that drug to stop the bleeding." She beamed at him. "I must say I don't feel unwell, so let's be grateful for that."

"You'll get the biopsy, though? Without it, they won't put you on a transplant list."

"Transplaaant! How horrid, taking someone else apart for spares. No, there'll be none of that for old Lil."

* * *

"Well done, Samil."

She slammed the door and the coral rattled on the outside. Sam lifted his gaze from the TV but kept on chewing a Cheezel.

"Cirrhosis!"

He wiped cheese bits from his fingers. "She did like her drink."

"She stunk of it, Sam."

"She said she was healthy."

"And look at this skin. Why, Sam?"

"I like Renoir women." He turned back to the TV. "And I thought it might slow you down a bit."

"Don't be a baby, Sam!"

The room hushed for a time, but for the sound of cricket commentators and the crunch of Cheezels.

"Anyway, you made the rule," he said.

She sat on the bed. "I know I made *this rule*, Samil."

"You usually do."

She sighed. "It was needed after Carlo. I will not be a baby sitter again. And that was *your* doing, not mine!"

Sam took another orange tube from the pack. "Anyway, from what I see, you seem to be doing okay. It certainly hasn't slowed you down."

"I have cirrhosis!" She handed him Doc's list of do's and don'ts. "Does this seem okay to you?"

He read the sheet. "You've had worse."

"Thank you for your concern, Samil."

"Look, I am sorry." He turned off the TV. "How long?"

"Un-pre-dictable." She sighed. "I brought the results so you could look at them."

And he did. "I'm guessing months, even before you get sick. But you can make the decision." He looked up at her. "Anyway, I've found someone who might be suitable."

"Oh, yes? Enlighten me."

"It's too early to be certain, but I'll be sure to give you plenty of notice this time."

"That's so good of you, Samil."

"Or maybe we should go back to the old way of choosing? I for me, you for you."

"No, Sam. You aren't ready."

"Says who?"

She leant over and pinched his cheeks with both hands, forcing him to face her. "Don't defy me, Samil."

And the room hushed back to the munch of Cheezels and the sound of leather on willow and nothing more was said.

CARLO

ONE

"*Stai calmo*, Carlo. *Stai calmo.*"

The boy softened his voice as instructed but kept on with the task.

"*Poco vibrato*. Let it come if it must, but don't force it."

He kept his eyes on the Maestro as he sung, and he knew he was pleased because his eyes were closed and his head moved like a feather floating on the bay. In time, the Maestro lifted his hand and opened his eyes with a smile.

"Rest, Carlo."

The boy sat by the window. Below him spread the Bay of Napoli splattered with ships, mostly without sails, lolling under the clear November sky. On the wide esplanade in front, pedestrians dawdled in the sun, horse-drawn buggies too, and indeed as the Maestro had said, life hadn't changed much at all, even though the Spanish were long gone.

The little studio was cold for the fire was always kept low. It was rumored that the Maestro was afraid of fire, but Carlo didn't mind since his own home was even colder, and he always came rugged up for his lessons.

"Picollo Ucello, bring us the tea," the Maestro shouted up.

Even though Carlo found it too bitter for his liking, he was the only member of his family who drank tea. Even Riccardo had only tasted it a few times. So he felt it a treat, especially since it was only offered if the Maestro was extra satisfied with his voice.

Picollo Ucello entered the room with a porcelain teapot and two matching cups on a wooden tray.

The maestro rubbed his hands. "A gift from Prince Phillip for my recent composition, which drew a well-deserved applause and his favor. Always remember, Carlo, look after the hand that feeds you. Isn't that true, Picollo Ucello?"

Picollo Ucello, or Little Bird, was one of the Maestro's favorites. He was given the name for his thrush-like tremolo and had become a novelty in the household of the Prince, where Maestro Porpora took charge of his private orchestra. Picollo Ucello was usually found in the company of the Maestro, sometimes little more than a servant, other times like a member of the family. The Maestro had said he was a gift from the Heavens, and there were rumors that his services might extend to activities of the more intimate, though Carlo thought this gossip came more from jealousy, for he had never witnessed anything that gave weight to it. Carlo liked Picollo Ucello, even though he never seemed to say much. But they had sung duets together, and he never seemed to mind if Carlo had the more dominant part, unlike most of the Maestro's protégés.

"Look at the musical instruments on the porcellana," the Maestro said. "The Prince said he had the design made especially for me. I think this was a fancy of his, but who knows."

"From China, Maestro?"

"Ah, what an intelligent boy you are, Carlo. No, this was made in Meissen. It is much in favor with those who can afford it . . . and we are fortunate to walk in the footsteps of those who can. The hand that feeds us, Carlo, the hand that feeds." The Maestro brought his fingers together like holding an invisible strawberry.

Picollo Ucello smiled.

"He has much to learn, this young boy of ours, doesn't he, Picollo Ucello?"

"He has the best teacher, Maestro."

"You are too kind." He bent over and pinched the cheek of the Little Bird and looked back to him. "Carlo, if you practice as often as Picollo Ucello, you will be without peer. This I can promise you."

He stared at Picollo Ucello, who took the insult—for not one of the Maestro's students would have taken the comment in any other way—as though it was simply a fact.

"And fortunately, in our profession, we are spared the vagaries of the changing of hands. Whether we are fed from Madrid or Vienna matters little to us. We, the Napoletano Maestros, are humble servants to all.

And we will watch them come and go as fate dictates, won't we my little doves."

He watched the Maestro bend and sip his tea, which was the cue he could do the same. Picollo Ucello sat with them, silent, without tea, waiting new instruction. The young man was now well in servant mode.

The trio hadn't moved when the knock came on the door, and before the Maestro could acknowledge it, the door flew opened. Carlo saw his brother Riccardo stand tall at the entrance, but faltering a bit, as if faced with a hidden obstacle. The concern on his older brother's face was clearly evident though, and Carlo thought he'd been crying.

"Apologies, Maestro Porpora, for the intrusion. But I must take Carlo home. Our father is very unwell."

"Salvatore? Of course, of course . . . I will come over later and see him, if he's strong enough."

"I fear . . ." His brother's voice faltered. "But we must go."

Riccardo took Carlo by the arm and hurried him down the stairs into the bustle of the esplanade.

And on the way home Riccardo told Carlo about the cut on their father's finger, which started as a small slice when he was scaling a garfish for Sunday dinner, but yesterday began to fester, and this early afternoon how they couldn't stop him shaking, his skin glistening with sweat, even though it was winter and the fireplace was well extinguished.

But Riccardo thought it best not to tell him how their father had taken his last breath just an hour past, with he and his mother and sister sitting at his side, because now, although only nineteen years of age, Riccardo was anointed the new head of the Broschi family. And if the truth be known, this was a greater responsibility than he was prepared to own. Indeed, if he had the courage, Riccardo would rather run into the Bay of Napoli and drown, than return home to all of the liability that would soon be his and his alone.

* * *

Carlo sat alone in the corner away from the fireplace and the solemn faces that cluttered around it. It was cold and dark in the corner, away from the candle-lit table, and every so often one of the solemn faces would come over and recognize him, though he kept his head down and pretended he wasn't there.

It's such a tragedy they would say, *God moving in ways that only He could fathom.* But there must be a purpose to it. There simply must be.

How could there not?

He had sung at the funeral Mass, alone, in front of the faces now fire-lit and standing away from him. At the church the altar boy swung the smoldering thurible as if it was a pot of berries for supper and didn't seem solemn at all. Carlo had watched the boy's face—of his age or thereabouts—and wondered why he couldn't be him, what he would do to be him, instead of singing out front with his father dead and his sister and brother and mother looking like they wanted to follow in the same way.

You sing like an Angel, Carlo, they said.

Your father would be so proud, listening up there.

So proud.

God moves in ways mysterious to us all.

From where he now sat the dim room was painted in shades of charcoal—the timber walls and floor, smoke stained, the black clad mourners, heavy coats, boots, all color hidden in the shadows except a tint of orange from the fireplace, a tint of yellow from the candles.

To Carlo, it seemed like it was raining inside.

He shifted his chair and looked over at them again. He had watched the Maestro talk with Riccardo at Church. He wasn't privy to the conversation. *Go to your sister and mother,* Riccardo had said, *they need a man by them.* He obeyed his brother but kept an eye on the talk—at first somber, but then more earnest, not like haggling over a fish, but something bigger, a house maybe, or settling a debt.

His father was always settling debts.

In the church Picollo Ucello stood a step away from the earnest talk––at a distance somewhere between a servant and son. He had watched his friend's face as he stood, but he couldn't tell anything from it, which was normal, so nothing was gleaned of the importance of the talk.

Carlo now sat and watched the three stand in the opposite corner of the room, gray lit—they, like him, stealing into the shadows as if they hid treasure. The Maestro's hands rose and tapped at something invisible, as he did after a prolonged applause or a gift from his patron. Riccardo wasn't as excited—his head shook then nodded then turned away from him and he couldn't gauge much from his manner. But it reminded him of his father who just a week ago agreed to terms for the rent of their house. And when the landlord had left, his father sat down and said that's done, let's move on and think no more of it.

And he hadn't until just now.

And he started to sob.

* * *

He woke to the warmth of her breath.

"Carlo."

His room was black, so her face was hidden but her lips touched his ear.

"Carlo, it's not my idea."

"Mamma?"

"You must understand . . . it's not my idea."

He shifted under the blanket and felt her heavy body hinder his movement.

"You don't have to, do you understand, Carlo? You don't have to do it, no matter what anyone tells you."

"Mamma?"

He felt her hands on his face and her staccato kisses warm, on cheeks and lips and forehead.

"Promise me, Carlo."

"Yes, Mamma."

The bed shifted and he felt the space free up again.

And he turned over toward her and felt her hand on his head and the whispered instruction how he should pray to the Madonna for protection. And so he did, though he wasn't sure from what danger he needed protection, except of course from death, that seemed to come and go as it pleased around him.

* * *

"It's all organized."

"And my brother?"

"It's best not to trouble him with details."

"But he knows what will happen? The result."

"All boys under my tutelage know of it, Riccardo. And Carlo is a bright boy."

They sat together with a view of the bay, though smeared from the rain that streaked down the little window. Tea from the Orient in fine Meissen porcelain. Impressing the brother with what he had to offer. Being the hand that would feed others.

"My family is not sure."

"They never are." He sipped his tea. "But, Riccardo, you are the head of the famiglia Broschi, and important decisions aren't made by the women."

The Maestro watched the young man bite into his lip. He put his cup down and shifted closer, touching his shoulder. "A voice like Carlo's comes only once in a generation. Once in a century."

"He is my brother, not a horse. Not a ram."

"You know the money to be made. With this short . . . inconvenience, the famiglia will be set for life. I have spoken to the Prince, and there are many others, of higher stature—" He lifted his hand and rubbed his fingers with his thumb, "—that will be waiting in line. I promise you."

"We have the immediate problem of the house."

"That is organized, I told you. A mere trifle, Riccardo." He took up his cup. "Look at this porcellana, the extravagant pattern. You see the detail? Look at the harps, even the strings . . . so fine . . ."

"When?"

"The day after tomorrow. Here in my house. I wouldn't have it any other way." He kept his eyes to the porcelain. "He will need to stay some days. Picollo Ucello will attend him. Night and day."

"We can visit?"

"Naturally. And, Riccardo, you must realize, from that time on and for the rest of his life, Carlo will be treated like a delicate egg. He will have the best food, the best wine, clothes . . ." The Maestro laughed.

"My goodness, look at the little sparrow on the handle . . . it's the first time I've noticed it!"

* * *

Carlo climbed the stairs and heard the sniggers coming from somewhere up above. He looked up and saw Giovanni and Pietro, arm-in-arm, and the smirk on their faces.

"Let us move to the side and let the little girl pass."

Carlo kept his head down and went on climbing.

"Pietro, he is not a girl . . . yet!"

Laughter filled the narrow staircase.

When he made it to the level of the boys, he felt an elbow dig into his ribs but he kept on and didn't flinch.

"Hey, Carlo!" The boys' taunts now came from the base of the stairs. "Hey, Carlo . . . Pietro wants to show you something."

He turned and saw the older Pietro with his strides down to his ankles, his hips moving back and forth into the empty space, his cock upstanding and his balls swaying. "Take a good look, Carlo. See what you're going to miss."

The other boy grabbed Pietro's balls in his hands. "Feel how heavy they are, Carlo. Come down and have a feel."

The boys squealed, rutting in the air, then suddenly stopped the charade. The older boy lifted his pants in a hurry and they twisted around and made for the door, and their sniggers all but disappeared.

Carlo turned and saw Picollo Ucello at the top of the stairs. It was the first time he had ever seen him angry.

"Come. You are late for practice . . . and you know how the Maestro doesn't like to be kept waiting."

* * *

He had just finished an hour's mirror tuition in front of the Venetian glass. *You have the face of an angel, Carlo, don't frown on that note, gli angeli non sono tristi, gli angeli non sono tristi.*

Angels aren't sad.

Picollo Ucello now sat next to him, and they both warmed themselves by the hearth. The Maestro had left them alone while he went off to attend to the Prince's orchestra.

"You are lucky, Carlo," he said. "You have something that I don't, and I'd give much for it."

"I don't feel lucky."

"Of course, not now. But you will . . . and I will be there to see it."

"Maestro says it doesn't hurt." He watched Picollo Ucello's face, but it didn't flicker a response.

"It is necessary . . . to keep the voice pure."

"Have you seen it done?"

"No."

"Maestro says I can talk to Senesino if I like."

"If that makes you feel stronger."

"He said Senesino would be nothing without it."

"Senesino is an insect compared to you."

Carlo heaved a sigh. "If I tell you something . . . promise not to tell anyone."

Picollo Ucello nodded.

"I would rather be dead than get it done."

Carlo watched his friend turn to him with an odd face, but what it showed he was uncertain.

"Don't wish for something unless you truly want it, Carlo."

"I'm not afraid of death."

"It will visit you in due course . . . so whether you are afraid or not doesn't matter."

"Are you afraid of death?"

"No."

"We are the same."

"No."

Carlo felt a quiver in his voice. "Why didn't you get it done, then?"

Picollo Ucello looked at the fireplace. "It would not have helped. I didn't have your voice."

"And if you did, would you have had it?"

"Yes."

"You're a liar!" Carlo started to cry.

"Believe what you will. But, I repeat, don't wish for something unless you want it."

He wiped his face. "I do want it! And I'll tell you something else . . . no one can stop me."

"You're being a child."

"That's what you all want, isn't it?"

"If you take your music seriously, you would understand."

"Then tell me it doesn't hurt."

"I can't do that."

"Then you can all go to hell!" He started to sob again. "I swear to the Holy Mother . . . I will be with her before morning."

Picollo Ucello walked over and tended to the fireplace, placing a larger log that would settle well before the Maestro returned.

"Well, Carlo, I must say that I gave you fair warning. Not that it matters, much."

* * *

The carriage tottered along the cobblestone path. Inside, the curtains were drawn, though there was much to be seen outside.

The doctor sat with his toolbox next to him, the instruments rattling with the uneven road. Opposite, his two assistants drew open the curtains an inch to catch what they could of the passing theatre. For while they had made the journey before, Napoli was a circus compared to the little provincial town of their birth.

"Have we time after, doctor?" one asked.

"Time?"

"To play?"

He frowned. "Why ask me that question when you know the answer. It irritates me."

"Just to visit the church, doctor."

The other assistant sniggered.

He looked over to the young men and realized he couldn't expect much else of them—they were from the South, with no special talents other than brawn, no more than laborers who could hold someone down and stand the smell of pain. His wife called them his *piccoli amici del Inquisizione*—his little Inquisition friends—and she didn't like being in the house when they were there.

This irritated him as well. For his wife liked the gifts that came with his craft, well enough to tolerate the means.

"They make the sacrifice for the Church . . . as a priest does in the flesh," he had told her.

"They are children. If you were a mother you would understand."

"They must be willing. We cannot force them."

"Don't be ridiculous. How can they understand what they give up? A priest may leave the Church. What of these boys when they are men?"

"You love to hear them, Rosa, you have said so many times. And I have watched you cry."

"I cry for what has been taken from them as much as for what they give."

It was the same conversation every time he was to depart. So he had gotten into the habit of lying about his quest—a difficult amputation for a nobleman with the gangrene, a tooth extraction for a little one, removal of bladder stones from a priest. But when his carriage was sent from Napoli, his wife would understand the purpose of his journey, and would keep on at him like a cat with a rodent. And as he entered the carriage she would say a not-too-silent prayer to allow him to do good work, without pain or festering or, even better, not to do it at all.

"May I, Master," his assistant asked. "Visit the church?"

"The last time you visited the church in Napoli, Paulo, you pissed pus for a week."

The young man grabbed at his crotch. "It still doesn't flow like it used to. I piss like an old man now."

"Well, one more visit to the *Church*, and you'll stop pissing at all."

"Then you'll need the doctor's hot wire," the other assistant said.

"I'd rather not piss than have the hot wire."

"Can that happen, doctor? What if he couldn't piss?" He shook his head but didn't reply.

"Maybe you would burst, Paulo. Or can you shit the piss out if it has nowhere to go. What do you say, doctor?"

"I say you're an idiot."

"I just want to learn, doctor."

"For the sake of God, please let me rest. We'll be arriving soon, and I've had little sleep as it is."

When they arrived, the carriage moved into a side entrance where the fishmonger had just made a delivery to the kitchen. He drew open the curtain a fraction and they seemed alone and well out of sight from the hustle of the esplanade. The coachman opened the door, and he stepped awkwardly from the carriage, the collar of his coat lifted to hide his face, and he arched his back that had become stiff from the long bumpy ride.

When he entered the house, it seemed as cold as outside and he declined the request of the servant to take his coat.

"They are waiting for you upstairs, doctor."

Maestro Porpora greeted him at the top of the stairs. "I hope your journey was pleasant."

"Pleasant enough," he lied.

"We have a little complication," the Maestro said. "My assistant, Picollo Ucello, and a friend of the boy's, has not been seen all day."

"I don't understand."

"He was to be attending the boy . . . after."

"Then find someone else."

"I fear Carlo will be upset with this turn of events."

"Believe me, Maestro, he'll have more things to miss than the presence of a friend. What of the family?"

"Impossible. The women are against it, you understand, and his brother . . . unable."

He turned to Paolo. "You will stay with the boy."

Paolo of the slow piss nodded.

"*My* assistant will stay with him. Of course there will be an extra fee."

"That is very generous of you, doctor. I will broach it with the boy . . . to see if it is suitable."

"He is willing?" He watched the Maestro's eyes turn down. "You have his consent, Maestro Porpora?"

"Yes. I am sure—"

"You don't seem sure."

The Maestro fidgeted into the air with his hands. "It's just that he has been very . . . quiet. I am worried."

"You must have his consent! I will not go forward without it."

"Well, he is here. But I haven't dared broach the formality of it yet, in case he has time to reconsider."

He sighed. "We have come a long way, and my fee will stand, whether or not the operation is performed." He thought that his wife's prayer may have been answered, but he swore not to tell her of it. Her faith was irritating enough as it was.

"Perhaps we could gain his consent . . . at the last moment, doctor."

"After he is under the opium, you mean."

"I understand, but I fear his strange behavior today. He might be . . . unpredictable."

"As you are aware, Maestro Porpora, the Church is conflicted about this practice already. But what is a clear directive, absolutely clear, is that the boy must consent in good faith. Without it I risk—you risk—too much." He had a vision of his wife kneeling before a statue of the Madonna lighting a candle. "And Maestro, could you tell your servants to heat the house, at least on the upper floor? It is in an unsatisfactory condition for this time of year."

They moved into the bathroom that was just as cold despite the iron hearth that sat by the tub and was well lit. Paolo had placed the instrument over the fire, but the metal had yet to brighten. The other assistant started to fill the tub with hot water dispensed from the kitchen.

"The boy?"

"He is waiting in the sitting room, doctor."

"He is attended?"

"He is alone. He wanted it that way."

"I will dispense the opium when he is in the bath. It will take effect more quickly."

Paolo came in with towels and placed them on a chair next to the portable hearth. The iron tong had started to color a lighter shade of gray.

Maestro Porpora returned to the room, smiling. "Good news, doctor, the boy has consented to be attended by your assistant." He played with the air. "When I find that Picollo Ucello . . ." and his voice trailed off into a mumble.

"Paolo will stay with him night and day." He looked over at his assistant. "And he is not to leave the house, even for *religious* duties, Maestro."

"We have a little chapel in the house."

"Do you hear that, Paolo. Your prayers have no need to leave the confines of the boy's care. And Maestro, I would like *you* to supervise the boy's opium. Paolo can sometimes forget his role, and has been known to transform into a patient."

The young man grimaced, and his fellow assistant strained to keep his laughter from erupting.

When the tongs had turned the color of the full moon, the doctor asked for the boy to be sent to the room. He had heard much of Carlo—news of the quality of his voice had travelled many miles from where they now stood. But when he appeared at the door, the doctor stared longer at the figure than was usual.

The boy stood in a white silk gown, loosely tied, and his long thin legs, speckled blue with the cold, fell down to matching slippers. This boy would be spared nothing, which gave him a comfort that was needed at this time.

"You must be Carlo."

The boy didn't flicker a response, and it was hard to discern anything from the blank expression on his face.

"Come over here, I need to examine you."

The boy came, and the doctor untied the gown that fell open. He noted the small tufts of hair that had just begun to sprout and realized, if the procedure was not performed today, it would never be. He lifted his hand and encircled the boy's sac with his thumb and finger. The boy didn't move an inch, even when he squeezed firmer to gauge the correct position for the tong.

"His voice has not broken?"

"It's as pure as the first time he cried for his mother's milk, doctor," Maestro Porpora said.

He felt the water in the tub, which was hot but not scalding. "Could you get in the bath, Carlo?"

The boy did as he was told, and as he submerged under the water the steam rose and his exposed skin went from mottled blue to the color of pink rouge.

"Do you know what I am to do, Carlo?"

The boy nodded but kept staring at the hearth and the iron tong that glowed wan on the fire.

"I am to remove the sac, not the cock. You will pee as normal, but you will never be able to make children, Carlo, as God intended. This is your sacrifice to Him." He looked up at the Maestro who stood jittery at the end of the tub. "Do you understand this, Carlo?"

The boy nodded but kept his eyes on the hearth and the tongs lit the color of the moon.

"I must hear it in your own voice, Carlo. We must all hear your consent."

The boy lifted himself up from the steaming water, his skin glowing pink, and carefully climbed from the tub and sat on its edge, parting his legs wide open. "Take them now, for I have no need of them."

"You need to take the opium, Carlo," the Maestro cried.

"Ars longa, vita brevis." Art is long, life is short. And the boy lifted his cock up and away from his balls. "I said . . . take them now!"

* * *

"The doctor will see you," Maestro Porpora said to Riccardo.

The sitting room hearth was lit high and Riccardo eyed the gray haired man hunched over the fire.

"Please, sit down," the doctor said, and Riccardo thought his words were slurred, even before noticing the carafe that sat nearby and a glass half empty next to it. "You are so young . . . my condolences on the death of your father."

Riccardo nodded but never bothered a reply. He knew he was young and was looking for more than condolences from the man.

"The procedure went as planned." The doctor smiled. "In fact, it was much easier than normal. I could have spared one of my assistants and cut the cost. But who was to know? Your brother—" The doctor looked up at Riccardo, "is a remarkable boy."

"We have high hopes for him."

The doctor took up his glass. "Well, I suspect those hopes of yours will be fulfilled." And he skulled his wine.

"You wanted to see me, doctor."

"I did indeed, Signore Broschi." He poured another glass from the carafe. "It is a matter of a delicate nature, perhaps one that should have been discussed before the event. But I left that in the hands of Maestro Porpora . . . which can sometimes be a mistake." The doctor raised his glass. "Fine wine, would you care for some?"

He shook his head.

"One of my little vices. Only allowed after the operation of course. My wife disapproves of wine . . . except at Holy Communion. So when I'm away, even for this short time, I indulge."

"A delicate matter, doctor?"

"Yes. I'm not sure you are aware, this operation is not exactly considered legal . . . by those who could make trouble. The Church, well, that is a more complicated matter. But the secular authorities frown against it."

"I'm aware, doctor."

"Excellent. Best to know before the cat jumps out of the bag as I always say." He gulped his wine. "But you see, we need an excuse to perform the procedure."

"Excuse, doctor?"

"An alibi of sorts. A story that you and I . . . and your family . . . will tell as required. Do you follow me, Signore Broschi?"

"I think so."

"And so what I would suggest, on this occasion, and what I have made note of in my log book, is that young Carlo had an accident yesterday."

"An accident, doctor?"

"An unfortunate accident, Signore." The doctor took another gulp from his glass. "Your family has a horse?"

He nodded.

"So it was, on the twentieth day of December 1717, young Carlo Broschi fell from his horse, and in doing so damaged, beyond repair, the glands that God gave him to be the seed of life . . . yet took away, for reasons that only He could understand."

"I see."

"Wonderful! Then that is settled. Are you sure you won't join me, Signore. This is an excellent drop, straight from the kitchen of Prince Phillip of Hesse-Darmstadt no less."

"I am eager to see my brother."

"Don't worry, he is sleeping with the angels. If you are that way inclined, I have plenty of the poppy extract to spare. But not to be mixed with wine, Signore Broschi. We must be sensible."

* * *

Paolo sat shivering on a chair next to the boy who slept sound in his bed. He cursed the Maestro under his breath again, for as soon as the doctor had left, the fireplaces had been tended so little that he felt his bones might fracture like the late winter ice in a pond.

He looked over at the boy, who stirred under the covers. It was only thirty minutes since he was given the extract, and for a brief moment Paolo wished he could magically swap places with the boy—just for an hour or so. But if it weren't for the cold, this task of his would be tolerable. The boy slept like a babe, waking only when the extract waned, and so was given another dose, under the supervision of the Maestro, who kept cursing this paltry burden of his, mumbling something about a little bird, whose death would be the only satisfactory excuse, or something of the sort. All Paolo had to do was help the boy piss in the pan, or feed him broth and quail's eggs, boiled so the yolks would just ooze a touch. And when the family came, the boy didn't seem eager to talk to any of them, despite the tears of the women—which Paolo could understand if put in his place, though at least he can piss proper, which was more than Paolo could do. But when the family did come he slipped down to the kitchen to chat with the cook, to whom he'd taken a fancy.

Paolo woke from a dream about snow and saw a woman standing by the bed. He glanced at the boy who was awake but seemed comfortable, if this blank face of his could ever be read.

"Paolo, leave us," the woman said.

He rubbed his eyes to focus better but didn't recognize her as one of the previous family visitors. And she was dressed like a washerwoman, so he thought she might be a member of staff.

"La Signorina, we have not met?"

"Yes, Paolo, we have not met."

He looked over to the boy who seemed not to have a care in the world.

"My instructions, Signorina, are to stay at all times unless a family member visits."

"Then you are excused. Run away. Off you go."

He looked at the woman who stared back at him like he was a dog. "I wonder—"

She put her hands on her hips. "Look, Paolo. I'm quite irritable today. In fact, let me say, to put this in some context, I am more irritable than I have been for as long as I can remember."

"I understand, but—"

"And so I strongly suggest you leave us . . . this . . . instant."

A high pitched voice came from the bed. "She is family, Paolo. You can go."

He looked over at the boy, who had kept his calm façade, though how could anyone be truly calm given the circumstances, despite the extract and the warm bed and quail's eggs?

"I will be in the kitchen if you need me, Carlo." He stood and felt a niggle in his back, the chair not the most comfortable place to sleep, and he went down to the kitchen, which he knew would be warmer if the meals were being prepared, which seemed to happen for most of the light hours of the day.

He was half way down the stairs when Maestro Porpora came into view. The man was adorned in his wig and velvets, and he guessed he was on his way to the Prince or something of the same importance.

"How is *il raggazo*?"

"He could not be better, Maestro. I have left him with family."

"Excellent, I need to see them about a matter. Come with me."

Paolo cursed the man to himself. It seemed the Maestro had mistaken him for a personal servant, and he was certain he now wouldn't take his break in the warmer confines of the kitchen, with all the delicacies that went with it.

When they arrived back to the boy's room, the Maestro became immediately agitated when he saw the woman. "What are you doing here? And where is Picollo Ucello?"

Paolo watched the woman turn, and the naked wrath on her face made him stand back a step.

"Is your brother sick?" the Maestro asked, in a more subdued voice.

"Is he sick? Yes, Maestro Porpora, Picollo Ucello—which, by the way, is a name that irritates me, since it's *not* my brother's given name, and is hardly a good description of him—is *very* sick." She took up the teapot pose again.

The Maestro touched the air with his fingers. "Well, I'm sorry. If I was to know before, your brother was ill . . ."

The woman sighed, though her anger seemed to linger. "Alas, it has just come to my attention as well."

"I am troubled by this. What can I do to help?"

"It looks like you are doing everything you can, Maestro."

Maestro Porpora looked at the woman with a perplexed face. "I don't understand. But, in any case, what are you doing here?"

Paolo heard the boy respond but couldn't see his face from where he stood. "I have invited her, Maestro."

He watched the Maestro fidget with the air again. "I see. Then that is in order."

"I would like her to stay, Maestro," the hidden Carlo said.

"Well, of course." The Maestro turned to Paolo. "Perhaps you could take a rest . . . well deserved, of course. Or perhaps you could accompany me—"

Paolo heard the boy raise his voice in a higher pitch. "I would like her to stay here *permanently*, Maestro."

The Maestro turned back toward the boy's bed. "I beg your pardon, Carlo?"

"I would like la Signora Lilit to stay with us. For as long as I breathe."

INTERMISSION

ONE

The peroxide host sat comfortably in the electric blue studio.

"There's been some shenanigans going on in the House of late. Shenanigans of the erotic variety. We all saw it again last night. At least those of you watching the streaming did—24/7 streaming if you want the action unedited." The peroxide blonde grinned a full set of teeth and crossed her legs, sultry like. *"So Big Brother thought he might share some insight of this juicy issue with you. So, here it is Australia—some heart to heart talk from Big Brother—recorded a few hours ago."*

The screen went blank for just a tad.

"Hi, Big Brother," a young, pretty woman said.

"Hello, Jessica." Big Brother's voice was deep though he was never seen.

"I just wanted to have a chat. Get away from the House for a bit."

"Feel free, this is what it's for."

"I'm getting so stir crazy. It's been how long now?"

"Two and a half months."

"Never leaving the House. It's so weird. And it's getting a bit much. With Blake and Amy, I mean."

"Do you like Blake, Jessica?"

"None of this will get back to anyone?"

"Jessica, the rules of the Diary Room are very clear. Anything you say will be kept in complete confidence from the House. And sometimes we don't even broadcast it."

Close up. *"Really?"*

"You should be completely at ease to discuss anything you wish. Big Brother will always be here to listen."

"Thank you, Big Brother."

"So tell me, Jessica, I have been watching you, and it seems to me you're developing strong feelings for Blake."

"You've noticed. I thought I kept it well hidden."

"We study the footage, we watch your eyes follow him around. You haven't done that with the others."

"Oh my God, you are so clever."

"But there's a problem. Blake seems to have developed a physical relationship with Amy. How does that make you feel?"

"I don't think there's much to it. Just a one-way thing. The physical stuff . . . well, it gets pretty boring in here. But I think I have a better connection with Blake. We talk for hours, we always have. He's been my best mate."

"You don't like Amy, do you, Jessica?"

Close up on her grimacing. "It's not just because of Blake. She's always talking about what she'll do when she gets evicted, getting her hair extensions, spa treatment. A holiday to Tahiti."

"You don't like those things?"

"Could never afford them, could I?"

"If you win, if you're the last in the House, you'll have plenty of money. That's important to you, with you being unemployed, isn't it, Jessica?"

"It'll give me a start. Buy a flat in Brissy. Start the beauty therapy course."

"There are only three of you left in the House. I don't have to guess who you want evicted, do I, Jessica?"

"I guess not."

"And I don't have to guess who Amy wants evicted."

"As I say, you're the clever one."

"But the question is, who does Blake want to be evicted? From what you're saying, even though he has a relationship with Amy, he might prefer you to stay in the House."

"He might. I don't know."

"Of course, it's strictly against the rules for Blake to reveal to anyone in the House who he wants to be evicted. It would make Big Brother very upset."

"We don't like upsetting you, so don't worry."

"But this situation is very interesting. So Big Brother is going to change the rules. But only if you agree."

"Agree to what?"

"Instead of the audience voting on the next eviction from the house, I'm going to let Blake vote."

"Oh my God!"

"But only if you agree to it."

"Oh my God! I . . . don't know."

"You believe that you could have a relationship with Blake, don't you, Jessica?"

"Maybe."

"You would like that, wouldn't you, Jessica?"

"Sure."

"More than the money?"

"I don't know. Yes. Maybe. I really don't know."

"Jessica, do you agree to Big Brother's new rule?"

"I don't know."

"Big Brother needs an answer now."

"Yes, all right."

"You agree?"

"Yes. Oh my God."

* * *

"Hello, Amy."

"Hello, Big Brother," said the other pretty girl.

"I've called you into the diary room to discuss your feelings about my proposed rule change."

"Blake is certainly happy about it."

"Of course. It means, unless he votes himself out, he would be one of the final two contestants in the House."

"Why would he vote himself out?"

"It would be a very selfless action."

"I don't know what selfless means . . . but it would be dumb."

"Big Brother has noticed you often share a bed with Blake."

"That's right."

"It seems like you've entered a new phase of the relationship with him."

"It's not against the rules."

"No, Amy, it isn't. But it is recorded."

"I think we've been pretty discreet."

"Every sound."

She laughed. "You make us sound like rabbits."

"How do you think Jessica feels about it?"

"I really like Jessica. She's such a good mate."

"Do you think Jessica might feel alienated by your relationship with Blake?"

"We do those things in the middle of the night."

"Jessica is in the next bed."

"I'll talk to her. We're best friends."

"Who do you think Blake will vote to be evicted?"

"I have no idea."

"Really, Amy? You're not lying to Big Brother?"

"No way. Obviously I would hope he would want me to stay."

"You were both single when you arrived?"

"Yes."

"Do you think the relationship will continue when you leave the House?"

"I think so. We're such good mates. Living on top of each other, never able to escape, that has to be a good test. Don't they say travel is the best test of a relationship? This is a million times harder."

"So it might seem strange that Jessica accepted Big Brother's rule change?"

"It was gutsy, I'll give you that. She is such a good mate. I really love her."

"And Blake, you love him in the same way."

"Not in the same way, obviously. But I love them both."

"If you win, how will it change your life?"

"I'm not thinking of winning. I just want to leave and lead a normal existence again."

"With Blake."

"With the world!"

* * *

A poolside chat between the two pretty young things, mike'd up for all Australia to hear.

"I dreamt about being in my own bed last night. At home. I woke up and mum was there and we had pancakes from Macka's."

"Wonderful! I could kill for Macka's."

"Can I ask you something, Jessica?"

"Go for it."

"You don't mind that Blake and I are . . . you know."

"Rooting?"

"Get out of here! But being in bed together."

"No problem."

"Because if you do—I'll stop. I mean it. I would stop right now. You are such a great mate."

"Really, Jess, I don't have a problem with it. Root away."

"Oh, my God! We haven't rooted yet."

"He must be good with his hands, then. You're pretty noisy."

"I can't help it. I've always been a screamer. God, I can tell you anything. You know something?"

"What?"

"When we're settled, when it's all over—"

"When you've stuffed yourself with pancakes."

"Stop it—you're making me so hungry! I love the creamy butter in those silly little plastic tubs and, oh, the maple syrup. Macka's drive thru. I swear I'll go straight from here to Macka's drive thru when I get out. But anyway, when we do get finally settled, let's all go on a holiday together. Just the three of us."

"Really? You want to do that? We've been together for almost three months."

"I'm so serious. But the winner has to pay for everything."

"That's expensive."

"We'll be loaded. You know, I have this feeling that Blake is going to win. So he can pay for the both of us. So let's make a pack—is it a pack or pact—anyway let's make a pack that if Blake wins he takes us both for a free holiday to Tahiti."

"He might not agree with that."

"He'll agree—otherwise no hanky panky."

"You are such a slut."

"Stop it! We haven't done the deed yet."

"Okay then, it's a deal. If Blake wins."

* * *

"Hello, Blake."

"Hello, Big Brother," said the young man. Pretty of course. Another pretty young thing sitting small on a red upholstered chair that sprouted curved red lips out and up, enveloping him like a beetle on a rose.

"I've brought you into the Diary Room to see how you're coping with our new rule change."

"Coping?"

"It's a serious task I've given you."

"I know."

"Have you come to any conclusions? You have to vote today."

"I think so."

"Interesting. Would you like to share your thoughts?"

"Not really."

"Big Brother can't force you."

"I wouldn't discuss it even if you could."

"I'm sure you would if you risked being evicted."

"Nope. I don't care."

"I guess that's easy for you to say, since you're not in that position."

"Nope."

"Four hundred thousand dollars is a lot of money to squander."

"Yep."

"Are you all right, Blake?"

"Yep."

"You sound distant."

"Do I?"

"Perhaps the pressure of deciding is getting to you?"

"Perhaps."

"The girls haven't been acting differently around you?"

"Nope."

"You are friends with both. It must be a hard decision."

"Yep."

"So how do you go about making such a decision?"

"As best I can."

"Big Brother was hoping for more details on your thought processes. Big Brother is a bit disappointed with the interview."

"Whatever."

"Your physical attraction to Jessica interests Big Brother."

"Okay."

"You understand why it would interest Big Brother?"

"Whatever."

"You seem close to Amy—in a more platonic sense."

"You're entitled to your opinion."
"You really are aggressive today."
"You noticed."
"I hope you aren't deliberately making Big Brother upset."
"Nope."
"Okay, Blake. You have one hour to make your decision on who you will evict."
"Whatever."

* * *

The peroxide host stood because this was prime time, the highest ratings ever, so how could anyone sit at a time like this. She teased the audience with the gold envelope that flapped in her hand. I know, but you don't. *"Okay, Australia. The time has come. Big Brother has verified the decision. Who do you think it will be? Come on, Australia, who do you think it'll be?"*

Screams from the audience. The banners wave. *We love Amy. We love Blake. We love Jessica. We love.*

"Amy's mum is here. Jessica's mum is here. And even Blake's mum is here! One of you will be seeing your child very soon. Who has Blake decided must leave the House?"

On the long white couch on the monitor, the two young women sit either side of the man, arms around each other.

The camera drifts across the faces of the audience, the banners waving hysterically, then back to the peroxide blonde—the host with the most.

"So I have looked at the answer on this paper . . . oh boy . . . it's time to go . . . it's time to go . . . Jessica!"

A flash to the ecstatic audience. Back to the couch. Jessica's face nodding. Kissing the man. The banners wave. The screams. A flash and back to the couch. Jessica stands and kisses them both. Long hugs. The banners keep waving. The peroxide blonde grins like a cartoon cat.

Then a deep voice above it all. *"It's Big Brother, Jessica. You have been evicted. It's time to leave the House."*

The elevator that isn't an elevator slides open. Center screen. Jessica walks out to the crowd, and the emotion scales up to a new level.

"Come on, Australia, here she is."

She walks down the long ramp past the crying banners. She makes it to the end and the close-up catches her wiping a tear.

"*Hello, mate.*" The peroxide host gives her a hug. "*You're devastated, I can see. Did you think it was going to be you? Did you?*"

The wailing banners keep on their chant.

"*Okay, Australia. This is Jessica's time.*" The peroxide host raises her arms. "*Come on, quiet all of you. Jessica, sit with me and we'll look at the highlights of your stay. And all of you, shoosh!*"

The screen goes back in time, the background music a *Looney Tunes* classic. The laughing House mates, funny dancing, pulling faces, jumping in the pool, carried on the back of a boy's shoulders, poking her tongue out, sleeping on the bed, sleeping on the couch, sleeping near the pool, a funny face again, dancing, playful, laughing, an almost sad face, talking with her mouth full of something, the sad face again. The funny face. And fade out.

The peroxide gleamed in the electric blue studio. "*You are amazing, mate! And you had a great time, I can tell.*"

"*It was something.*"

"*Special.*" The peroxide displayed a full set of teeth.

Jessica wipes a tear away.

"*Tell me, and all of them out there, did you think it would be you?*"

The banners yell up an answer.

Jessica says, "*I wasn't sure. But yes. I thought it would be me.*"

"*We know it's been hard. Sleeping near the recent late night shenanigans of Amy and Blake. And your feelings for Blake, we know about that. We all do, don't we? But does he know?*"

"*God, no.*"

"*Well, soon he'll be out and perhaps you can . . . confess.*" The screaming banners erupt. "*This lot is loud tonight. Australia, you are really getting the full Big Brother experience, right here, right now. And all because of you, mate.*"

A close-up on the crying audience.

"*It's all because of you.*"

* * *

"*I can't stand it. I just want it to end.*"

A poolside vigil with the last two survivors.
"You and me both."
"Blake, you're gunna win, I just know it."
"I don't think I care anymore."
"Remember our deal . . . the holiday in Hawaii."
"I thought it was Tahiti?"
"Same thing. Anyway, I feel so sorry for Jess. It'll cheer us both up . . . when you win."
"I wish you wouldn't keep saying I'm going to win."

She bent over and kissed him. The pool a sunlit crystal blue. The high fence that kept them away from the great outside that watches their every movement.

Amy said, *"I think we should plan what we'll do when we're out. Day one."*
"Eat and drink for a week."
"Where?"
"I'm not sure," Blake said.
"Come on, cheer up."
He looked at her and smiled.
"Do you think we can . . . you know . . . what we planned?"
He held her hand. *"I don't know much at the moment."*
"It's this place . . . I don't either. It'll be different when we're out."
"I don't know about that."
"What do you mean?" Amy said.
"I think outside is just like in here, only bigger."

* * *

Cut to a message from our sponsors.

A bulky man sipping XXXX Gold with the Hills Hoist behind—and the gold of the sun—down and low after a hard day's yakka—you bloody beauty . . .

> You have all read the beautiful stories
> Of the countries far over the sea
> From that which came our ancestors
> To establish this land of the free
>
> There are some folks that still like to travel

To see what they have over there
But when they go look . . . it's not like the book
And they find there is none to compare

Oh beautiful beautiful Queensland
Up where the wildflowers grow
We're proud of our beautiful climate
Where we never see ice or snow

You can live on the plains or the mountains
Or down where the sea-breezes blow
And you're still in beautiful Queensland
The most wonderful State that I know

* * *

"Hello Blake."

"Hello, Big Brother."

"Tonight, Australia will be casting their final vote. Either you or Jessica will win the money. So I thought we would have a chat, perhaps to help them make a final decision."

"Sure, whatever."

"I warn you, though, this is going live to air." In the corner of the screen the hostess sat with her short skirt and waved to the camera. Waved to Australia. *"Do you have any final words, Blake?"*

"Nope."

There was silence for a bit. *"You've been a bit aggressive of late, Blake."*

The handsome boy did not answer.

"Amy opened her heart to Australia just a few minutes ago. I don't expect that of you. But sharing your thoughts might be beneficial to us all."

"Too bad."

In the corner of the screen the hostess threw up a sad face to Australia.

The handsome boy looked down at his lap.

"Big Brother is disappointed, again."

The boy kept his head down.

"Blake, nobody knows your secret but Big Brother."

"I really don't care."

"You can walk out now if you really don't care."

"I know I can."

"Well."

"I don't want to bump up your ratings."

Some more silence. *"That's a bit nasty, Blake."*

"Whatever. You'll probably edit it out."

"I told you, this is going out live." In the corner screen the hostess waved again to Australia.

"Really, then why don't you go—"

And the screen went black except for the hostess in the corner who lifted her fingers to her ears and pulled a shocked face to Australia.

* * *

"Let's welcome our two finalists. Come on . . . here they are, Australia . . . Amy and Blake!"

They came out along the silver walkway, slapping hands with the faceless crowd. Banners, glitter, sparkling lights.

"Come on, Australia!"

Giant teeth smiles from all.

"Come here, you two." The peroxide blonde held them both. *"Well done. Well done . . . this is all for you."*

"I can't believe it's over." Who cares who says it? They are both interchangeable by this time.

Cuddles and hugs. Cuddles and hugs.

"You both look . . ."

"Happy!"

Pan to screaming heads and banners.

Close up to our host. *"Believe me, Australia, I can feel the excitement hitting me in the face."* She grinned with teeth that had been whitened again for the event. *"While we settle ourselves, let's see how these two spent the months . . . just for us!"*

Camera fades out. Then—Blake laughing. Amy laughing. Piggyback rides. Jumping and laughing and those funny faces. Blowing out her cheeks. Lifting a skirt with shorts underneath. Naughty naughty. Look at the belly buster in the pool. Wam, bam, thank you, Mam. Whipped cream on their faces. Whipped cream on her tits, covered with that tiny bikini. Naughty naughty. A cake in the face. A little nookie in green cam darkness. Aren't you naughty things. Just like those at home who are watching. Oh, bring it on, you ragamuffins. Bring it on.

Cut.

"That hasn't settled us, Big Brother!" The peroxide blonde laughs, and her whitened teeth sparkle sparkle. *"That hasn't settled us at all."* She winks at Australia. *"Where . . . is . . . that . . . check?"*

Screams as bikini-clad lackeys bring out the green check the size of a windscreen.

"Count the zeros, Australia!"

They count at home and the tension is brutal.

"Well, you two." She beams. *"Come here you rascals."* And she hugs them both like long lost friends.

"One of you will be carrying this great big check away . . . and you, Australia, have chosen who that someone will be!"

I love Blake. I love Amy. The banners claim to know the winner.

"You know what, Big Brother? I'm just going to cut to the chase. I'm not going to go through any more preliminaries. I . . . want . . . the . . . envelope."

Screams and screams as the gold envelope makes its appearance.

"Ladies and Gentlemen . . . are you ready for this? Seriously. Are . . . you . . . ready . . . for . . . this?" Close up on that white teethed grin. *"The winner of this year's Big Brother is . . ."*

She lets time tick on.

The screams choke on themselves and fade into a whimper.

"Blake!"

The tumult explodes. Gold rains down on them all. Let's get this party started.

Amy screams for joy. Hugs Blake. Hugs the peroxide host. *"I knew you'd win, you are amazing . . . I'm just so happy."* Blake lifts Amy up in his arms. Glitter sprinkles all over them.

"Congratulations, Blake!" The peroxide pulls a face at Australia. *"We have had our moments, you and I. But you have been chosen . . . oh yes, you have!"*

He grins, though not as white as the hostess.

The 'I love Blake' banners flap a frenzy.

She raises her arms. *"But maybe just one more . . . Settle down, Australia!"* She laughs with those teeth. *"What am I goin' to do with you?"* She lets the audience settle themselves in their own good time, letting flop those skinny little arms of hers. *"If you have the energy out there, maybe just one more surprise for you all. Let's bring out Big Brother's secret. Hey Blake, what do you say? Let's bring out Big Brother's little secret he has kept from us all."* She pulls one of those famous faces of hers. *"I didn't know. I didn't!"*

Close up on a wide-eyed stare from Amy. An odd face. Perplexed. And a downcast look from our handsome Blake.

"I didn't. I swear!" Whitened teeth looking so fine. *"Let's bring out Blake's little secret, hey?"*

The camera pans to the long silver walkway, and out pops a well-groomed boy. A Blake look-a-like. Same hair. Same color. Same old, same old.

Pan to an open-mouthed Amy.

He comes down the walkway. Pan to the peroxide's funny face. Pan to the waving crowd.

The handsome boy comes to the end of the walkway and takes Blake in his arms. And the boys kiss, open mouthed.

Close up on the kiss.

Close up on Amy.

Close up on the peroxide host with her hands clutching her face. With that Oh My look of hers. *"Were you ready for this, Australia?"*

The audience looks at one another as if to ask who farted. The waves at the camera continue, although some appear to be drowning.

"And before we say goodbye, Australia, I want to say thanks to this great State of Queensland for giving us the opportunity to look at ourselves year after year . . . a celebration of who we are . . . and learn, learn, learn!"

The learned crowd sung up a cheer but still some can smell the fart.

"And what do you want to say, Blake, to this great country who picked you. Picked you, my boy—I don't think he can believe it—but picked you out of all these talented housemates of yours!"

Handsome Blake takes the microphone in one hand and his good-looking boy in the other.

Close up.

"I want to say, Australia . . . thank you for choosing me. And Fuck You All!"

STRAYADAY

ONE

It was Tuesday, and the folks of Guburnburnin were festive. Some were seen driving with little red, white, and blue flags flapping from their sedans, some walking the streets wrapped in the same, like beach towels, some with yellow kangaroos in red boxing gloves instead of the Southern Cross and the Union Jack in the corner.

It was Tuesday but no one was working in Guburnburnin—except at the pub—for it was the 26th of the first month of the year. Australia Day.

"Have you ever seen so many flags before, Sam?" Lil said.

"Not as garments."

"What a strange land this is."

They sat on stools at one end of the bar packed with flag draping patrons singing off-key.

"What is chunder, Sam?"

"Vomit."

"So they're singing they come from a land . . . where men vomit?"

"Sounds like it."

"Not an expression you'd find in that Wordsworth of yours, Sam."

"It appears to be the national song. In this town, at least."

"Shamayim!"

Pete came over to them whistling merrily, for it never got busier than Australia Day, and the till was already looking healthy. "What'll you have, ladies and gent?"

"Our usual, luv."

"Not even a beer on Strayaday, Lil? How unpatriotic."

Lil looked him over like an insect she might like to add to her collection. "Tell us, luv . . . why do they wrap themselves in these flags, 'ey?"

The publican turned downstream. "Jimmy, Lil wants to know why you're wearing the Ozzy flag?"

Jimmy lifted the flag from his shoulders like Batman's cape. "We fought for it, Lil."

"Did you, luv?"

"Well, not me, myself. But my grandfather did."

"Against the bloody Japs," another flag bearer said.

"And the Germans."

"And the Turks."

"The Turks aren't bad. They like us, you know."

"Bloody Churchill fucked us up with the Turks."

"Did he, luv?"

"You need a history lesson, Lil?" Pete said.

Sam lifted his dark eyes to the publican. "How did those wars turn out for you then?"

Pete swung his gaze to the bar in a full arc and grinned. "Well, we fuckin' won!"

"Good one, Pete," someone said from afar. And they all laughed.

"Not in Vietnam we didn't." A lone voice in the brown surrounds.

The publican turned to the dissenter. "No, Mickey, but we weren't fighten' for the flag in Vietnam."

"Weren't you, luv?"

"You takin' the micky, Lil?"

Sam kept his gaze on the framed picture of King Wally, as if something important could be gleaned from it. "I noticed a monument in Banga . . . a statue of sorts, in the middle of the road."

"Yeah, the war memorial," downstream said. "My Pop's name's on it."

"What's your point, Nightingale?"

"There seemed to be a lot of names carved in it."

"It was the Great War," Jimmy said." Half the men of Banga never came back."

Sam lifted his lemon, lime and bitters and took a sip. "So you're celebrating their deaths?"

Jimmy wrapped the Union Jack and the Southern Cross over his shoulders like he was cold, but it couldn't have been below 30 Celsius. "Not celebratin', you fuckin' idiot."

"Settle down." Pete poured a schooner. "It's a holiday."

"Rememberin'. That's what we're fuckin' doin'."

Sam went back to his drink. "It rather looks like a celebration."

"Rememberin' or celebratin' . . . who cares?"

"They killed the horses, you know."

"What the fuck are you talking about, Mickey."

"They killed a lot of horses after World War One . . . couldn't afford to bring 'em back. Bloody good horses they were. Walers."

Sam took another swig. "Dead horses and men. Sounds very successful."

The bar turned to Sam as one, and Pete came over wiping a glass, bent over the booze-soaked bench like a sick relative, and whispered, "You better watch yourself, Nightingale. Some of these boys are pretty tanked, and I won't be able to control them."

Downstream sung up. "You been too busy singin' to fight in a war, mate!"

The brown surrounds laughed up.

"Oh, we've seen our fair share of fightin', luv."

"Who with, Lil? Your old man? Wherever you mighta buried him?"

Low mumbled sniggers fell over the bar like a sun shower.

"Steady on, Jimmy, that's your last drink for an hour." The publican watched Sam turn a fraction toward Lil with a smirk on his face and say something that he couldn't quite catch. "Don't get me wrong, Sam, everyone has a right to their opinion. You a love-not-war type of fella, hey?"

Sam swung his gaze at the brown men drinking their brown ale. "You are mistaken. We are not against war. It's what you do best . . . without any help at all."

"What do you mean *you*, mate?" Jimmy said.

Sam held his stare at the flagman. "I mean *you*."

"We might sit out back," Lil said in a strange voice.

Pete tilted the King Wally photograph back to level, like adjusting flowers at a gravestone. "Don't be fussed by them, Lil. Anyway, it's too stinkin' hot. The breeze wouldn't blow out a candle out there." And he stared down at Jimmy, who pulled a face but kept quiet all the same.

The door of the pub swung open, the bright sun flashing gold across the patrons, and the crouched-over heads twisted to it. Some followed the source stealthily with their eyes, one or two turned on their stools without bothering to hide their interest.

And Pete said under his breath, "That's all I need."

The cause of the turned heads went over to the pokies and sat in front of the machine closest to the door. His black curly hair. His black curly beard. His black shiny skin.

"Yep, bloody good horses were Walers," Mickey said.

The bar fell silent and the digital tune of 'yes we have no bananas' started up as the Aboriginal man fed the slot machine a few coins. Before anyone could lift their XXXX, the sound of falling metal fell down on the place like a hailstorm.

"Fuck me, I'm goin' bankrupt with that pokie."

"On Strayaday . . . there can't be a God, can there, Pete?" The Southern Cross cape flapped on Jimmy's shoulders like a breeze had come through.

The black man took a plastic bag from his shorts and a stone from it that was shaped like a biscuit, scratched with odd symbols, and put it in his pocket. He scooped the coins from the trough into the bag and came over to the bar. "I'll have a beer." His voice was deep.

Pete filled the schooner but kept his eye on Jimmy as he did. "Hot enough for ya?"

The black man nodded, watching the amber rise.

"Passing through, mate?"

The man took the glass and gulped half down.

"D' ya mind using the coaster? I just had a coat of varnish put on."

Jimmy squirmed on his stool, grinning a full set of teeth. "I love Strayaday, don't *you*, Pete?"

The publican didn't respond.

"I like any day off," Mickey said.

"Nah, that's not why I like it." Jimmy lifted his glass. "Give us a beer, Pete."

"I said you're banned for an hour."

"It's not fuckin' right. I'm a regular . . . and others are drinkin' just off the street."

"Do you want to go home early, Jimmy?"

"Fuck, keep ya hair on. Anyway . . . I didn't tell ya why I like Strayaday."

"We're all ears, Jimmy."

The flagman lifted his empty glass and studied it. "It's not so much the wars we won . . . but it's how we took over the country."

Pete shook his head. "Steady on, Jimmy."

"Well it is! Captain Cook arrived, didn't he?"

"You know Captain Cook wasn't buried when he died," Mickey said.

"Was he cremated, Mickey?"

"No. Eaten."

"Bullshit."

"It's true. After he was beaten to death . . . the natives ate him."

"The Abo's ate him?"

"The Hawaiians," Mickey said. "Anyway, Australia Day is about the First Fleet landing, not Captain Cook."

"Yeah, he was well eaten by that time."

"I love Hawaiian pizza . . . Captain Cook and pineapple."

The bar laughed, and Jimmy lifted his empty glass to the men. "We still took over the place . . . it's all about that."

The black man skulled his schooner, took more change from his plastic bag, and nodded for another.

"Invasion Day, some people call it."

"Mickey, you're a real historian, you know that?"

"Bleeding bloody hearts call it that," downstream said.

"Fucking basket weavers."

"You can understand their point of view," Mickey said.

Jimmy flapped his Australia flag like he wanted to take off. "What do *you* reckon, mate?"

"Jimmy, you lookin' to get banned for the day?" Pete said.

"I'm askin' our *traditional owner* over there—that's the right word, isn't it, Mickey—I'm askin' the opinion of one of the *traditional owners* of this fine land of ours, his opinion." Jimmy said 'traditional owners' like a galah.

But the man kept to his schooner, not even bothering to lift his head.

"I like the Aboriginal flag," Mickey said. "Might be ours one day."

"You . . . are . . . fuckin' . . . kiddin'."

"Might be. It's already an official Ozzy flag."

"Not in fuckin' Queensland."

The bar swelled in agreement.

"Well, the colors remind me of Australia more than the one we have."

"My fuckin' grandfather died for that flag, Mickey."

"And so did mine," Mickey said. "But I still prefer it."

The flagman looked down at his empty glass like he was willing it to fill. "We still haven't heard what our friend has got to say for himself." He turned to the publican. "Is that polite enough for ya, Pete?"

Pete watched the black man look over to Sam and Lil, who seemed attracted to the chatter more than usual. He even thought he saw Sam smile, which would have made twice in one sitting, but thought the better of it. "You here for the harvest, mate?"

The man shook his head.

"Jesus," Jimmy said, "it's a bit rude not to answer my question, wouldn't you say, Pete?"

"There's a couple of pubs open in Banga, Jimmy. Why don't you visit them?"

"What's the matter mate, don't you love Austraya?"

The black man kept his gaze at his schooner. "Australia ain't my fucking mother."

A few sniggered and a few expletives floated upstream and down.

"Is that the flag on ya back, mate?" a man draped in a boxing kangaroo asked.

"Good spottin', Billy," Jimmy said. "That's the Abo flag . . . isn't that right, Mickey?"

"Yep. The colors of the earth and sun."

"What's the black then?"

The man with skin of the same color answered deep and loud but kept his eyes down to his XXXX. "The people."

And the bar fell silent for a spell. If someone had just come in from the hot outside, they might think the place was in prayer.

But in the little town of Guburnburnin, silent vigils never had legs.

"Well, mate, I'm lookin' round the bar, and there's only one black sittin' amongst us. So—if I might be permittin', Pete—I would be suggestin' the flag be red, yellow and . . . *white*."

Some of the bar raised their glasses but none voiced their opinions.

"Suggestion noted, Jimmy," Pete said. "Now I think I can hear your mother callin' ya."

"Might not be her, Pete, since she's been dead for three years."

"Well someone's callin' ya."

The Aboriginal man took a swig of XXXX and wiped at his mouth. "What about green?"

"What was that, mate?" Jimmy said.

The man lifted his head and stared in front at nothing in particular. "What . . . about . . . green?"

"It's supposed to be the most relaxing color to look at," Mickey said.

The black man drained the dregs of his glass. "Thanks for the drink." He lifted himself off his stool and took himself and his bag of coins out into the heat of the day, the door swinging brilliant yellow across the brown surrounds.

The bar twisted back to their hunched-over selves and 'yes we have no bananas' kept on its song.

Jimmy looked over at the swinging door. "Well, who or what the fuck was that?"

"He's got to be here for harvest, though he's a bit early."

"Or gone walk about."

They laughed and the amber liquid kept getting poured and the pub settled for a while.

It wasn't until mid-afternoon, the insulation and the aircon just managing to keep the place from sweltering, before the alarm was heard.

"You feelin' alright, Jimmy?"

The flagman shrugged. "Good as gold."

"You look a bit strange, mate."

"If you give me a beer, I'll brighten up."

"I swear, Jimmy, you look like you need a lie down."

The patrons all turned. Some of them frowned and some wiped at their eyes.

And the flagman noticed the odd complexion of his hands, turning his palms over to face the light of the overhead fluorescent to gain a better look.

"Jimmy, you're the color of Mickey's shirt."

Pete looked over the man. "Jesus, Jimmy. I think it's your liver. I seen it before. For Christ sake stay off the booze."

Some came off their stools and touched the flagman's skin, tentative, like they were testing the temperature of a bath.

"Is Doc workin' today?" one of the examiners asked.

"I feel fine, I'm telling ya."

"Pete, give Doc a call. Jesus!"

And as they spoke, the flagman's skin turned from the color of a pale honeydew to the flesh of an avocado, and then to the skin of an overripe lime.

And it continued that way until Doc finally arrived, for he had been hard to chase down, with Jill Riddon's baby and all. And he confirmed it was Jimmy's liver, maybe alcohol, maybe hepatitis, but thought the final diagnosis would be down to the coroner. Though the autopsy results wouldn't be back for a week or two.

* * *

Outside, the ocean groaned on the rocks. The tent fluttered like a sail, and the salt air within the cave of canvas was fresh and warm.

Bob turned over on his airbed, facing the flapping door that threw open a strip of clear sky. He stretched out and gave the morning a grunt, rolled back over and drifted off to sleep again. When he woke the wind had settled but the sky had kept the same way.

His tent was perched on a grassy dune at the northern end of the beach. A thick forest of gums protected the platform behind. In front the dune fell down to a little sandstone plateau that the ocean etched like a laced doily. As he stood on the dune, bare-chested, he watched a lone surfer weave his board along the crest of a wave, the rest of the little sandy beach devoid of any human company.

He had no idea of the time. He loved it that way.

He was hungry or not. Tired or not. And when he was, he ate, or slept. And when he wasn't, he did everything or nothing. And he liked both just about the same.

The gas flame lit, the bacon crackled on the pan, an egg fried.

The surfer twisted to and fro.

And the blue-scape kept on as far as he could see.

He walked down to the sandstone shelf, the surface pockmarked with tiny pools left from the outgoing tide. He bent down and touched the cool water, and a hermit crab raced just under the surface, disappearing into a narrow corridor that joined to another caramel pool. He followed it, hopping over the coarse rock that scraped at his feet, until it scampered into a deeper hole. He wondered where the crab went when the tide came back, whether it just floated away with the ocean or managed to stay sheltered down in a pocket in the stone, waiting for the tide to head out again, to leave the place as it was now, shallow and full of life.

He went to the edge of the shelf and sat facing the ocean. The froth of the waves washed his feet, the water cool on his skin, the sun warming as the water receded.

The surfer waved at him. Bob waved back.

They'd never spoken a word but Bob felt he knew him just the same. The sharing of the place, morning after morning, fashioned into a companionship of sorts. He had slept too long to see the fishermen, a father and son by the look of their mugs, who stood ankle deep when the tide was high, close to where he sat, the bucket and bait and spare rods dry up on the dune. They had left him a fish more than once, wrapped in newspaper just outside the flap of his tent. The white meat tasted like nothing on earth, the skin crisp off the pan. They had never spoken either, fishing and sleeping being the quiet pastimes they were, though he left them a bottle of wine the next morning, which was gone when he woke.

Bob slid off the shelf and walked out into the ocean, jumping as the wash came to him, salt spray rising, a cool ache in his groin as the water came up, and he dived, the rush of cold thrilling his skin, splashing his arms into the surf before lifting his head, shaking the water from his mane, his beard, the sun streaming down to warm his face.

He swam two easy laps, to the southern tip of the beach and back. Sometimes he did four, his record was six, but on this day he was tired—just a bit—with the bacon still high in his belly, and the warm salty air and all that went with it.

So he went back to his little canvas tent and slept again. And when he woke he had no idea of the time.

But he felt hungry, so he had something to eat.

***

"Knock, knock."

Little Jamie looked up from the kitchen table at her.

"Anyone home?"

Sharon peeled her rubber gloves off and went down the hall to the screen door that let a bit of breeze into the place. The sun streamed on her face but she made out the man who stood at the entrance. "Robbo?"

"Just passin', Shaz. Thought I'd drop in."

She straightened her hair and thought about taking the apron off but didn't. "I never heard the dog bark."

"He's sleepin' down by the gate. I don't blame him. He'd need double rations to work in this heat."

She opened the door and Robbo came in tentatively, round shouldered.

"Tea, Robbo?"

"Ta, Shaz."

She watched him pull up a chair next to little Jamie. "I'm sorry about your wife, Robbo. The kids still up?"

"Nah, back at school."

"It must be quiet. You been okay?"

"I have my moments."

She watched his round-shouldered glance drift around the room, though never at her. "Quiet around here too, Shaz?"

The water whistled and she poured two cups, the Earl Gray bags floating to the top. "Milk and sugar?"

"Nah . . . just as it comes."

"My mother would like you, Robbo. *It's not meant to have milk and sugar, Sharon!*" She mimicked her mother's high-pitched whine.

"How is the old lady?"

"Just the same, Robbo. Just the same."

They sat together and little Jamie went back to his drawing.

"Sorry to barge in and all."

"You don't need an invitation. And I'm sorry I missed the funeral. There was no excuse, but with the chaos around here . . . I'm no farmer, Robbo . . . but I'm sorry."

"It's nothing, Shaz."

"It bloody well is!" Her voice faltered and they both kept quiet for a spell.

"You heard from him yet?"

"Nothing. He's alive, credit card ticking away. Hec said it might have been stolen, but I told him to look at the purchases . . . camp stove, petrol at the same place on the coast, 7-Eleven goods, nothing flash. It's got Bob written all over it."

"He could have called, though."

"Yep. He could have called." She looked up at him. "You wouldn't like a glass of wine, Robbo?"

The slouched-over man grinned. "Well, if you're twistin' my arm."

She went over to the Kelvinator and took out a bottle of white. And she noticed that little Jamie had wandered off, maybe to play with the dog.

"I thought you might need a hand around here, Shaz."

"That's sweet of you."

He twisted around with his gaze not as hidden as before. "You keep the place nice." He lifted his eyes to her for the first time.

She smiled. "A man's castle."

"He'll be back before harvest, Shaz. It's pretty straight forward now. Irrigate every few weeks because of the drought —you doin' regular soil moisture tests?"

She nodded.

"Pests shouldn't be a problem since Bob uses chemicals. I'm the only dickhead around not doin' that. And I had a squiz before knockin', and you've got less weeds than in my tomato patch. No doubt about it, Shaz, this is the best property for two hundred miles. So, as long as it doesn't pour, and there's bugger all chance of that, you should have a good harvest."

"Even a woman couldn't stuff it up, hey, Robbo."

"Well, I wouldn't like to challenge you." He lifted his glass. "I'm not normally a wine drinker, but this goes down well."

"It's a chardonnay. And you're drinking it like water."

"Sorry, Shaz."

"Sorry nothing. There's another couple of bottles in the fridge. And, as you say, the farming is easy goin' before harvest, so we might as well relax while we can." She watched him empty his glass. "You like farming, Robbo?"

"It's all I know. This land might be big and flat, but in the scheme of things it's a real shit place if you want to grow anything other than weeds."

She filled his glass again.

"I heard Bob had a chat with the gas company. Not that it's any of my business."

"This place suffocates me, Robbo."

"They make an offer?"

"A good one." She sipped her wine. "Not that it's any of your business, but would you take it?"

He frowned. "If I had this farm, probably not."

"The best in two hundred miles."

"Maybe more."

"And when they make you an offer?"

"Probably not." He swigged his glass. "As I said, it's all I know." He grinned. "But if I can't stop this bloody bollworm, and the drought doesn't lift, you put in a good word for me, okay."

"Deal." She stared at him. "Robbo, have you got a drinking problem? That's two glasses in as many minutes."

"You make me nervous, Shaz."

She laughed.

"Always have. Even at school."

"You were always a shy one." She thought about filling his glass again but decided against it. "I never knew Molly to talk to, more than the weather that is. She was from Brissy?"

"Toowoomba. I met her at the Brissy Show. She had a blue ribbon in the Dark Rich Fruitcake competition. I got a red for my Murray Grey. She was always better than me . . . if I won a bronze she'd win a silver. Ma said she thought she'd come down as a present from Heaven. *Don't you lose this one*, Robbie, she told me when we were married. *Don't lose her.*" He sighed. "But that was harder than it looked."

She changed her mind and filled his glass.

"You know what the name of my Murray Grey was?" He smiled. "Don't get riled up now." He took a swig and wiped his mouth. "Elsie."

She laughed. "Not a bad name for a bull."

"He was fiery. Shoulda won, except his brisket had a double chin. That's what the judges told me."

"I can't wait to tell mum."

"Don't you dare, Shaz."

"Why, you're not still scared of her, Robbo?"

"Course I am." He lifted his glass. "She came to the funeral, which was good of her. Molly kept to herself and all. She was a family girl, not much socializin'. I don't think they ever met, but she came. We had a bit of a chat. Said she knew what it was like to lose a partner."

"Did she?"

"It sort of helped. More specific advice than pats on the shoulder."

"And what advice did she give."

"Time."

"That's hardly original."

"Guess not. But it means something when it's told by someone who's been through the same thing."

She emptied her glass.

"You got a drinkin' problem, Shaz?"

"I aim to get one, Robbo. You want to help?"

And little Jamie decided to keep away for the rest of the afternoon.

* * *

The toad croaked twice, and Gordon looked up at the young blonde who stood at the entrance. "We're full up, Sally."

"If you keep this up, Gord, you might make some dough."

"Let's not get excited now."

She put the bucket and mop down by the door. "Well, if people keep fallin' off the perch, you'll need to build extensions."

"Jimmy's wake got a fair crowd. I never knew he was so popular."

"Jimmy was a dick, Gord. People were there to gossip."

"What's the latest theory?"

"It seems like it was a classic case of bone pointing."

"Ah, we haven't had one of those for a while."

"And people are keeping their eyes open for the black fella."

"A posse?"

"Not really, no one's game to front him. They just want to stay clear of the bloke . . . and his bone. Even Doc looked convinced. Apparently the autopsy didn't show any cause of death, even though he looked like a watermelon. Some fancy guys from Canberra were called in. They talked about quarantining the pub and all that were in it."

"Jesus."

"Doc said it'd be too late now, so they decided not to, but he looked worried."

"Doc's not one to worry."

"It's back to the bone pointing theory. Anyway, I better get to the cleaning."

"Before you go, Sally, I've been meaning to ask you. You know those suitcases in Lil and Sam's room?" He watched her drop her gaze to the bucket. "It seems like they think you've been snoopin' around."

"Something missing, Gord?"

"No, no. But they think you've been taking a look at their stuff."

"I'm too busy scrapin' down the loos to bother with someone's bags, Gord."

"I told 'em that. But I also said I'd pass the message on." He watched her eyes that had kept to the swill.

"Messaged received."

"Sally, do you mind shutting the door for a second."

And she did as he asked.

"What's in the bags?"

"Gord!"

"Yeah, I know. What's in them?"

"If you're so interested why don't you take a look yourself? I'll keep watch."

He smiled at her. "Well, it seems I don't need to, since you've beaten me to it."

"If you are saying it's for security purposes, Gord, like they were terrorist suspects, the laws are different, so I believe."

"You're only protecting the community, Sally."

She pushed the bucket next to the door and lowered her voice. "I only had a quick look, I swear."

"Of course you did."

"Besides the usual stuff there was something odd wrapped in a rag . . . in both bags, his and hers."

"Something odd?"

"Well, I'm no expert, Gord, but it was made of rock, about the size of my hand, maybe a bit bigger. And on it, it had old writing, like from a museum, like the Rosetta stone, I've seen pictures. They were pretty similar, in hers and his, I didn't have them next to each other to compare, but only a few of the squiggles if any were different I'm sure."

"I feel like I'm in a Secret Seven novel," he said.

"I loved the Secret Seven . . . read them all as a kid. You can be Peter, and I'll be Janet."

"Well, Janet. Just to add to the mystery, I'll share something with you." He stared into her. "As long as you keep it to yourself."

"The Secret Seven are sworn to secrecy, Gord."

He opened the desk drawer and passed the sheet over to her. "It's my bank statement."

She studied it. "Not much in it, Gord."

"I'm aware." He pointed to the underlined credits. "That's our lodgers' payments. Notice anything unusual?"

"Regular payment, nice for a change. Hold on, Peter . . . the account number on the details of the transactions are different."

"Good one, Janet. But they use the same card."

"Another mystery." She lowered her voice to a whisper. "Listen, I know a bank teller at Banga . . . I can make some enquiries."

"Already have."

"Good going, Peter!"

"They say they can't go into the details, for privacy reasons, but the money is certainly real."

"Interesting. I might have a word with my bank teller friend anyway."

"No, Janet. They're good customers. And the customer is—"

"Always right!" She smiled. "You're not as much fun as you used to be, Peter."

"Gettin' old, Janet. Gettin' old."

She picked up the bucket and mop and opened the door. But before she left, Sally turned back, though she kept her eyes low. "Just supposin' I happened to have photographed those rocks with my mobile, Gord? Just supposin'?"

"Fuck, Sally, do you want me to lose this place? It's hard enough getting customers as it is. If word gets around we're photographing their dirty laundry . . ."

"Don't worry, Gord. Janet's got you covered."

"Delete them, Sally."

"But what happens if they're stolen, culturally sensitive artifacts?" She looked up at him. "And there might be a reward."

"Delete them, Sally."

"Jesus, Gordy, a fine Secret Seven member you've turned out to be."

* * *

With Jimmy gone, the Guburnburnin Hooters were down to eleven, including the Nightingale. Jimmy had been a bowler, a leg spinner—just like Sam. And on this day, the Hooters lost the toss and had to bowl first.

It was a stinker, and the baked pitch had started to crack like a broken mirror. With an over before lunch, it was none for eighty-seven, and both the opening bowlers looked like they were in need of an ambulance.

"Go on, Nightingale," Pete said. "Let's see what you're made of."

Sam took the ball from Pete, and the Hooters clapped, and so did the sweating few that sat under umbrellas to watch their men. Even the opposition gave up a clap, for the legend of the Nightingale had spread far. Some shouted for him to give them a tune.

"Whoo whoo," Sharon poked her tongue out at Pete, who crouched behind the stumps, punching his gloves.

Sam strolled from his mark and swung his arm over in an easy roll. The ball spun off the wicket and the batsman didn't get close. And neither did Pete's glove, the ball rolling down the slope of the short boundary for four byes.

The batsman nodded his head to Sam and gave him a grimace. And Pete kept his gaffe to himself, smacking his gloves harder this time.

The Nightingale walked back to his mark and strolled down to bowl in the same easy way. The batsman charged down the pitch but didn't get close, and the ball missed the stumps and Pete's gloves as well, the stumping chance gone, and the batsman didn't bother to run, the principle of it all, and said good ball to Sam, who didn't seem fazed by the wicketkeeper's blunder.

"That was a stumpin' for the takin', Pete," Teddy shouted up.

"You want the gloves, Ted?"

"Maybe stand back a bit? Sam's moving it like Warney."

Sam rubbed the shiny half of the ball against his white flannels and went back to his mark in the same effortless way, rolled his arm over just as easy. But this time the ball came off the pitch in the opposite direction, hitting the stumps that rattled behind the batsman, who lifted his head up to the sky.

"Got him with the googly!" Teddy shouted up.

The Hooters ran in and patted Sam on the back, and the batsman lifted his bat to acknowledge the Nightingale before heading off the field. Sharon ran over and patted him too, and the dark haired man may have smiled but she wasn't sure.

"Got him with your googly," she laughed—maybe a bit too eager some would have said, what with Bob away and all.

In the next deliveries Sam mesmerized the batsmen. "You're playin' with them," Teddy kept up, and the stumps rattled again and again. Pete stood back as far as seemed fitting, even managing a stumping or two, which raised his spirits, for he kept a sour look most of the time, which Sharon took great pleasure in riding him for. And her eagerness never abated. She was heard to shout up, "Show 'em your googlies" all throughout the innings, to the amusement of the Hooters and the onlookers, who seemed to swell as the word got around.

But the innings didn't last long. For, on this sticky summer's day, the Banga Buccaneers went from none for eighty-seven to all out for a hundred and six, thanks to the Nightingale, who was now given the moniker of the Guburnburnin Googly, in addition to his more cultural nickname.

And indeed, the town talked about nothing else, even snubbing the hot topic of Jimmy the Grape for the rest of the weekend. And for a few days after that.

ALL THE PRETTY FLOWERS

ONE

As the heat of summer was lost to autumn, and the land kept moist by rain or bore, the cotton could be harvested and wheat seeds planted. And if all went well, the folks of Guburnburnin could rest a while and let nature take its course.

At the end of this summer the rains did come, not too harsh, just enough to hold off irrigation for a spell. And the local blue grasses drank and flourished, as did the African Lovegrass and Cotton-tails. But that didn't matter, even though in the strictest sense they were weeds, though some even debated that, since the livestock would eat them if no other food was available.

And amidst the land full of promise, pretty little flowers with red petals and plump lime stems were seen around the place, first within the sprouting wild grasses, and later in clumps of tall slender lovegrass and fluffy Cotton-tails. Sarah McConachy even brought some home for her mother, who thought them beautiful, and made a display on the dining room table. Nothing so red ever came to the town, she said, except for the dirt that was the color of rust and not bright and alive like the petals.

Nature had its way and the little red flowers started to blossom in and around the cotton shrubs, and within the weeds that had flourished on the land where the wheat would be planted. For the soil had been nurtured well by the rains, and much hope was held for the sowing time that grew near.

They don't grow by themselves, Mum, Sarah McConachy had noted. She was a bright little thing her teacher said, and she was right. The pretty red flowers only grew where other things did, for they needed the roots of a living host to bud. And when their tiny tubes penetrated the roots of their neighbors, they could suck the nutrients from them, and live happily ever after, each plant producing up to half a million seeds that looked like dust, and floated like dust, and could lie dormant for a decade in the soil, just waiting for other unsuspecting neighbors to sprout nearby and help them on their way again.

The pretty red flower was *Striga asiatica*, better known as Witchweed. And the Queensland Biosecurity Team was called. And no one was allowed to leave their property, man or machine, without their permission. And over the months that followed, a concoction of gas and chemicals was sprayed over the land that enclosed the little hamlet of Guburnburnin, so that every plant—both pest and ripe, promising crop—was completely destroyed.

* * *

The sound of the gravel, the car door closing, not too loud, not too soft, the front door opening and closing with the same thud. Same old, same old, familiar despite five months' absence.

Sharon looked up from the kitchen table and saw him standing slender, his curly beard full and painted with gray streaks, the skin of his arms and legs bronzed. He didn't smile or grimace or do anything. He just stood and stared at her, and she felt like a bus driver ready to issue a ticket.

If he had come an hour earlier she wouldn't have been tanked. The bottle of chardonnay was nearly finished now, little Jamie fast asleep in her bed. Jamie usually disappeared when she drank. Best not to see bad habits.

But Bob came when he came, and there was nothing anyone could do about it.

"What the fuck are you staring at?"

He kept his gaze but didn't glimmer a response.

"Are you fucking deaf?" The words came out from her harsh and loud. She shook her head and laughed. "But please, how rude of me, you must be eager to have a tour around the property." She stood up, staggering just a little, and went over to the sink. "Come over here, Bob, and you can get a feel of the place just by looking through the kitchen window."

Bob didn't move.

"The place is looking a little barer since you were here last. If you look you'll just see . . . nothing. The dirt is still there, it's not as if we were flooded, the land is dry. But you see, Bob, even though the soil is still here, I've been told it won't grow a fucking thing, for quite . . . some . . . time."

"I'm sorry, Shaz."

"It will be weed free, though, that's one silver lining. Let's be thankful for small mercies, as my dear mother would say."

"I only found out yesterday."

"Yesterday, Bob? I gather you've not been watching the news. A disaster area, I think they called our town. We had a visit from the Premier three weeks ago. All very exciting. He nearly made it up the drive, he was supposed to, Hec had rung to give me the heads up, he was supposed to come and visit . . . little . . . old . . . me. But he had to leave earlier than planned. Important Government business to attend." She looked back at him. "But you only found out . . . yesterday!" She shouted the words and spittle sprayed from her mouth.

"I haven't been in front of a TV since I left."

"What did happen there? It's been quite a while and I can't remember all of the details."

"I'm sorry, Shaz."

"It's Sharon, Bob. I don't like being called Shaz." She laughed. "I never told you that, did I?"

"Do you want me to stay at the Coral?"

"Hold on, Bob. Not so fast." She went back over to the table and sat, emptying the bottle of chardonnay into her glass. "We have some business to attend to, you and I." She reached over to papers that were sitting in a fruit bowl in the middle of the table. "Here they are, Bob. For you to sign. It seems that little old me can't simply sign away the place to Chingasco—that is, the China Gas Company. You may have forgotten, but we need your signature as well."

"I'll go to the Coral and come back in the morning."

"No, no, no, Bobby." She laughed. "Do you like being called Bobby?" She shook her head into the chardonnay as if expecting a response from the glass. "I don't think you do. But, Bobby, I need your signature."

"Sharon, let's talk about it tomorrow."

"Are you deaf, Bobby? I need your fucking signature!" And she flung the papers at him.

They flared and landed at his feet. She watched him stare down at them, then turn to the corridor and make for the door.

"Don't you fucking run away from me again, Bob!"

And when the door thudded in the same old, same old, she started to cry.

And she kept on crying.

And felt weak for doing so.

Weak as tea.

* * *

"I thought this time it was my turn to cook breakfast?"

"You do look rested, Bob, but I'm very particular how my eggs are done."

"Let me give you a tip, Gord, eggs are best fried with seasoning from the ocean air."

"Very poetic." He turned the bacon strips over on the pan. "I don't have to tell you I'm bloody jealous of your grand adventure."

"It's your turn next."

"But I've got to warn you, I think you'll be needing room number 2 for some time."

"She's pretty riled up."

"Rabid, Bob. She's been like this ever since the Witchweed."

"Funny, I thought she'd use it as an excuse to sell."

"Seems like, according to the local telegraph, she was getting excited about the harvest. It was meant to be a bumper crop."

"Her first, I guess."

Gordon scraped the bacon strips from the pan and placed them next to the eggs, poached so the yolks oozed slow when cut. He took both plates and sat at the table with Bob.

"I must say it was nice to have a shower. I'd forgotten what fresh water feels like."

Gordon dug into his breakfast.

"I've been a dick, Gord."

Cut the bacon fat away.

"I know I should have . . ."

"Phoned?"

"Come back for harvest. And phoned."

"Yep, would have been easier. But you weren't to know."

"That's hardly an excuse."

"No, it isn't." He looked up at him. "Eat your breaky, Bob. You look like you can do with a good feed."

And the two men ate a while without saying much, but when the plates were clean started up again.

"I reckon this might be the end of the town, Bob."

"Insurance will cover a lot of it."

"True. But as you know, most of the farms are dry, and there's talk that cotton is just too water-intense for these parts. You're lucky, with the irrigation. Not to say you haven't played your cards well."

"I don't feel lucky at the moment."

"Fair enough. None of my business."

"We've been through that before, Gord. Me sittin' here eating your grub makes it your business." Bob scratched his beard. "Even the wheat has done it tough over the years . . . and the one year that rain came at sowing time? Fucking Witchweed."

"It's supposed to be tropical. No one can figure how it got down here."

"Well, it's all a bloody wasteland now."

"And Chingasco are coming in with their check books."

"Very generous of them."

"And the aquifers are pretty sparse around here, so the threat of opening a coal seam isn't as bad as it might be. According to the local telegraph."

"This is shit land, Gord. Always has been. God knows why we ever came here."

"Cheap, I guess."

"And plentiful."

He watched him rub at his beard. "Sharon knows you're here? I thought you might've had a call by now."

"She's real riled up."

"I'm not sure it's my business—yeah, yeah, you're eating my grub, but still I'm not sure it's any of my business. But the local telegraph has been heard to say . . ." He paused and feigned to scrape some fat off his plate.

"Spit it out, Gord."

He looked out the window and the sky was clear and he guessed it would be twenty Celsius or a touch more. "You know something, Bob, it's a bloody beautiful day. It always is this time of year. Rather than being stuck inside, you go and see that little wife of yours. And for God's sake take some flowers." He smiled at him. "Only not if they're red."

* * *

He thought about knocking but didn't. And when he entered the house Sharon was sitting in the same spot he left her last evening.

He stood at the entrance to the kitchen and waited.

Sharon kept her head down at the Gazette but spoke easily. "Take a pew, Bob."

And when he went to sit she said, "Not on that chair. Over here," which he thought was strange, even under the circumstances.

"I'm sorry, Sharon."

She turned the page and he glimpsed a picture of the Premier with the Banga Mayor.

"I'll try and explain . . ."

"I don't want an explanation."

"You deserve one."

"I don't want it!" She closed the newspaper and folded it in half. "I just want to move on."

He bit his lip and waited. Her mother would say he was too weak to take charge. But the fact was, he didn't have the right.

"This is your farm—now don't interrupt, Bob." She held her hand up and he saw her mother in her. "This is your farm, has been in your family's hands for a century. So, the decision is yours to make." She tilted her head just like Elsie before a sermon. "As I see it, you can either sell to the Gas Company or . . ." She looked up at him. "You can pay me out."

The pit of his stomach sunk, and he thought he might bring up his bacon and eggs. "How can I pay you out?"

"I don't know, Bob. We can get a valuation. With everything that's gone on lately that might be tricky, the gas value being a lot more than the farm. But Tillie Brydon did it last year, when they parted ways."

"Ted Brydon went bust after that."

"Well, Ted Brydon isn't the issue, Bob. If you want to keep the farm, then I want my share."

He grabbed at his beard and felt the tug on his cheek smart.

"I assume you think I deserve a share, Bob?"

"Of course." He took the newspaper but never looked at a word. "Why can't we settle a bit before making a final decision?"

She nodded. "I thought you might be leaning that way. But, Bob, I've had plenty of time to settle. You see, time is pretty plentiful around here these days. You know, they even stopped playing cricket. Everyone was scared to come through the Bio border, and no one wanted us coming to them for fear we might contaminate their land. Which was understandable." She chuckled. "But I was getting good at cricket. Sam said my batting had come on leaps and bounds. I practiced with him down the park, you know, with all . . . this . . . time on our hands."

He unfolded the paper and flattened it with his hand. "If we sell, do we still have a chance . . . you and I?" Water brash pooled in his mouth and his sick innards sunk further down.

"I'm surprised you asked . . . flattered almost. But no, Bob. We have no chance."

He looked over to the fruit bowl and a strange numb feeling came over him.

And he looked around the room and sighed. "Have you got a pen handy?"

* * *

"Well I never." The publican stared at him as the saloon door swung back and forth.

The pub was full, since in Guburnburnin drinking time now started early and never seemed to end.

"Who do you remind me of? Don't tell me . . . Joe Cocker. Doesn't he look like Joe Cocker, Mickey?"

"Or ZZ Top," downstream said.

"She's got legs . . . and she knows how to use them."

"Good one, Pete."

And the brown bar started up the song but kept their stare at him.

Bob knew he had it coming, he'd been expecting it. So without taking the bait, he sat when upstream gave him a stool.

"It's good to see everyone hasn't lost their sense of humor," he said.

"First one's on the house." Pete poured the XXXX. "Full strength okay?"

"Full strength it is."

Some of the men came over and huddled around. Boredom sat heavy in the little town of Guburnburnin, and no one wanted to miss out on any entertainment, scant as it was.

"I must say, Bob, you're lookin' pretty good. Lost some weight, I see."

"And a little more hair."

"Tanned and all."

"The little woman must be excited to see you back," one of the huddled shouted up.

The chuckles rained spiteful over the place.

"Now, now, give him some room," Pete said. "You lot are like fuckin' blowflies around a turd . . . must be your color, Bob."

The huddle laughed and some sung She's Got Legs again and all waited for the story to unfold.

"You passin' through or stayin'?"

He sipped the XXXX. "Is this truth or dare, Pete?"

"Don't go a dare. We don't want to see your willy!"

Pete laughed, and so did everyone else. A stranger in town might think they were celebrating a lotto win or Black Caviar's last race, even though the land still wept of ethylene glycol and herbicides that no one could pronounce.

"Truth, then." He lifted his schooner. "I'll stay until the property is settled."

The brown surrounds kept their stares, though now open mouthed.

"Fuck, Bob," Pete said. "You too? Three generations and all."

"It's got to end someday. Might as well be with me. Anyway, we haven't any kids to make it four, whether we stay or not."

"Shaz is still young. You shootin' blanks?"

"No, Pete. But I'm not doin' much shootin' these days."

The audience pulled faces at each other—the tale giving them all it promised and more.

"So . . . where the fuck have you been?"

"You look like you're doing good business, Pete."

"Booming, you're right about that. So—"

"It's your turn." He took a swig and wiped his mouth, the froth settling on his beard. "Truth or dare, Pete?"

"My turn? What do'ya want to know?"

"I've been away for a while. I'm sure you have something you could tell me." He heard the snickers from upstream and down.

"Well, you heard about Jimmy."

"Yep. I'd like to say he'd be missed."

"Fuck, Bob, you've got bloody nerve! He was one of us."

And some of the huddle mumbled their disapproval as well.

He took another swig.

Downstream shouted up, "You seen Robbo around, Mickey?"

And the brown surrounds giggled like schoolgirls. There it was.

"Come on fellas, don't be pricks," Pete said.

"I bet he's not at home," upstream said.

And the giggles came at a higher pitch, and some of the stools hid their faces or slouched over so far they nearly touched the timber slab.

Pete lent forward and kept his voice down to a whisper. "You stayin' for dinner, Bob?"

"Not sure." He lifted his glass and took a good measure. The alcohol felt warm since he'd kept dry for most of his trip away. "What news of Robbo, Pete?" But he said it not in a whisper at all.

The bar hushed for a spell.

"Well, his missus died around Christmas."

"I'm sorry to hear that."

"Yeah. He took it hard . . . with two kids and all."

"He's takin' it hard now," someone said from behind.

And the giggles from the hunched-over patrons made his guts squirm, like they had for most of the day. And the water brash felt sour in his mouth. And he thought he might spew.

"Why don't I get you a steak . . . medium rare, just as you like it? On the house. I'll set you up out back, it's bloody beautiful there."

"That's good of you, Pete. I might just take you up on that."

He lifted himself off the stool and went out to the garden, where it was bloody beautiful, the sun low and orange on the land, the cool breeze, the quiet. And he sat and drained the dregs of his XXXX.

And he started to cry.

*　*　*

"You want the heads up, Bob?"

He still sat alone in the beer garden and hadn't moved up to closing time. He was drunk but not chundering drunk. Nicely pickled his grandfather would have said. And his grandfather would have known. The first generations knew how to drink.

"Do I want the heads up? You tell me, Pete, do I?"

Pete wiped down the table with a sponge that soaked up the XXXX. "Well, I'm offerin' if you do."

"Sit with me." He staggered back on his chair and it scraped on the slate. "You know something? I don't think you're appreciated as much as you should be . . . the long hours and all. The same old faces every day, most of them drunk."

"Certainly by closing time they seem to be."

"Exactly, Pete! When you are most tired, the day is done, you have to sit and listen to drunks like me. And if you're unlucky they might spew on you—sorry about that little incident a while back. I never said sorry, did I?"

"Occupational hazard."

"That's exactly what I mean . . . you ain't appreciated for what sacrifices you've made for the town." He sat up and the world spun a touch. "Tell me, when was the last time you had a holiday?"

"A real one?" The publican lent back in his chair. "Can't say I've ever had one. Went to Tamworth for the festival a spell back. A week it would have been."

"A week . . . the longest in fifteen years?"

"I know, I deserve a medal."

"I'm serious, Pete, you and I have never been friends—don't pull a face now, we aren't enemies, but you know what I mean. But we, or I, don't give you enough credit."

"Thanks, Bob. Maybe you can put me in for the Queen's honors. Sir Pete. It has a nice ring about it."

He watched the publican look out at the dark land, and he felt a strange liking to him. But maybe it was the booze. "I'm telling you, I wouldn't do the job. And I don't know many who would, except the drunks. The town would be shittier than it is without this place. So thanks, Pete. If it wasn't closing time I'd buy you a drink." He grinned. "Anyway . . . I'm getting off the topic. Do I want the heads up?" He sighed. "Well, it seems like the boys having a laugh at the bar have already done that for you."

"Actually, Bob, no they haven't."

He looked at Pete, who dropped his stare down at the sponge. "What, my little woman isn't rooting Robbo?"

"Well, yeah, she is. But that's not what I was going to tell you."

He laughed. "Well, let's see. The land is fucked for years, I have no kids, my marriage is over . . . it's going to be very interesting to see how you can top that."

"You're better off without her."

He watched the publican lift his gaze from the sponge and up to him with a blank face.

"Look, Pete. I know you've been sweet on Sharon."

"You're wrong, Bob. Well, maybe ten years ago, but not for long even then, and not since." Pete smiled. "Don't get me wrong, I've never found the right girl . . . probably she doesn't exist. But I'm tellin' ya, I would prefer the loneliness any day to Shaz." The publican laughed. "I know what you're thinking, sour grapes. But it's not true. Robbo had a fine girl, Molly. I would have given my right arm to have someone like her, I don't mind admitting it. But not Shaz. And I pity Robbo if she gets her hands on him. Just as I pitied you."

He closed his eyes and drifted a bit as a cool breeze came off the land and onto his face. Gordy was right, it was a beautiful time of the year, even though the land was dead.

"Stop me if you want, Bob, but Shaz has always been up herself. Like she's better than us. I know school buddies of hers, and they say the same thing. She's no royalty, but she thinks she is." The publican took a wheezy breath. "Now you stop me if my opinion is not wanted."

"I'm still here."

The publican feigned to wipe down the table, and the smell of stale beer oozed from the sponge and over them. "She's always been a cock tease. She's a looker, no doubt. But she knows it, and she uses it."

He wished his beer wasn't finished. "Anything else?"

"Well, you were right that Jimmy was a prick, though maybe you shouldn't have said it out there, so close to him carking it. But even though he was a prick, what he said, he would do. Right or wrong, he was always straight down the line."

"So I should'a married Jimmy instead?"

Pete laughed. "Not sure about that. But unlike Jimmy, I wouldn't trust Shaz as far as I could throw her."

His thirst came on sudden, and his innards shifted a tad but the feeling wasn't like before, in the bar, when upstream and down sung up their spite.

"That's quite a list you have there."

Pete stood and took up the tray of empties. "I'm closing in ten, Bob. Last call."

He closed his eyes but the world kept still this time. And the breeze kept on his face and he thought he might need an extra blanket to sleep.

He wanted sleep, sweet sleep taking him away from the barren land and all that went with it. "Thanks for the heads up."

Pete moved away with his tray. "And do me a favor, Bob. Try not to spew before you get out the door this time."

* * *

He didn't spew.

Bob went out into the beautiful night and walked the two minutes down to the Coral. He went past the office and the lights were out and he thought about knocking, but even the courage of his drunkenness didn't get the better of him and he kept on. He saw a flicker come from the window of room number three, the TV going. It was easier to hear from the quiet outside rather than through the double brick, and he staggered with his key, not finding the hole, and the light kept flickering from number three like candles on a birthday cake.

So he knocked, and his guts moved a bit as he did.

The door opened just a slice.

"Sam, old man. I saw your light on and thought you might like some company."

The dark eyes looked at him, and he smiled sheepishly at them. "But if you're wanting to go to bed, I understand."

The dark eyes opened the door wider, and he thought he was welcome but wasn't too sure.

"We're neighbors now, as Gordon probably told you. I apologize for the intrusion . . . but I'm a little . . . drunk. So please, you make sure you send me on my way as soon as I get annoying."

He watched the eyes for some direction, and when it came he went over and sat in the chair, the only one in the room, and the world spun more than it should.

"Your room ain't no different to mine, except for the picture of the Barrier Reef. Mine is of a sandy beach of no known location. But it gives me a nice feeling, anyway."

The dark eyes lay on the bed and turned the TV to mute.

"No need to turn it off, Sam. What you watchin', Big Brother? Can't see the point of it myself, but the little woman loves it." He looked around expecting to see something of interest but nothing came forward. "She tapes the shows, watches them in the daytime. She's religious about it." He shut his eyes and the bed swirled so he opened them again. "Have you seen my little woman lately, Sam?"

The dark eyes stared at him blankly.

"You being in the same cricket team." He pulled at his beard. "Let me tell you something funny—no need to interrupt until I'm finished, but I think you'll get a laugh from it." He chuckled but didn't feel happy at all. "I think . . . the little woman . . . might have a crush on you."

The dark eyes never gave a hint of anything.

"Don't laugh it off, Sam. You're an attractive man, anyone can see that. And the little woman is an attractive woman. You got to admit. Like attracts like." He lifted himself higher in the chair. "Like . . . attracts . . . like." He nodded at the picture of the Barrier Reef. "But, a warning to you, Sam. She just might be interested in another as well. Again, a nice guy, no doubt. What my mother-in-law would call salt of the earth."

He looked at the dark eyes and the grin that came forth and even his drunkenness didn't calm his disquiet. "My head is spinning, Sam. It's very wise you don't drink. I wish I had your constitution." He shook his head but it made it worse. "You know something, I like you, Sam. You are straight down the line. Yep, you are straight . . . down . . . the . . . line." He squinted at the TV. "What do you see in this show, Sam, if you don't mind me askin'?"

The eyes looked over to the screen. "It's like stale bread. All manmade."

He laughed so loud that he held a hand over his mouth. "It is, Sam! Jesus, it's like a moldy old loaf. My grandfather used to toast moldy bread. Scrape off the green, we had to do it in the depression, he said, and put it in the toaster, then layer it with butter, thick like cheese. He never made *me* eat it though. It reminded him of worse times past, he said." He pointed a finger at Sam, or thereabouts. "You make sure you tell Shaz when you see her next. Don't you forget, now? Big Brother is like my Pa's moldy old loaf!" He labored in the chair and the world moved to catch him. "Where were we? Oh, yes. The little woman."

"You don't have to worry about me, Bob," the dark eyes said.

"I'm not. I thought I'd just give you the heads up. We like doing that in this town of ours, very community minded we are." He smiled at him. "You been here for one hell of a time, Sam. I hope Gordy has given you a special rate. But I reckon you and Lil have broken the record for the longest stayers by a long shot."

"We like it here."

"You do?" He shook his head. "Can't see the attraction myself. This Witchweed has turned the land like my grandfather's bread."

"A wasteland."

"That it is, Sam. That it is." He stood uneasily from the chair. "But I can see you're too much of a gentleman to tell me to go to bed. So I won't overstay my welcome. Thanks for the visit."

"Goodnight, Bob."

He staggered over to the door and fiddled at the knob, but before he went out he proffered one more opinion. "I don't understand. If it's like stale bread why do you watch this show?"

And Sam switched the control from mute and the room filled with nothing of importance. "I already told you. It's one hundred percent . . . man-made."

* * *

After the herbicides and pesticides settled, the land was laid to rest. It wasn't ploughed under; this would chance movement of the tiny seeds and cause more strife further afield, so everything was left to stew in its own waste, decomposing where it lay, cotton and wild blue grass, Cotton-tails and African Lovegrass, and any wheat that hadn't made it to harvest. All festering together in a giant cemetery.

The best view of it was high up on Robbo's farm. From his gate he could see a lake of decay, etched into the land like a child's picture crossed out by thick pencil marks instead of erasing. The fester spread out in a wide circle as ordained by the Agriculture Department, with the main street of Guburnburnin near its center, then fanning out for twenty kilometers or more, into the region of desolation that Robbo looked at now.

It was pretty in an odd way, with dawn smearing light over the wasteland and turning it into a vast orange lake. If he could paint, maybe like the Impressionist exhibition he saw with Molly in Brisbane, he would do it, set up his easel every morning, the light much the same, for the clouds had all but gone this time of year, covering the canvas in quick brushstrokes. That's what Molly said the Impressionists did, capturing the light just when it hit, and he'd get up each morning until the job was done. For he couldn't shake this early waking of his, the farmer's lot, even though there was no more farming to be had.

It had taken him a while to work out what was even stranger about the place. He could see it now, looking out at the wasteland—a mute electric blue that faded into the ginger sunrise. Silence. The chemicals had killed all the bugs, they could carry the seeds it was said. And what fed on them fled to all compass points. And so, where he now stood, high and above it all, the heavens fell down on him without any skerrick of life to it, the sky a moonscape, like lying under a heavy blanket. He had only realized how noisy the land was when it stopped its singing.

Robbo thought again about being a surveyor. He had toyed with the idea when he was younger, you could even do it by correspondence. And if he was a surveyor, he might start by mapping out the wasteland, to take advantage of being up so high, which would keep him well occupied during the daylight instead of trying to fight the boredom of it all, making the trip every hour out to the gate to see if any visitors were in sight—mainly of the female kind.

And, though he didn't realize it, if he did map the desolation, he would find that the epicenter wasn't exactly in the main street of Guburnburnin as it seemed, but a kilometer southwest at the McCarthy farm. And if he was particularly accurate, using laser instruments of fine quality, he might pinpoint it in the rear of the wheat field, in a little circular clearing where nothing grew, even before the chemicals were sprayed.

TWO

"How you feeling, Lil?"

"Good as gold, luv."

"You haven't noticed the change in the color of your skin and eyes?"

"Not like that poor soul a while back. My goodness, he was like an unripe banana, 'ey."

He shuffled the blood results, underlining the liver tests with a green marker.

"You look worried, Doc."

He looked over his glasses at her, this flaming beacon of woman, with a grin that showed not a care in the world. "Well, every test is worse than before."

Lil laughed. "Don't hold back now, luv."

"It's serious, Lil."

"How long have I got?"

"You need to get on that transplant list."

"We've been through that, Doc. Too ghoulish. Just tell old Lil how long."

"Maybe a year, if you're lucky. But it could be tomorrow if you weren't."

He watched her frown a touch, like she was trying to remember something.

"That's a shame. I quite like it in your tidy town." She laughed. "I see you think I'm a strange one, luv. And the truth is, you just don't know."

He pushed the file aside. "The added complication is that the Health Department will want to see you. You were there at the pub when Jimmy died. And you have deteriorating liver function tests. I don't believe your problem is related—"

"To Jimmy the banana?"

"Yes."

"He was giving my Sam a hard time just before it happened. But we never hold a grudge, Doc. Even went to the funeral. I don't mind admitting I had to twist my Sam's arm to go, but he was a good boy. He usually does what he's told." She cackled. "But he was a bit naughty . . . everyone was in black but he wore green." She shook her head. "Little things amuse him. I tell him he's got to grow up, but he's my little boy and I guess I'm stuck with him. We never saw you at the funeral, luv."

"I never attend a funeral of one of my patients."

"I understand, Doc. It could be a bit tricky. But don't you worry, we all make mistakes, luv. We all make mistakes."

And she laughed so much he thought she might burst.

*　*　*

Billy sang the falsetto 'ooh to ahh', up and down, up and down.

"In the middle of the throat. Let it come from there."

Billy stopped before reaching the high note. "You say that all the time."

"Then why don't you do it?"

"I'm tryin'."

"Don't whinge."

He kicked at the dirt. "I'm tired."

"You said that already."

"Then why don't you let me rest?"

Sam lifted his hand and the signal to stop was greeted by the boy with a sigh.

Billy shifted the soil with his shoe. "Why do we have to practice out here? Dad says we shouldn't play outside, the chemicals might be bad for us."

"We won't be disturbed out here."

"We could use the hall. Mrs. Shipping said we could, anytime."

"The sound is pure, out in the open."

"What sound?"

"Exactly."

He kicked at the dirt again. "I don't seem to be getting better, do I?"

"Your voice is good." Sam touched his skull. "It's what's up here is the problem."

He sighed. "You say that all the time, too."

They stood alone like scarecrows in a vast field of nothing. The sun was low, and the chill of winter had started to bite.

He looked up at Sam who stared at him even more oddly than usual. "Mrs. Shipping says it's rude to stare."

But Sam didn't stop. "Tomorrow we rest."

Billy nodded. "It's not that I don't like to sing. I do. And mum keeps on about the skolship. Even Dad likes the idea . . . not that he's got much say in it." He patted down the broken soil with the tip of his shoe. "Paul Hanahan says I'm a poof because I like singin'."

"Why do you care what he thinks?"

"I don't. Sissy kicked him in the balls when he said it. He wasn't ready for it but I knew she was gonna do it. She's done it to me before, she lines them up with her eyes."

"Well, that will teach Paul Hanahan."

"Mum says I need to go to Brisbane if I want to be a famous singer like . . . Pavrotti."

"You won't sing like him."

"But do I need to go to Brisbane to sing good? Can't you teach me?"

"I won't be here much longer."

"Well, I can go to Brisbane when you go away."

Sam never responded, and the boy saw the strange look in his eyes again.

"Paul Hanahan said Billy Elliot went away and then he was a poof."

"What is it about this place and the fascination with poofs?"

"I do like singin', but I just miss playin'. Sissy gets to . . . and teases me about it. And Rusty goes to her now, which makes me mad 'cause he's really my dog."

"Then tomorrow we play."

"We?"

"After school we can go for a ride."

"And jump?"

"Yes."

"Can Rusty come?"

"But no one else."

"Paul Hanahan says he can jump over Harris's hedge, which is taller than me, when it had leaves. It's dead now, so it won't spook Mr. Ed so much. Can we try and jump it?"

"Maybe. But I want to go back to our old jumping spot first."

"Deal. We can start with the little jumps before tryin' Harris's hedge."

Sam nodded but he still had that odd look about him. "Remember, Billy. It's our secret."

"I know, I know. The contract." He hugged himself. "It's gettin' cold. It might be bad for my throat."

"Well, we wouldn't want that, would we?"

And he watched Sam grin and this strange look of his kept on, even up to the time they parted company outside of Billy's house, just before the sun fell below the drab horizon.

* * *

Just beyond the edge of the wasteland, some twenty kilometers from Guburnburnin, the fauna mushroomed. Insects made the migration first, then those that fed on them—Wrinkled and Littlejohns toadlets, the Crucifix and New Holland toad. Then those that fed on them—Kites and Kingfishers, Eagles and Kestrels. Then those that fed on them—etcetera, etcetera—etcetera, etcetera. Indeed, unbeknownst to the farmers that found their properties on the untouched side of the Government's red pen, this prosperous fauna created such an assortment that the pests were kept away, without the need for chemicals of any sort. A silver lining to the Witchweed's cloud.

And in amongst this soup of life, the snakes fattened like never before. Bandy Bandy and Orange-naped, Collett's and Speckled Brown. Their bellies bulged like plump sausages, and they bathed in the winter sun knowing more tucker was ready whenever they pleased. Which is why it was so odd that one Olive python, a real beauty of three or more meters, that usually preferred caves to the open night, and in the day ambushed bats and spinifex pigeons when it couldn't find larger prey, would make its way beyond this smorgasbord into the wasteland, and keep on going, further and further, toward the center of the desolation.

* * *

The sun was low but warm, and the sky was splattered with clouds carrying no rain. They rode side by side, for the rotting ground made paths redundant on the flat land. The black mare, five hands taller than the old gray, sidled its companion, and every so often they touched, like an old couple walking down the aisle of a supermarket.

A crow came circling down near them, squawking loud, and the gray pricked its ears, but the mare kept on without flinching.

"Nothing to eat around here for you, Mr. Crow," Billy shouted up.

"He's not hungry," Sam said.

The boy looked around. "Keep up, Rusty."

The dog, with its tongue flapping, followed behind them, for there was little to chase in the dead earth.

"Mum told Mrs. Shipping that my meetin' for the skolship is in three weeks. I got to work out what to sing for them."

"You'll impress them no matter what you sing."

"Can you come?"

"Maybe."

"It's in Brissy."

"Maybe."

"They said I can look around and see where I'll sleep . . . if they let me in."

"They'll let you in."

"Maybe I should sing Lusha key-panga."

"Maybe."

The boy heaved up a deep breath. "I still don't know why I can't stay here and sing with you."

"This place isn't worthy of you."

"I told Paul Hanahan that I might be jumpin' Harris's hedge, but he never believed me."

"I thought I told you not to tell anyone."

"Well, he was teasin' again, and Sissy was gettin' riled up. I could see her lookin' down at his . . . you know what." He laughed and gave Mr. Ed a gentle nudge with his stirrups. "Sissy's still sore about not bein' able to sing with us. I said she could practice with Mrs. Shipping in the hall, and she came a few times. But when Mrs. Shipping said my songs were too hard for her and she had to start easy, she stormed off home."

"She has plenty of time to learn. You don't."

"I'm only eleven."

"You're still a boy. That won't last."

"I know all about that!" He twisted on the saddle to face Sam. "And we had a talk in class . . . just the older kids. Sissy had to go out and play and she spat the dummy and said she knew all about it 'cause Paul Hanahan had shown everyone pictures on his iPad. And so Paul Hanahan was banned from bringin' his IPad to school, and his parents were called up, and there was a hell of a blue."

"A boy's voice changes. A girl's, not so much. She has time to develop it. You only have a window that will soon close."

"Mrs. Shipping says I might be able to sing at the Opera House one day."

"You will."

"Which was the best place you sang at?"

"For *El Aprendidas*."

"Where's that?"

"Not where. Who. The King of Spain."

"Man . . . a king! Did you hear that, Mr. Ed?" He gave the gray a pat. "Were you nervous? I was real nervous when I sang at the Christmas concert. But I'd be shittin' myself if I had to sing in front of a king."

"And the Queen."

"You *must* have been shittin' yourself."

He turned to Sam and saw him smile in that odd way of his. "It was not who they were, for they were nothing. But they understood. They could have been stable-hands for all I cared. The audience means nothing if they don't understand, Billy."

"Dad says he doesn't know why you would come from those fancy places to Guburnburnin. I shouldn't say, but he thinks you might be runnin' from the police. Mum says she doesn't care as long as I get the skolship. Are you runnin' from the police?"

"No. Not from the police."

"Did you kill someone?" He watched Sam gently turn the mare toward the falling sun, Mr. Ed following without the need of instruction.

"Too many to count."

He laughed. "You're kiddin' me, aren't you?"

"No."

The boy looked at Sam, whose gaze kept on straight. "Were they bad? Did they do somethin' nasty to you?"

"Sometimes."

"You're pullin' my leg."

"I've been told I have a temper."

"You gotta be pullin' my leg."

"You have a right to know."

"I don't wanna know. Well . . . I do. But I might get in trouble. I might be a assory."

"Accessory."

"Yeah."

"I don't think that's likely."

The boy turned around at the bare land and his pulse quickened. "Who'd you kill last?"

"I thought you didn't want to know."

"I changed my mind."

"Depends what you mean by kill."

"Dead. Not breathin'."

The boy watched Sam lift his eyes up to the cloud-spattered sky. "Doing the killing myself? Or simply responsible for the death?"

"You're pullin' my leg."

"Let's say doing it myself, then. Lilit would say there's no difference between the two, but I see a difference."

In the distance the crow fell from the sky, just like hunting for mice, though he knew there was nothing to hunt for miles. But it was only a fleeting distraction from the talk at hand.

"It was in Nevada, I think. We were sitting on the roadside. And a truck driver thought he would have some fun with us. There are some bad people out there, Billy, and sometimes we run into them."

The boy kept his stare, and the chill of winter came on all of a sudden.

"Lilit understood. *Keep the streets from trash*, she said."

"What'd you do to him?"

"Well, we are not in the habit of getting our hands dirty. But let's say he tried to become a speed bump on the highway. With his head."

"You're pullin' my leg! Paul Hanahan said he saw a dead body down by the creek, floatin' face up, with maggots comin' out its mouth. He even went to show us, but the creek was dry, which stuffed his story right up."

"I'm looking forward to meeting this Paul Hanahan."

"We might see him at Harris's hedge. But it's a bit far from here, and I don't want Mr. Ed to be tired when he tries it. But no more pullin' my leg stories, okay?"

"Okay."

And the black mare and old gray stopped together, their ears pointed and flicking. And the timber jumps lay ready for them like discarded toys in a great backyard of nothing.

* * *

Crows have an eclectic diet—insects and small animals, cold blooded or warm, fruit and grain, carrion and scraps. But when this crow fell from the sky, it took on a three meter Olive python, a nice snack for a snake that had spent the night and most of the day slithering over the dead land without a morsel in sight.

It's true to say this attack was highly unusual—not from a feral cat or fox, or a gun carrying farmer mistaking it for a Brown—for there wasn't a bird in the land, even a Wedge-tailed Eagle, that would take the python on. Which was strange as nature can be, since a Wedgie would take a cat and fox if given the chance.

So the python was surprised when the large black bird came down from the sky, and maybe because it had used much of its energy in its travels, or maybe it simply wasn't used to striking at a bird that flew at it rather than away, the crow managed to remove a chunk of flesh from its head.

The wound was far from fatal, though.

The crow flailed its wings, screeched up, and retreated a safe distance from the wounded giant. And there they both kept to themselves, for any crow, and this one was certainly no novice, knew it had one opportunity and that was gone. And so it went up into the safety of the sky again and flew away.

But not too far.

* * *

From Lil's bed the only sound came from the soft purr of the road, the fifty-kay speed limit strictly observed, or from a closer human source—footsteps, a shutting door. Idle chatter was rarely heard outside.

Tap tap tap.

She rolled over and let her tired bones rest into another position.

Tap tap tap.

When she first heard the sound, she thought she'd been dreaming, but the second time reminded her of a charming little restaurant, though of limited menu, way back when? Some time ago. And she smiled as one does when reflecting on events that tickled their fancy.

Tap tap tap. Tap tap tap.

She lifted her heavy body up from the mattress and arched her back. Since her last visit with Doc, she had started to feel the yellow color of her eyes had moved to the sinews and gristle of her joints. And she knew the time was near.

Tap tap tap.

She went over and opened the door, and the coral rattled against the timber like it always did. And she looked down at the black bird that stood gazing up at her with large white eyes.

Lil raised her head to the Heavens and sighed. And she knew the time was nearer than she would have liked it to be. Since she liked it here, in this tidy town of Guburnburnin.

* * *

"You take the jump first, Billy."

"Mr. Ed gets more confident if yours does it before him." The boy grinned. "I think he's in love."

"If you're going to show . . . what's his name . . . you jumping that hedge, then he's got to do it alone. Best to start easy."

"I guess." Billy lent down and cuddled at the gray's neck. "You ready, Mr. Ed?"

Sam watched as the boy trotted toward the smallest of the jumps, but the gray hesitated, so Billy went around it and started a gallop in a wide circle before facing it front on again.

As the horse moved in, the python glided out from the hollow log of the jump.

And the old, gentle gray reared up on its hind legs, kicking wildly, with Billy landing with a thud on his back, striking his head against the dead soil.

Sam steadied his mare, who had turned sharply with the chaos, and eased himself off the saddle. He went over to the boy who hadn't moved, though his breathing was easily made out in the quiet.

"Sometimes an innocent is taken," he said softly.

He knelt down and rolled Billy over onto his back. An egg had already formed hard on the boy's skull, but the skin wasn't broken, and he knew he didn't have much time.

He unhinged the top button of Billy's jeans, pulling the zipper open, and dragged his pants down, undies and all, as far as the boy's boots would allow. Sam examined the boy's privates, the little tuft of hair—the time was indeed short—the small sacs that he took between thumb and forefinger, as was done to him three hundred years back.

He lifted himself up and went over to the hollow log, the python retreated but available, and brought it over and placed it under the boy's bare thighs. And he went over to the mare's saddle, taking the hard rubber mallet from a pouch, and drifted back, kneeling again, encircling the sacs with his left thumb and forefinger, the soft skin of the boy's scrotum positioned against the rough of the bark.

"*Ars longa, vita brevis.*"

He raised the mallet up high in his right hand.

"No, Samil!"

The loud command came over his shoulder, and the dead soil shifted like a sand storm, but there wasn't a breeze to be found.

He paused in mid swing, the mallet clenched hard in his fist.

"Don't defy me, Samil!"

The command that came from the red mop of hair wasn't human; rather a cavernous growl, like a massive bear—a Grizzly protecting its territory. And when it came again, and the earth shifted as before, Sam loosened his grip and the mallet slipped from his fingers, and onto the dead soil.

THE METAMORPHOSIS

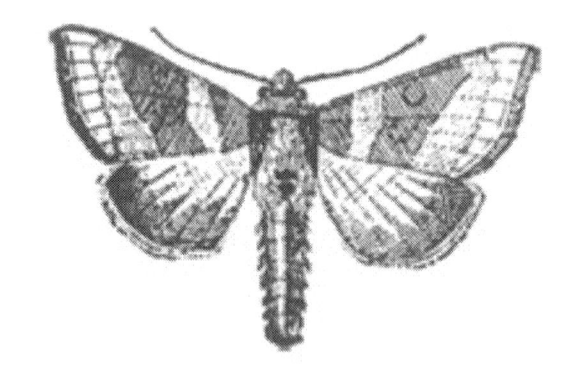

ONE

Little Jamie hadn't been seen since she was told the news. He'd just plumb disappeared, like he'd gone out to play and had never come back.

A dingo has taken my baby.

The famous mantra was well known in these parts. It had been a favorite debate in the land of the Queen's for years, long before Hollywood turned it into a movie and popular culture turned it into a joke. And in Guburnburnin, where time slows like dribbling winter honey, it still goes on.

The bitch killed it. Hang her.

But fortunately, for the mother of the taken baby, they don't hang'em Down Under. Indeed, the land of the Queen's was the first to stop it way back in the twenties.

But given the chance . . .

It was late afternoon, and Elsie had popped in for tea, but there were no Iced VoVos to be had.

"The problem with you, Sharon, is that you have to learn to forgive."

"I'll add that to my list." She rested her hand on her tummy and stroked the soft skin through her top.

"There's no need to get snooty, now. But every man deserves a second chance. It's not like he was *unfaithful*." She said the word like greeting a long lost friend.

"Why don't you say exactly what's on your mind, Mum?"

"Well, it's not my place."

She poured the Earl Grey and put in extra milk and sugar for good measure—but not in Elsie's, of course.

"But I have heard stories . . ."

"Are you telling me, if my husband leaves for six months, without a word, I have no right to seek companionship elsewhere?"

"Six months is hardly a lifetime, Sharon. Your father—"

"Please, don't bring Dad into this."

Elsie picked up her cup and winced. "It's weak, dear. Let it draw longer."

They sat silent for a bit. Sharon watched her mother shiver in her cardigan and thought about putting on the fire but decided against it.

And she thought about telling her the news, but decided against that too. It was too early to be sure. And Elsie would make such a fuss.

Elsie lifted the now drawn tea to her mouth. "Ah, that's better." She kept the cup and saucer in her hand. "Men are the weaker sex, my dear. They go off half-cocked, cause a to-do, realize the foolishness of it, and then, for good measure, try to sweep it under the carpet. It's who they are. And whether we like it or not, it's what we're stuck with."

Sharon sipped her tea and wished she hadn't put so much milk in. "I've got Lemon Crisps if you want."

"Too sweet for me, dear. But you have some. You've lost some weight. And, no matter what the tragedy, we women know how to prepare a meal. But the men—"

"Eat chocolate and chips." She laughed. "You want to stay for dinner, Mum?"

Elsie sipped her tea. "Will we be eating alone?"

"You'd like Robbo."

"What do you mean, I'd like him? I've known him since he was high as that chair." She pointed at little Jamie's chair.

"He's scared of you."

"Not another weak man, Sharon. Spare me that, at least. I can say one thing about your father. Weakness was not one of his faults."

She stood and went over to the kitchen window, the low-lying sun fashioning the ground into the color of nutmeg.

"What do you think about us selling the property?" she said.

"Keating was right. This land wasn't meant to be farmed."

"You turning into a Labor voter now, Mum?"

"Hardly. But it is an undeniable fact. And I'm not so *stubborn*, that I don't change my mind." Stubborn was Elsie's new long lost friend. "I assume the deal is good. I trust your judgment in such matters, even more than Bob's. He's too attached to the land. And you have never been attached to anything in your life."

"Well, thanks, Mum."

"It's true. I watched you when Terry was killed."

"I was shattered."

"Pooh. We buried that dog in the garden, you had a cry, then wanted to know what was for dinner."

"I was no more than seven or eight."

"And there was Birdie."

"Birdie wasn't my pet. You made me change the paper in his stupid cage, but he wasn't mine."

"In many ways I wish we had another child to keep you . . ."

"Yes?"

"Not so spoilt."

"Thanks again, Mum."

"Or self indulgent."

She laughed. "Oh, much nicer."

"Well, it's just my opinion. And in my daughter's house, surely I have the right to it."

"Anything else while we're on it, Mum?"

"At least Robbo's a step up from the publican."

"For God's sake—and don't pull that face—will you ever forget Pete? That was when I was a child."

"Twenty, actually, and you were hardly a late bloomer, Sharon." She poured another cup. "So what's your plan?"

"The property will be settled in three months or so."

"I wouldn't let it drag on. Bob's liable to change his mind. Who are you using for lawyers?"

"Bilson's."

"Good. They're no bunnies." She put her cup down. "I might have biscuit. And what about the divorce?"

"I haven't decided."

"You'll get a fair slab. Not half, but a fair slab."

"Why won't I get half?"

"The farm is three generations, Sharon. You've come onto the scene late in the piece."

"Perhaps they'll call you as a witness for Bob."

"I'm just saying what others will think."

"Again, I am so *grateful* for your opinion."

"Not a Lemon Crisp, dear. Haven't you something plainer?"

"Jatz."

"Well, if that's all you've got. And then what will you do, when the money is in the bank?"

"I haven't decided."

"But you've thought about it."

"It's too early, Mum."

"You can stay with me, of course."

She laughed. "I'd kill you within the week. Or you me."

"I'm just offering."

"Don't pull a face, Mum, I appreciate it. I'll knock on your door if necessary."

"Are you thinking of shacking up with Robbo?"

"Shacking up . . . very sixties, Mum."

"I had my time, Sharon."

"Oh, yes. The Country Women's Association must have been swingin' back then."

"Before your father, dear. I'm not the prudish wallflower you and your father, God rest his soul, thought me."

"Damn, now my nipples are erect."

"Sharon!"

"Save it for later, Mum. I couldn't do with any more excitement."

"And have something to eat. I hope you aren't becoming anorexic again. Such a trial should never be placed on a mother twice in a lifetime."

* * *

"Put on some of that lovely music, handsome Gordon."

"Bach or Sade?"

"Bob, why don't *you* choose, luv."

"I know nothing about music." Bob went over to the CD player. "Are you sure you don't want to invite Sam, Lil?"

"No. He's in disgrace at the moment."

"But he's just in the room by himself."

"He can go to the pub for dinner." She cackled. "Or he can starve, 'ey."

"Sent to his room without any dinner, hey mum."

"Exactly, Bob. I can't remember when he's been so naughty. I'm partly to blame, bringing him out here. He gets so fidgety . . . But sometimes he deserves a damn good smack."

"Mothers and sons, Lil. It can be tricky. What are you pulling a face for, Gordy?"

"Yes, handsome Gordon. Are you looking for a smack as well?"

"Any time, Lil."

"You cheeky thing."

The central light in the dining room came from two tall candles. Their faces were painted as well with a touch of vermillion rouge, fashioned from the well-tended fireplace. Besides that, the place was without light—a cave of a space. A sanctuary from the dead outside.

"I must say it smells wonderful, Gordy."

"Pot roast a la Guburnburnin."

"Are *you* a good cook, Bob?"

"If I keep it simple, not so bad. But I'm no chef like Gordy."

"There's nothing to this. Good produce, thirty minutes preparation including braising the meat, then cook it slow in its juices for six hours."

"You're making me all wet, Gordon."

They all laughed in the cozy space, smelling of garlic and butter and braised beef.

"You are one of a kind, Lil."

"That I am, luv."

"I'd love to see you drunk."

"Lil has liver problems, Bob."

"I need a new one, 'ey. Care to donate?" She laughed. "Don't you worry, luv. It takes more than that to stop old Lil." She reached over and pulled at Bob's face. "And tell me, when are you going to shave off that beard? You gotta think of the women, luv. The itch after is horrible."

They laughed together, their faces blushing into a deeper shade of scarlet.

"You are a wag, Lil. But I'm telling you there's not a woman in sight for me."

"You and me both," Gordon said.

"Oh, both of you could have anyone in town you want."

"Yeah. They're just lining up as we speak." Gordon went over to the kitchen. "I'm going to open the Shiraz as well, it'll go nice with the beef. It's okay, Bob, Lil is used to me drinking."

She laughed. "I like it better when my men drink. It loosens their tongues."

"Jesus. This place won't be the same when you leave, Lil."

"Or you, Bob."

Her face and hair lit up vermillion with the candlelight. "You leaving us, young Bob?"

"Not much to keep me here now."

Gordon tended the pot roast with a ladle. "With you both gone, the Coral will go back to being its old lonely self again."

"Plenty of customers when the gas company moves in, Gord."

"Who knows, I might even be able to sell it."

Lil lifted her glass. "You young boys need to get out of this place."

Bob raised the bottle. "A road trip, Gordy, just the two of us in my Statesman. Unless, of course, Lil wants to join in."

She grinned. "Where will you boys take me?"

"Anywhere you want. We'll be your servants. Bob'll cook and I'll drive."

"And you'll both fuck me."

"Jesus, Lil. I don't know we'll have the energy."

"Speak for yourself, Bob."

"See how his tongue wags when he drinks."

They all laughed and more wine was poured, though Lil kept to her sparkling water.

"I'm still feeling sorry for Sam."

"You are a thoughtful one, Bob. I don't know why that little woman of yours doesn't see sense."

"She has another buck to keep her warm now."

"Oh, Robbo won't last, luv. He's a nice boy, but his head is all over the place. Shave that beard off and get over with a nice bunch of flowers. Isn't that what women around here like?"

"She prefers a good bottle of wine."

"Gets her tongue wagging too, 'ey luv?"

"Sometimes it's more of a lashing."

Lil took a sip of her water. "I can imagine. She might do better to stay off the wine like old Lil does."

Gordon spooned mash on his plate. "It must be easier though, Bob, without the complication of having kids."

"In some ways, yes." He emptied his glass. "In other ways, no."

"Let's not talk about children, boys. It bores me so."

Gordon lifted both his arms in the air. "Well then, Lil, we kneel before you . . . at your command."

"You are a flatterer. Pass the mash over, there's a good boy."

And with it the copper pot of beef, carrot, celery and mushroom, rosemary and thyme.

"If you don't mind me asking, Lil, Gordy and I were wondering—okay, Gord, *I* was wondering then—this nomadic life of yours must add up, and it isn't as if staying at the Coral hasn't cost you some."

"Are you trying to lose me a customer, Bob?"

"Well, you are too shy to ask, so I'm doin' the askin' for you."

"How do we travel the world and stay in such palatial surrounds?" She grinned. "I believe Sam says it's compound interest, luv. I have no head for money, I leave that to him, 'ey. But we have put away a little nest egg—I think that's what you call it—over many many years. And it just gets bigger and bigger. Until one day, it just . . . might . . . burst."

"So big it needs more than one account?"

"Gordon, you probably know more than you should. That smack might be coming sooner than you think."

He grinned. "I don't care where you get it from Lil, as long as it stays here."

"Ah, you have a bit of the scoundrel about you. Which, I must say, I like. But I wouldn't ask Sam about it. He's touchy about things like that."

Bob took another swig of wine. "But for the life of me, Lil, I can't see why anyone would stop in Guburnburnin for so long."

"You did, luv."

"I was born here."

Gordon sighed. "But I wasn't, and I'm paying for it with every breath I take."

The Well-tempered Clavier mingled nicely with the pot roast. The fire-place blazing. The wine and sparkling water. A place painted with sepia brush strokes applied quickly to the canvas.

"This food is something special, luv."

"Unbelievably good, Gord."

"What about giving us a poem after dinner?"

"Wordsworth?"

Lil grinned. "You see, Bob, I'm trying to make an effort for my Sam."

"Let's call him in then and he can read to us. If he impresses, we might let him come on our road trip together."

She laughed. "Just forget him for the moment. The food is going cold on your plate." She turned around on her chair. "I like your log fire, Gordon. There's nothing like the smell of burning timber."

"These last few nights have been bloody cold. The frost was an inch thick this morning."

"Jesus Gord, the earth is dead *and* frozen."

Lil went back to her stew, stirring the beef into her mash. "I'm telling you boys—and I promise not to repeat it—but you have to leave this place. Take old Lil's word for it."

But because the hamlet held them in such solace, there seemed little reason to heed Lil's word, at least until the taste of stew was gone, and the sour land crawled back over them, like it always seemed to do.

* * *

"Here he is, the Nightingale!"

The brown surrounds raised up their welcome.

"Take a pew, Sam." And he watched the dark eyed man sit in the center of the bar. And when they all raised their glasses, he took a swig of the Johnnie Walker he kept under the cash register.

Only the regulars were still around—those that would stagger off to the little women after a session with their mates, if they hadn't yet been abandoned, of course. Those from farther afield would be given a ride home by the least pissed, not that there was traffic to dodge. Even at the height of harvest nothing much moved through the town at such a late hour, except a roo caught in the high beam, frozen God knows why, and they were all taught don't try and dodge, hit'em square on, it's when you dodge'em you hit a tree. Then say goodnight, Gracie.

"It's late for you, Nightingale. I've still some Bolognese out in the kitchen. It's not a problem to heat it up."

The dark eyed man shook his head.

"Lemon, lime, and bitters on the house." He poured the lemonade into a schooner glass.

"I'll have a scotch."

"Jesus, Nightingale. It's about time."

"Why don't you give him yours, Pete?"

"Fuck off, Brucey."

"Black label it is. On the house."

The dark eyes nodded.

"The boy will be okay," Pete said. "Just a bump on the head. I don't see what the fuss is about. He wasn't jumping in the Grand National."

"Superman broke his neck on a horse."

"Well, Mickey, Superman was a bloody septic tank. Out here, riding is part of the deal."

"I'm not judging, Pete. Just sharing information."

"I know, you're a fucking encyclopedia." He looked at Sam. "Steady with that scotch, Nightingale. That was a double shot you skulled down."

"How many shots you had, Pete?"

"Not as many as you, Brucey."

The brown surrounds laughed up, and Brucey grinned. Someone gave him a pat on the head.

"I was wrong about you, Nightingale," Pete said. "Or rather, I *did* you wrong. So, because of this wrong doin' of mine . . . you get drinks on the house. But only tonight. I don't want these bastards getting the idea I'm a saint." He poured another double shot into Sam's glass. "You're a fine cricketer, and I was a dickhead not to give you more of a spell."

"And he's a better singer."

"When did you hear him, Brucey?"

"I was at the concert. My niece was playin' the piano. She's fuckin' hopeless, but him . . . Just when I was driften' to sleep, the old lady diggin' in my ribs, off goes the Nightingale . . . and fuck me dead!"

Pete took another swig of scotch but kept the glass on top of the counter, for it was late and no one could care less.

Brucey raised his glass to the dark-eyed man. "It was something fucking special . . . no doubt about it."

"Well, I wasn't there. But I haven't seen spin bowling like his since Warney did the Poms."

"You are a multitalent."

"There you go, Nightingale. High praise from encyclopedia Mickey."

"Mickey," Brucey said, "why didn't you become a school teacher rather than a drunk."

The brown surrounds laughed.

The encyclopedia scratched his head. "You lot are my class. And a miserable bunch you are, never doing your homework."

Pete took another swig. "Set us some then Mickey. I miss school. Funny, I didn't seem to like it at the time."

"Youth is wasted on the young . . . George Bernard Shaw."

"You *are* an encyclopedia. You should go on 'who wants to be a millionaire'. Or what was that show where you picked a special subject?"

"Mastermind," the encyclopedia said.

"That's it, welcome to the show, Mickey Green. And your special subject is . . ."

"Being a fucking drunk!"

They all laughed.

"I should've got married. That was my mistake."

"Did you get close, Mickey?"

"Not really."

"Why don't you get a mail order bride?" Brucey said. "One of those good lookin' Asian gals . . . or Russians."

"Oh yes," Mickey said, "coming from the other side of the world to lovely Guburnburnin to shack up with an old drunk who just scrapes even in a petrol station in the back of whoop whoop."

"Well, we still luv ya."

"Give us a drink then."

And the publican shook his head and took another swig of scotch.

The saloon door swung open, and the hunched over heads turned to its direction.

"Another surprise customer! Take a pew, Bob." The brown surrounds raised their XXXXs and the publican noticed a sway in Bob's gait as he sat next to the Nightingale. "What'll it be, Bob?"

"I'll have what my friend is having."

"A double scotch. This is a night of firsts." The cork popped like a fart from the bottle. "Well, at least you boys don't have far to go home. And take it easy, Bob. I just cleaned the carpet."

* * *

"Look at the size of those stars."

They staggered down the edge of the road in the still night.

"It reminds me of the telegram to Harry S. Truman, Sam," Bob said.

"Try and walk in a straight line."

He placed each foot more carefully, keeping as close to the imaginary line as he could—like stepping on the cracks in the pavement of his childhood. "In M.A.S.H., Sam. I loved that show, especially the early episodes." He turned to his buddy. "Did you ever see the show? They're smack in the middle of the Korean War."

"No."

"Well, no matter. But they're smack in the middle of war, and Hawkeye, he's the hero of the show, sends this telegram that makes it all the way to the President's desk. And we laugh because of the guts he has to do it. And we laugh because it's funny." One foot swayed a touch and he missed his aim. "And it's such an obvious question, but somehow nobody has dared to ask it."

"And?"

"Four words." He lifted his hand and counted them. "Why . . . are . . . we . . . here?" He watched as Sam turned to him but he couldn't quite make out the expression on his face, for the moonlight was veiled in a wisp of cloud.

"Depends on who *we* is, Bob."

"Just for this conversation, let the *we* be *me*, Sam."

"You haven't got any say in it. So best not to think about it."

They stumbled down the road together and kept quiet for a while, their shuffling gait scattering bits of bitumen at the road's edge.

Bob eventually strayed from the line despite his careful steps. "I don't mind telling you, Sam. I'm pretty lost."

Sam said nothing.

"Lost my land, lost my wife, lost my will."

"Get out of this place, Bob."

He laughed. "Your dear mother said the same thing to me not two hours ago."

"She would know."

Bob looked up to the heavens again. "My God, these stars are like headlights." He swung his head down and the world swung with him. And he hunched over, bracing himself with his hands on his knees, and tottered with the swirling sky. "You hold you liquor better than me, Sam."

"Thank you."

He lifted his neck and looked at Sam, who stood high above him. "Lil tells me you two will be leaving soon."

"Maybe."

"Well, I hope you're still here before I head off."

"Can't promise it."

"Tell me something . . . do you like my beard?"

"Yes."

"Because . . . your mother doesn't like it."

"Keep it."

"Keep it I will." Bob laughed. "I used to like the smell of the salt in it . . . keeping with me wherever I went, to the shops, to the loo."

"Why don't you go back?"

"Be a beach bum, hey?" He raised himself up from his knees. "I don't think I could, Sam. I've got to do something more substantial. Just playing doesn't seem right. You know what I mean?"

"Yes."

"Your mother, though . . ."

"Only plays."

They both kept to the straight road lit softly by the stars and moon.

"Now, what does old Elsie say about sluggards?"

"Sluggards don't plow in season, so at harvest they look but find nothing to eat. Proverbs."

Bob stopped in his tracks but Sam kept on. "That's what she says, Sam! By God, you *are* a wonder."

"Lilit would say that's His great curse. He won't let you play."

"Lil might have something there, at that." He quickened his pace to keep up and looked around. "Why . . . we've walked right past our little home away from home."

Sam didn't reply.

"It's getting cold. The booze must be wearing thin. I guess we should turn back."

But Sam didn't respond, and Bob kept on with him, swaying back and forth from the asphalt to the dead earth.

"You want to know something, Sam?"

"Yes."

"That curse might be the reason I stayed away so long. I mean, even as a kid I had chores. Every fucking day." He slipped on the edge of the gravel. "You ever lived on a farm, Sam?"

"Yes."

"Well you know what I'm saying, then. It never eases up. There's always something needed to be done, even as a kid when I should have been swimming in the river rather than mending the fence. That bloody fence was never completely right, it was a noose around us kids' necks. Even the weeks after harvest my Grandfather would say to me, *Go and fix that bloody fence.*" He stopped and looked up at the moonlit sky. "My sister—"

"I never knew you had a sister."

"She was the oldest. *It'll be yours one day if you want*, my Grandfather would say to her all the time. She was the favorite, no doubt. Well deserved too. It's a great thing having an older sister, Sam. When things aren't going right, with a girl or something more complicated than fixing the bloody fence, I could go into her room and seek her opinion. She was four years older. I was her little lamb, she called me. *Come and put your head on my lap, little lamb, and tell me what the problem is.*" He stopped and lifted his hands up to the sky. "By God, the night is beautiful, Sam. Look at it . . . everything is dead around us but the sky just keeps on as if it couldn't give a shit."

"Maybe it doesn't."

"Well, why would it, hey? Why the fuck would it?" He knelt down on his haunches and the sparkling lights through his shut eyes swirled and rolled. "Where was I, Sam?"

"Your sister."

"My sister! She told me once—I was pining over a girl at school—Amy Henderson . . . she married a lawyer in Banga and has three kids, so Pete tells me . . . Anyway, *What's the matter with my little lamb* she says. And I told her I was in love with Amy Henderson. But she didn't love *me!*" He pointed into nothing. "She didn't laugh, you know that? Any boy would have, but she didn't. And she got me over, and I lay on her lap, and she told me what I had to do the next day to get Amy Henderson to love me." He put his arms around Sam. "And you know what? It worked! I came home and my sister was waiting and I almost cried I was so happy." He stopped and lifted his hands up high. "Amy Henderson, where are you now, my angel?"

"With a lawyer and three kids. Or so says Pete."

"Don't bring the romance down, Sam." He laughed. "I like you, you know that, right? I really like you. But you are the least romantic person I've ever known. And if you've lived in Guburnburnin all your life like I have, that's bloody saying something."

"I'll take that as a compliment, Bob."

"I told you my Sharon was keen on you. And I know I had nothing to worry about. And I didn't, so don't you worry. But I watched her give you her best shot, I did, Sam. She made her favorite dishes for the cricket, got dolled up—who wears lipstick to play bloody cricket? And you know something, I didn't give a shit."

"Good for you, Bob."

"Jesus, the sky is beautiful. How about us going back to Gordy's, waking him up, and have us a night cap?"

"Maybe later."

"Okay, Sam. I'm holding you to it . . . a deal is a deal." He stopped all of a sudden. "For Christ's sake, look at Trevor's place with the 'sold' sign. Trevor knows more about wheat than anyone on the planet. What a fucking waste." He went over and pulled at the sign that was tied to the front gate of the property, but it didn't budge an inch.

"Leave it, Bob."

"But it's a fucking waste, Sam! You got to see it's such a fucking waste." He kicked at the closed gate that shuddered in the silent black. "Wait on a step, Sam. Where are we going anyway?"

The road raised a slight incline, but not enough to slow their lazy pace. It was cold, the frost starting to fashion crystals on the dead earth. And in the hour that they had walked, nothing passed them in either direction.

"What happened to your sister?"

"She up and went away. And then she did the darndest thing. She died." He kicked the gravel and laughed. "She told my family one Christmas dinner that farming was not for her, that she was going to do marine biology. I remember smiling because she picked a profession that was so far removed from Guburnburnin, she might as well said she was going to be an astronaut. I swear it killed my Grandfather—he was dead within a month, a stroke when he was fixing the bloody fence. Anyway, so she went off and did marine biology at UQ. And got leukemia. And died."

"I'm sorry."

"Tell me the point of that, Sam. Elsie says there was a purpose for her in this world. What do you reckon?"

"I don't reckon anything."

He shivered. "It's getting fucking freezing, Sam. Let's make a deal, the next car that comes in the direction of town, we wave down."

"Deal."

Bob stopped and lifted one arm. "There is my Sharon's man's house. Over there, you can see the light on. Just up that hill."

"I see it."

"She was a good sort, Molly. Another one taken in her prime." He stopped again and lifted his arm in Sam's direction. "I'll tell you a little secret, Molly made Sharon nervous. She was so good to Robbo. To the kids. Sharon always said she never knew Molly to speak to, which was bullshit. I saw them both in a café at Banga once . . . I was picking up a motor and they were sitting in the Inferus together. I never said anything to her later. Never met her, she says to this day. Women like that make women like my Shaz very nervous." He shivered. "Fuck, it's cold. Aren't you cold?"

"No."

A breeze came up and brought with it clouds that covered the moon and stars in a curtain. And before long, the only evidence of themselves was the sound of their feet against the road and their breath, for the road was drowned in ink.

"I wanted to tell you, Sam . . . but I got sidetracked somehow. I wanted to tell you why I stayed away so long."

"I'm here."

"I never fully realized it until you said about that curse that Lil spoke about." Bob stopped in his tracks. "At the beach . . . I played, Sam. I played and played and did nothing else." He started back and quickened his stride to catch up to his buddy. "I broke the curse, Sam! For the first time in my life, I broke old Lil's curse."

"His curse. But, well done, Bob."

He sighed. "But where to from here, Sam?" And he held himself in his arms. "By God, it's bloody cold. I'd give my right testicle if a truck came by right now." He shivered and looked over to the footsteps that shuffled next to him. "But tell me something, Sam. Why the fuck are we still walking away from town?"

* * *

Robbo felt the warmth of her body next to him, just inches away—the slither of air between heated by both of them. But it was cold, and he knew he could get warmer if he held her. She wouldn't wake because she slept like a log, snored a bit, which was funny really. Princesses don't snore, at least in storybooks.

But the Prince turned away from Sleeping Beauty, and the warm air vanished like a puff of smoke.

Jesus, what was he doing?

He'd been dreaming not long ago. Molly was holding up a blue ribbon for her cake, he a red for his bull, and they smiled together for the local rag, and the light from the flash made them giggle. It was before the girls were born. He didn't know why, but it was. What do you want to say to the folks of Guburnburnin who are watching on TV, live via satellite? And they laughed and held each other and kissed—not passionately—they kissed each other like only those who were in love could. Don't try and describe it. You know it or you don't.

Then he woke to the Princess, and the spell was broken.

She is a fucking looker, Robbo! They said it more than once down the pub. And they were right. Brucey McInerney never let up. *You have struck gold, Robbo, and she's got dough. Well, will have. You're a lucky cunt. And so say all of us.*

He got out of bed without a stitch on and went down the hall, past the family portraits of dead soldiers, into the cold kitchen, and through the door that welcomed an even colder outside.

His skin was numb, and he could see it too—standing directly under the porch light—a mottled bruised blue forming little rivers on his white hide. His body seemed shrunken, too, with the cold, his cock like a frankfurter trying to find a way out of his pubes.

The porch light was on because Molly was dead.

Bring on the psycho!

It would only be justice, Ivan Milat popping in for a quick snack, Wolf Creek style, taking them in their beds and burying them in the earth that didn't grow a fucking thing.

It would be a fair result for Molly. A suitable death for the cunt that he was.

Come and get me, Ivan. I ain't gonna give you any resistance.

The cold was such that he couldn't feel anything at all. Nothing spoke to him—the land drifting from a yellow halo into a great black empty.

And then for a second he thought he heard some voices far off. So he kept still for a spell but heard nothing more except his shivering skin.

Why had Shaz cried before they slept? Maybe it was women's problems. Molly used to have them on occasion, nothing he couldn't handle, he'd just tiptoe around the place for a few days, take out the garbage without being asked, keep the toilet seat down, though he never understood why it should be put down, he never got angry when he had to lift it up to piss. But he always kept it down around that time of the month.

And Shaz kept looking at something that wasn't there. *I don't want to talk about it* she said even though she cried in the bed. So he didn't. She rubbed at her tummy—*I don't want to talk about it*—looking at the empty space next to him.

If you don't tell me what's upsetting you how can I understand, he said.

I don't care if you understand or not.

So he never understood, and that was just fine by him.

Fuck it was cold.

The night sky was now a blotched black. Might be rain coming, not that it mattered. If you water the dead earth, it would still stay dead.

But there was a trace of something moving down by the road. Something that came and went with the light of the blanketed moon.

Come on, Ivan. If you're out there come and get us—the girls all safe in their beds at boarding school. Molly was right to send them away.

But she was always right.

He couldn't feel his fingers. They were dead pencils that couldn't write a word.

The flicker of something came again and he wanted to shout out to it.

But it just dawned on him—if he stayed outside he would die. They would say he went mad with sadness . . . and he just wandered off into the freezing night and perished like the lost did. It can be warm during the day Down Under but, Jesus, by night you don't want to get caught outside. He could just hear Brucey. How could he kill himself after snatching such a looker? His farm is stuffed, his wife is not long buried . . . but she is such a doll. Miss Guburnburnin.

Crying seemed pointless, so he didn't.

But just as he turned to go back in, something came up from the path. He heard it, he was sure this time, his shivers and cold breath couldn't disguise it.

And he was ready, though he didn't know what for.

A NEW DAY

ONE

"It shouldn't be long now."

Sam turned to her. "You said that already."

They sat at the edge of the road, the only paved within a hundred kilometers or so, the land on either side painted with every color the earth could muster. Northern bluebells, yellow-flowering cassias and wattles, purple mulia-mulias, and banksias the color of lipstick. On one side, a range rose from the flat land, the slant of the afternoon sun forming blue branches in the iron rich rock, the clouds above that had brought the rain gone, though not far.

"What a pretty place this is."

Sam kept staring along the gray stretch of road.

"These flies are annoying though." She swiped at her face. "We need to get that repellant, what do you call it?"

Sam never replied.

"Samil, stop sulking . . . you're making me more irritated by the second."

Still he said nothing.

"I told you, I'm not going to be a baby sitter again."

Sam stared, implacable, down the road.

"Anyway, I am pleased with my choice."

"Why Robbo?"

"Bob had broken His curse." She picked at her forearm. "What do you think of this, then." She lifted her arm under his face.

"Stop picking at it."

"And it will go away?"

"No it won't."

"Is it dangerous, doctor?"

"Hopefully, yes."

"Charming, Sam." Lil turned her head, but the road showed no sign of life. She flapped at something that flew at her face, and must have made contact because the large winged thing fell down to her feet. "But it's a pretty place, you have to admit that."

"Wait until the rains come."

"I'm not a fan of rain, Sam. You know that."

"What do you expect me to do about it?"

"Nothing. But I'm not a fan . . . that's all I'm saying."

"Then bring an umbrella."

"How long before it rains?"

"Three months."

"Shamayim! I wanted to stay a while this time."

"You always say that."

She swiped at her face. "Well, why don't you listen and do something about it."

"We could have stayed at Guburnburnin."

"The tidy town? How, Sam? The Doc said it could be at any time. I don't like it when I die. At least I'm healthy now, though no thanks to you."

He twisted his face to her. "Well, you've made the choice for both of us . . . so it's on your head."

Lil kicked at the insect that looked to make a recovery. "We've been through this . . . you broke our rule."

"*Your* rule . . . and I didn't break it."

"You gave it your best shot."

"You are sounding like a local more and more, Lilit."

"Don't change the subject. You gave it your best shot. You know I don't like children. So, to teach you a lesson, I have chosen for both of us this time. If you behave yourself, we can go back to our previous arrangement, like the old days before Carlo."

He turned to her. "You mean I can choose for *myself?*"

She nodded.

"That's very good of you, Lil."

"Why, thank you, Sam." She turned to him and smiled. "I've been thinking about the old days more and more of late."

"How old?"

"I don't want to get you into a sulking mood again."

"How old?"

"Our time at the start."

"Not before?"

"See, you are getting sulky." She reached out with her foot and squashed the bug that had nearly managed to crawl a safe distance. "Sometimes I think about before, but mainly after."

"Ah, before ... Genesis Chapter 2. So you have been breaking our rule."

"*Your* rule."

Sam smiled. "Don't get sulky."

"Well, I've never understood, Samil, this insistence on never mentioning anything before Chapter 3."

"It irritates."

"I know it irritates, Samil, and I know why it irritates. But it was a long time ago. Shamayim! Let's move on."

"Move is what we've always done."

She swiped at a fly. "At least that fucking raven hasn't followed us."

"Crow."

"What?"

"They call them crows here."

"I don't care what *these* people call them, Sam. You and I both know it's a raven."

"Whatever."

She swatted at another insect that sidled her face but missed. "And if that ... *raven* ... stays away, maybe we could go to a city next time."

"Where?"

"Your choosing, Sam."

"Melbourne?"

She turned to him. "But you'll have to behave, or we'll never find our way out of this place."

"I thought you wanted to stay longer?"

"I'm just thinking of you, Sam."

He turned to her but didn't say a word.

"Don't give me one of those looks." She touched his shoulder and huffed. "Be a good boy, which I know you can be, and you'll get your holiday in a big city. Okay?"

"Okay."

"But you must admit, Sam, it's very pretty around here." She scanned the rainbow-colored land and turned back to him. "Let's play a game! Are you ready? I spy with my little eye . . . something beginning with . . . A."

"Asshole."

"Charming as always, Sam."

"A face that only a mother could love."

"Ah, that's what's upsetting you. I knew it was something else. I think you look fine."

"All wind and piss."

"I don't even know what that means."

He smiled. "Angel."

"No. But thank you for playing properly."

"Give me a hint."

"It's close by."

"How close."

"Less than ten feet."

Sam arced his search a full 360 degrees. "I give up."

"No. It's too early to give up!"

"Arm-candy."

"What's that?"

"You, Lilit."

"Well, thank you, Samil. I think I approve of . . . arm-candy. No. But you are warm."

The sun threw their shadows charcoal on the asphalt in front, their suitcases like rectangular benches, their shoulders hunched over. And the westerly that took the clouds away kept on, and with it the heat of the day.

"What will we do in Melbourne?" Lil said.

"Eat better. Ant."

"No. I happened to like the food in Guburnburnin. Gordy was good."

"It helps when *you* have a live-in chef. Angry."

"No, but good try. Well, if you make an effort, Sam, get to know the locals, you might find yourself a nice chef too."

"I don't want to fuck everyone I see."

"If you must know, I didn't fuck Gordon."

"Congratulations. Amber."

"No. Where is the amber?"

"The soil is the color."

"Getting colder." She turned to him. "We won't be able to stay long in Melbourne, you know that of course. But you'll get to go to the theatre."

"I want to go in summer. To watch the cricket."

"Oh, Sam, I thought you shook that interest of yours."

"I'm out of practice. And, thanks to you, not in the same shape I was in."

She cackled. "I thought it might slow you down."

"Argy-bargy."

"You aren't playing properly now—you know full well I don't know what that means." She turned to him. "Anyway, *I* like you. And that's all that matters. And—"

Sam kept his eyes on the wildflowers out front.

"Well, Sam . . . do you approve of me."

"I used the term 'arm-candy' remember?"

"I do like it when you talk nice."

Sam flickered a smile.

She laughed again. "We've never had a fight in all these years, Sam."

"We got close this time."

"That little warning? No, you silly boy. It'll take a much bigger event than that for us to come to blows."

"I don't want to talk about it."

She leant over and kissed him on the cheek. "Do you think we'll ever fight, you and I?"

"I thought I said I didn't want to talk about it. Apocalypse."

"No. And I've used that so many times . . . this is new, Sam." She turned back to the colored land and laughed. "Shamayim! It would certainly give Them something to talk about, wouldn't it. There'd be a plague of ravens if you and I fought, Samil. Those fucking *crows* would come from everywhere." She grinned. "Go on, who do you think would win?"

"Anus."

"You're not playing properly, so I win."

"Congratulations."

And Lil sighed. "It shouldn't be long now."

* * *

He saw them a hundred yards away and pulled the truck into second gear. A diesel plume belched from the exhaust as he reached over and turned down the radio. He lolled the truck into first and it spasmed to a halt in the middle of the road.

"You folks need a lift?"

He watched the woman spring off her case. "You've taken your time, young man."

He grinned. "This is a pretty big taxi, but you'll find it comfortable, at least an improvement from sitting on the tarmac."

"Will we fit in front with you?" the woman said.

"You could ride out back with the meat, but unless you're an Eskimo, it might be a bit more pleasant in front." He looked at her companion who had kept seated on his case and thought him a strange lookin' bloke.

The woman laughed and opened the door. "Get up, Sam, our Prince Charming has arrived." And she bundled in with her case on her knee and he felt the warmth of her leg touch his. "I better be careful of this gear stick. Goodness knows what damage I could do."

He felt a tingle on his skin and his cheeks flush up. He usually didn't take hitchhikers, especially if there were two of them, but he was real glad that he had. "Where you headin' then?"

"Surprise us."

"I'm going all the way to Broome."

The woman turned to her companion who shook his head, then turned back to him. "Why don't you take us to the first town that has a nice place to stay. Who knows, we might fall in love with it. It's so pretty around here."

"I never get sick of driving this route in spring. It's God's garden around here."

"You here that, Sam, it's God's garden. How appropriate." And the woman smiled though he wasn't sure how genuine it was and he started to feel a bit uneasy.

He felt her hand on his thigh.

"Take us, Prince Charming. We're ready for anything."

He eased the truck into first, the road stark against the painted land, like a gray tie on a Hawaiian shirt. And he turned up the radio, and raised his voice above it. "The news is coming on soon. Did you hear about that guy who stabbed the TV presenter? He was a bloody dole bludger . . . and she was just doin' her job. What's the world coming to?"

The odd-looking companion made first contact. "What *is* the world coming to?"

He felt uneasy again even with the warm touch of her hand that hadn't left his thigh.

"Don't you worry about Sam, he's in a cranky mood."

"He's got a right to his opinion. But they keep playing the episode over and over on the TV. You must have seen it. Okay, she riles him up. She was damn good at her job. Some say she was too hard . . . neighbors' quarrels can get out of hand . . . dogs do bark, hard to stop them. But you don't go and kill someone for just doin' their job."

"And what job was that?" the odd man said.

"A TV presenter, mate." He was starting to get testy and knew it was a fault of his so he toned his voice down a bit. "She's just reporting what's goin' on. She's on our side . . . or was."

"Whose side is that?"

"Sam, stop bickering with our Prince Charming." He felt her hand squeeze his thigh. "Tell me, something—"

"Ron."

"Tell me something, handsome Ron. Do you think my brother is a good looking man?"

That uneasy feeling came back to him like a slap on the face and he felt his stomach churn.

The woman laughed. "Don't take it the wrong way, Ron. I'm just asking for my own interest."

He turned and looked at the steely-eyed man. "He's alright." He thought it best to lie.

"He *is* alright! Did you hear that, Sam?"

He turned his gaze to the man who didn't seem to flinch a response. And as he looked back to the road he noticed a spot on her arm. "You seen someone about that?"

She picked at it. "Should I, Ron? I was just asking Sam the same question but he didn't give me any opinion worth repeating." She leant across and lifted her forearm in front of her companion's face. "I spy . . . with my little eye . . . something . . . beginning . . . with . . . A." She laughed and the truck and the rainbow land seemed to all laugh with her. "Australia, Sam! Here, look at it, Ron. Tell me the truth, it really does look like a map of Australia, doesn't it? But there's no Tasmania."

EPILOGUE

Dear Sally,

Thank you for your email. I can confirm that the tablets are written in Akkadian, most likely somewhere between 1300-1000 BCE (BC) in Mesopotamia (Assyria or Babylonia). We know this because of the similarity of the text to a very famous version of The Epic of Gilgamesh. You may have heard of this, since earlier versions are considered to be one of the World's first great literary achievements. Fortunately, this much-studied and more complete later Akkadian version allows our translation to be more confident than would normally be possible.

I understand that the images you sent us are to be considered private and in confidence, which we have respected. Nevertheless, examination of such complete tablets are important to understanding the culture of that time, and, for that reason, we would very much like the opportunity to investigate the provenance of these rare artifacts. If you have time, I would like to discuss how we could proceed with this, while preserving the privacy wishes of the owner. Perhaps an initial phone conversation could start the ball rolling.

And so to the translation. Both clay tablets are identical in content, and clearly scribed by the same cuneiform hand. They state:

> Let the holders of these tablets walk together in a place of desolation, a soulless land, though made from the hand of man. And let there be warning to those who meet them on their path, for if the land is not desolate when they arrive, it may become so before they leave.

ACKNOWLEDGEMENTS

As always, my heartfelt appreciation to the readers, both professional and lay, who facilitate the massaging of the text. And a special mention to AB for his Italian and North Queensland linguistic skills, 'ey.

ABOUT THE AUTHOR

PTG Man lives in Sydney, Australia. He is the author of two other novels, *The Scent of Daisies* and *Of Love and Guilt*.

Made in the USA
San Bernardino, CA
09 October 2016